BED OF NAILS

BED OF NAILS

Antonin Varenne

Translated from the French by Siân Reynolds

MacLehose Press
New York • London

MacLehose Press
An imprint of Quercus
New York • London

© 2008 by Éditions Viviane Hamy
Translation © 2012 by Sîan Reynolds
Originally published in France as *Fakirs* by Éditions Viviane Hamy in 2009
First published in the United States by Quercus in 2014

This book is supported by the French Ministry of Foreign Affairs as part of the Burgess
Programme run by the Cultural Department of the French Embassy in London.
www.frenchbooknews.com

Liberté • Égalité • Fraternité
RÉPUBLIQUE FRANÇAISE

ISBN 978-1-62365-125-1

Library of Congress Control Number: 2014948383

Distributed in the United States and Canada by
Hachette Book Group
237 Park Avenue
New York, NY 10017

Manufactured in the United States

2 4 6 8 10 9 7 5 3 1

www.quercus.com

[. . .] So it is as if the torturer had let the victim take over the job of continuing his work of annihilation. But the case of this man, a former torturer who has become his own victim—both physically in his own person and representatively of others—is a striking illustration of what I have called the Saint Sebastian Syndrome: the inversion of the object and subject of torture and its behavioral consequences. This case study will be both the object and the subject of this study on war-related trauma, from the point of view of the torturer. So among the questions to be considered will be whether other forms of torture exist, separately from the "institutionalized" form [. . .] We shall see clearly that the answer is no. Like suicide, chosen as a subject of study by the earliest sociologists, torture is a social phenomenon. To paraphrase Durkheim and his famous demonstration on voluntary death, we may conclude this introduction as follows: every society is predisposed to produce a given contingent of torturers.

John P. Nichols, PhD thesis

The burned hand was heroism pure and simple; as for cutting off his ear, it was entirely logical, and I repeat: a world that day and night, and increasingly, eats the uneatable, in order that its ill will may achieve its ends can, on this point, simply shut up.

Antonin Artaud
Van Gogh, *Suicide and Society*

1

Lambert was gnawing at his fingernails.

The half-light shrouded the three other policemen in a shadowy space and time, neither day nor night. The cramped office reeked of alcohol and stale tobacco. Their fatigue could be heard in their voices, still hoarse and unprepared for the day, although it was already late morning. Huddled around the TV screen, they were chain-smoking, but no one in Paris Police HQ was about to quote the rules at them.

"What the fuck's he doing?"

"Taking his kit off."

"Is that it? Where's this come from anyway?"

"It's one of Guérin's files. Lambert's treating us to a film show."

Berlion, grinding a cigarette between his teeth, turned to the back of the room. "Hey Lambert, don't you want to watch it again?"

Lambert glanced at the door. The cigarette shifted to the corner of Berlion's mouth, and the filter tip scrunched under his premolars.

"Don't worry, Guérin's not around!"

They guffawed with scornful laughter.

"Look, look!"

The three of them were now glued to the small screen, breathing out thick clouds of cigarette smoke.

"Bloody hell, he's running through the traffic!"

"Where is this?"

"Porte Maillot, under the bridge. Closed-circuit TV."

"Hey, it's like he's looking up at the camera!"

"Get out of here, he doesn't even know he's being filmed."

"Hung like a horse, eh?"

"Don't get too excited, Roman."

Roman elbowed Savane.

"Piss off."

Lambert was working out the damage. Not difficult. The worse ideas he had, the more he blamed himself. If Guérin turned up now, he was for it.

"Oh my God, that Peugeot nearly wiped him out."

"He won't make it."

"Jeez, look at the pile-up, ten cars, more!"

"And this nutcase galloping up the road."

On the black-and-white screen, a young man, naked and waving his arms in the air, was running up the inside lane of the *périphérique*, the inner ring road around Paris. Cars were swerving to avoid him, scooters were smashing into the crash barriers. Privates on parade, the man was running toward the oncoming traffic with a beatific smile on his face. Shouting something that couldn't be heard, and looking unmistakably joyous, he was exposing his bare flesh to the hurtling metal bodies. At the foot of the screen, a digital display recorded the date and time: 9:37 a.m. After the minutes, the seconds crept by, much more slowly than the man's running steps. He was thin and pale skinned, with the elegant profile of a heron taking off across a pool of oil. The crashes, shocks, and broken glass were all happening in total silence.

"He's shouting, what's he saying?"

"Lambert, what was the guy shouting?"

Lambert didn't reply. He had been a fucking moron to try to curry favor with these three brutes.

According to a witness, the runner had been shouting "I'm on my way!" That was all. Lambert thought it was quite enough. Not for these three, though. By not replying, he was redeeming himself slightly in his own eyes.

"Ah, what's happened, where's he gone?"

"Wait, it'll be on the next camera."

The camera angle changed. Now they were viewing the man from behind and could see the cars coming toward him. He emerged from under the bridge while the traffic, like a black stream, flowed around this white pebble with its hairy backside.

"Doesn't give a damn, does he?"

"He's been going, oh, two hundred meters now, must be a world record!"

Savane nudged Roman, his darker alter ego.

"Easy to tell: got a stopwatch going!"

Another burst of throaty laughs. Lambert opened his mouth to protest, but the three of them intimidated him.

"Shut the fuck up; look at the screen!"

"Berlion doesn't like people talking when he's watching a film."

"Shut it."

Roman, Savane, and Berlion. If you were in Homicides, you could do a good job and still be a complete cretin. As they amply demonstrated, three times over. They fell silent now, sensing the end approaching, their gallows instinct awakened. Ash from their forgotten cigarettes fell on the tiled floor, and the only sound was the whirring of the tape in the video recorder.

A large sedan headed straight for the kamikaze, center screen. The young man spread out his arms as if in crucifixion, thrusting out his chest, like an athlete breasting the tape. The car swerved at the last moment and missed him. But behind it, a heavy truck was thundering along.

Soundlessly, the runner was drawn under the truck, his insane race stopped short. Then absurdly, it began running in reverse. The radiator of the truck was now spattered with a circular bloodstain from the man's pulverized skull, and the rest of the body had entirely disappeared under the cab as the trailer, its wheels locked, started to slide across the road.

The video squeaked, the tape stopped, freezing on a final image of the truck skidding sideways and the driver's horrified face. At the bottom of the screen, the numbers of the digital clock had stopped.

Berlion stubbed out his cigarette, burned to the filter, on the tiled floor.

"Eeurgh, that's gross."

"I told you it was crazy as hell."

They went on staring at the screen, caught in midbreath, sickened and disappointed.

Savane turned toward the dark corner where Lambert had taken refuge.

"Hey, Lambert, what's the verdict, then, suicide or a serial killer?"

They all collapsed laughing, and Savane, gasping for breath, piled it on further.

"Think your boss has arrested the truck driver?"

They were practically pissing themselves at this when the door of the TV room opened. Lambert drew up his tall body, as if guiltily standing to attention.

Guérin switched on the light. His three colleagues, emerging from the smoke-filled twilight, were wiping their eyes. He glanced at the screen, then more slowly at Lambert. The anger almost immediately faded from his big brown eyes, dissolving into weariness.

The expressions of Berlion and his sidekicks moved from laughter to aggression, with the facility of men used to questioning suspects.

They filed slowly out of the room, passing in front of Guérin. Savane, probably the most vicious of the three, snarled quietly as he went past:

"Hey Colombo, your raincoat's dragging on the floor."

As he went off down the corridor, he added more loudly,

"Don't drag it in the shit your little mutt leaves around!"

Lambert blushed crimson and stared down at his shoes.

Guérin ejected the tape from the machine, put it in his pocket, and walked out. Lambert, like a lamppost with no bulb, stood without moving. Guérin put his head back around the door.

"Coming? We've got a job to do."

He almost said "I'm on my way," in a jokey voice, but something stopped him. Dragging his feet, he followed the boss along the corridors. He tried to guess from the figure in front of him whether it expressed rage but could only discern the eternal fatigue in which the raincoat draped it. A dog that needed no lead to follow its master. Unlike Savane, he didn't find the idea degrading. Lambert considered it rather as a sign of trust.

The boss had carried on as if nothing had happened, without a word, but Lambert knew what to think. Being nice wasn't a quality required in this building. Indeed, one had to admit in the end that it was of little use. Any niceness you had, you got rid of as fast as possible, feeling a bit ashamed, like losing your virginity to some broken-down hooker. Lambert wondered if the boss—forty-two years old, thirteen of them in the job—was perhaps making this unnatural exception in his case only. Another reason, he told himself, not to act like a complete dickhead. One, it was a privilege, and two, Guérin was certainly capable of the opposite.

Trainee officer Lambert, who sometimes pursued his thought to its exact limits, wondered whether the boss wasn't in fact using him as a sort of lifebelt, a refuge for his feelings. When he lost himself in these hypothetical ramblings, generally after a few beers, the image of the dog and its master came back every time. In the end, it summed up their relationship pretty clearly. For the humble, humiliation is the first step toward recognition.

Lambert pushed open the door of their office, meditating on self-esteem. That delicate thing the boss was trying to get him to cultivate.

Guérin, silent and inscrutable, had sat down and plunged straight into the file on the man from the ring road. His ancient raincoat flopped around his shoulders like a sagging and discolored scout tent.

What was the name of that character on the *périphérique*? Lambert had already forgotten. A complicated name, double barreled. Impossible to remember.

"So, young Lambert, what would you say about him? I agree with you, it wasn't a very user-friendly way to commit suicide." Guérin smiled to himself. "You saw it, too, did you, how he was waving at the cameras?"

There was no sound or movement in the office. Looking up at his junior encouragingly, Guérin was waiting for some word, some approval. Lambert was busy picking his beaky nose. He looked fascinated by what he was extracting and sticking on the underside of the chair.

"Lambert?"

The big, fair-haired junior jumped, slipping his hands under the desk.

"Yessir!"

"Could you go and fetch us some coffee, please."

Lambert trailed off down the corridor, hoping not to meet too many people. On the way, he once more wondered why in the quai des Orfèvres no one ever used first names. They said things like "Roman's divorced again," "Lefranc's depressed," "That dope Savane is in trouble," "Guérin is completely nuts," and so on. No first names. To his mind, it was odd to talk in such a detached way among supposed friends.

Guérin listened as the trailing footsteps of his colleague died away and stared into the distance. Invariably, the sound of old sneakers dragging along on the floor reminded him of holidays and the luxury hotel for middle-income tourists in Morocco where he had once booked himself into a room. A palace with unreliable plumbing, where the waiters, with drowsy zeal, walked around slowly, dragging their feet, as they brought trays of mint tea. A week spent sitting on the hotel terrace, looking at the sea, into which he had not once dipped a toe, just listening to the waiters' footsteps. Lambert's shoes, echoing in the corridor of HQ, reminded him of the sound of the waves washing over the beach. There was a direct link between his junior and the Atlantic tide. A link, one of many, that nobody had ever made. As the sound of the sea grew fainter, he wondered why Lambert went on calling him "boss" or sometimes "sir," like the Moroccan waiters, whereas he had told him a hundred times just to call him Guérin.

He suddenly realized that there was another undeniable link between people being called "sir" and *vacations*. Hadn't it been his own boss, Barnier, who had advised him to take that break? *"Guérin, why don't you just get away from Paris and the squad for a bit? Things will have calmed down by the time you get back. Are you listening, Guérin, just take some leave, go away somewhere, anywhere."* So the words "sir" or "boss" really had no business in the workplace. Guérin plunged into the file again but was distracted by these exotic images and the direct connection he would always make from now on between disciplinary leave and Islam.

Lambert came back with two plastic cups of coffee: he put one on his boss's desk: black, no sugar. The other one, frothy and heaped with half a ton of demerara, he put on his own desk. Before sitting down, he went over to the wall and smartly tore a little sheet off the calendar. In red figures and letters, it now said: April 14, 2008. He went back to his seat and started to drink his coffee, still looking at the date.

Two years earlier, when he got back from Morocco, Guérin had been directed to this poky office. Two desks, a strip-light, two chairs, a few electric sockets, and two doors, as if the way in and the way out were not the same. In fact, there wasn't really a way out of this office. Behind one of the tables, a long thin strand of white coral with a human head sat facing a wall without a window, calmly contemplating the future. Since that day, it had seemed as if Lambert had never budged from his seat and that the future had definitely postponed its arrival until some later date.

The office was at the very end of the building, at the western point of the Île de la Cité, in central Paris. To reach it you had to go through half of No. 36, or use a side entrance and an old service staircase. Barnier had handed Guérin the keys, giving him to understand that going through the other offices to get there would be a wasted effort. *"Your new assistant,"* Barnier had said. *"Your new office. Your new job. Suicides. Guérin. From now on, you're Suicides and Suicides is you."*

The second door opened into a much bigger room, of which their office was the antechamber. The archives of all the suicides in Paris. Or part of them anyway, the ones that ended up in the prefecture of police. Why they had been chosen, he and Lambert, as guard dogs for this endless vista of shelves and files, was a sign he had not yet interpreted. But he was a patient man.

The archives were no longer consulted these days; they were the anachronistic remains of files now kept on computer, the paper copies made for insurance companies and rarely requested. Almost every month the question arose of chucking them out onto a rubbish dump. Guérin was now the only person who added to them or spent hours looking at them, apart from the odd sociology student who came from time to time to investigate social behavior. It was these students who allowed the archive to survive. The University of Paris had declared the deposit a research resource, and getting rid of it would cause a row. The oldest files went back to the industrial revolution, a time when suicide, as a sort of counterbalance to progress, had embarked on its golden age. Guérin, during the two years since he had listened to the waves on the beach, had become something of a specialist on voluntary death. Ten or so cases a week, hundreds of hours in the archives. He had become a walking encyclopedia on Parisian suicides. Any aspect you could think of: methods, social categories, seasons, family situation, time of day, trends, legislation, influence of religion, age, district—you name it. After the first week spent rummaging through these dusty boxes he had almost forgotten why he had ended up in this dead-end job.

Suicides was a dreaded chore at the Criminal Investigation Department. Not really an established service, but an aspect of police work that had a natural tendency to be separated from the other kinds of case. Every presumed suicide was the subject of a report, confirming or contesting the facts. Where there was any doubt, an investigation was opened: in almost every case, it was simply a matter of checking off boxes. If there was an investigation, it was taken out of Guérin's hands to land up with characters like Berlion and Savane. The hierarchical powers that sent you to Suicides could only be overturned by even more powerful forces, of whose existence nobody was certain. The only exit paths out of Suicides were retirement, resignation on account of depression, committal to an institution—or even, and these cases were more frequent in this branch of the police force than any other—ending it all with a service revolver in the mouth. All these options, with varying orders of preference, had been wished on

Guérin. The only one no one had anticipated was that he would take to it like a duck to water.

But that was what had happened.

As a result, Guérin had added a new layer to the preexisting hate of his colleagues: the visceral repulsion inspired by perverts, who, when plunged into something everyone else thinks revolting, actually seem to be enjoying themselves.

Two years earlier, Guérin, age forty and a top graduate from the officer training school, had already had both admirers and enemies. But everyone respected his competence, choosing to ignore certain odd aspects of his behavior. Then there were the incidents, more and more frequent, outside the usual field of thinking and the classic methods of investigation. The incidents were put down to his Nobel-sized brain, which people hoped was working, even if it was not always easy to follow. But two years later, his career was over, he was personally disliked, and his assistant was universally considered a halfwit.

After the fall, Guérin had undergone psychological tests. They had tried to find something physically amiss as well, so that he could be fired. But no valid reason for early retirement had been discovered, either physically or mentally. If there was anything like madness in his makeup, it fitted quite easily into the checkboxes for normality. Dr. Furet—an independent psychiatrist who had been consulted because of some administrative slip-up—had put a note in Guérin's file that had inspired some gossip: "The subject, in a perfectly reasoned way, seems to think, just as some people see God as a concept unifying everything else, that the world can only be comprehended and explained; in other words, that the subject's police work can only be accomplished, if the idea is accepted (is that so absurd?) that *everything is connected*. No event can be understood or conceived in isolation without losing sight of its meaning, causality, and effects. The subject is perfectly sane, and fit for police work."

Furet had also said to Barnier, who was gently pressing him to reconsider his diagnosis: "He may make mistakes, like anyone else, but sack him from the force and if you're going to be logical, you should resign at the same time. And you could change the Minister of Justice while you're at it."

Guérin had stayed. In Suicides.

Poised on the edge of a landslide away from objectivity, the little lieutenant was still concentrating on the case of the kamikaze nudist, which seemed more and more suspicious. Looking for support from his junior, and anxiously rubbing his glossy bald head with one hand, he asked the question again.

"Really, what do you think?"

Looking up at the ceiling, Lambert spoke slowly.

"I didn't hear it rain in the night."

Guérin didn't catch his meaning at first, then looked up, too. The pink stain had, indeed, gotten bigger.

Their office was on the top floor, under the attics. Or, more precisely, under the drying room. The roof leaked, and rain tended to seep inside onto the clothes hanging up there, then started dripping, now laden with blood. The rainwater collected in a pool on the wooden floor, and trickled between the planks into the plaster in the ceiling below, where it created a rose-pink stain of variable shape, expanding and shrinking above their heads, depending on the amount of rainfall. Every time the stain shrank, it left a series of concentric tawny rings, like a cross section of amethyst. It had rained that night and into the morning. Heavy rain, announcing that spring was on the way. The pink stain had got bigger, a living amethyst, the mineral pulse of dead victims, whose clothes, stiff with blood, were stored in the attics. Police evidence, which in summer gave off an unbearable stench.

Guérin looked at the stain in silence. The sound of the waves, Lambert's sneakers, the truck's wheels skidding on the wet asphalt, the blood-tinted stain on the ceiling . . . all merged into a kind of three-dimensional and stereophonic idea: modernization would never be able to do without these large rooms with their crammed shelves. Everything had to have its place.

He stood up, opened the door to the archives, and walked in between the rows of files. At the end of the room, he pulled down a large box from a shelf and put the ring-road dossier into it, along with the videocassette. Polishing his head, like a housemaid cleaning a silver soup tureen, he walked away from the murmur of the archives, cellulose sediments whose music he alone could hear.

He sat back down in the office and, like Lambert, looked up at the stain again. The imperceptible movement of water and blood, spreading slowly as if by capillary action, was accompanied by the regular scraping of their chairs on the ground, as they shifted their buttocks backward, anticipating the deluge.

The telephone rang several times before either of them heard it.

It rang on average about one and a half times a day, with two extremes over the year: the peak was in June and early July, when the sunshine increased social agitation like a chemical reaction affected by heat, and the lowest point was from December to January, when the cold seemed to make life move sluggishly, depriving people of the energy to harm themselves.

Guérin looked at his watch, answered the telephone, and took down the details in his notebook; then the faded yellow raincoat stood up, like a ghost.

From the doorway he looked back at his junior, who was still absorbed in gazing at the ceiling.

"Coming? We've got work to do."

Lambert followed Guérin, who was rubbing his head again awkwardly.

"You've got to stop showing things from our files to other people. I told you to watch the tape, not to organize a film show. Do you understand?"

Red faced, Lambert pulled up the zip of his tracksuit top.

"Yes, sir."

White clouds on a blue-gray background were streaming across the sky, propelled by winds at high altitude but leaving the world below at rest. As he emerged from their isolated staircase, Guérin paid them no attention.

While his assistant started the staff car, he thought once more about the TV programs he had watched the night before in an effort to relax. He racked his brains to try to find the link, because he knew there was one, between the vanished civilization of Easter Island and trout fishing in Montana. A little exercise to distract him from his lack of desire to look at the dull eyes of a corpse.

Lambert started whistling "*Le petit vin blanc.*" He liked driving, feeling the engine doing all the work while he made no effort.

As they drove along the bank of the Seine, Guérin wondered if the inhabitants of Easter Island—since thousands of them must have been employed in carving those stones as high as houses to please their chiefs—had perhaps fished the local waters so much that they ended up starving to death. It made sense, since there was no longer a tree left on the island to produce so much as a single nut, once they had finished putting up their statues. The last of them, since there was no more wood to transport them, had even remained in the quarries. Deforestation, soil erosion, overpopulation, running out of food, overfishing the sea, and you were back to square one: zero population. As for the fishermen in Montana, they were complaining about the cutting down of forests, land degradation, and the pollution of the rivers from copper mining. The trout were dying out, decimated by parasites that flourished in waters where the ecological balance had been disturbed, and now young people were emigrating from the state because there was no work for them on unproductive farms without crops. So the link was the trees. The cause in one case was the carving of great rock sculptures, in the other the timber and mining companies. And the result: the end of an outdoor sport and the wiping out of a whole civilization.

Besides, when the giant sculptures had appeared on television, Churchill had cackled with laughter. He never missed a chance to mock humans whenever they deserved it. In conclusion, Guérin told himself, nowadays it was no more reasonable to swim in the sea than to dig the ground, since Man, an unbalanced species, had already buried countless pieces of evidence of his crimes in the earth. More even than were left on the surface.

•

The young woman was twenty-four years old, a literature student. On her bedside table was an empty tube of powerful barbiturates, no doubt prescribed by a doctor who had irresponsibly handed out sleeping pills to an oversensitive student with insomnia. Since she had left no note, which seemed unusual for someone of a literary bent, Guérin concluded that this was a suicide attempt that had got out of hand and succeeded better than intended. The telephone, still grasped in the hand of the young woman on the bed, was the clincher. Category: "cry for help," subcategory "unintentional irreparable damage."

The small apartment was full of whispers, sobs, and choking sounds. The police did their work in silence. Cries of "No, no!" or "It can't be!" were heard, tearing into people's consciences. They came from the mother, whom the father was clasping tightly in his arms to stop the poor woman from entering the room. Her daughter, white faced, with purple lips and eyes already clouded with postmortem cataracts, could hear her no more.

Guérin sometimes found it hard to share the grief of suffering families. Such awkward and belated displays of concern made him uneasy.

Lambert—as happened every time the suicide was a pretty young woman—was in tears alongside the parents. Lieutenant Guérin, embarrassed himself, silently thanked him for it.

The police might hate letting their emotions show, but the public didn't mind at all. Families adored Lambert. Guérin had always needed a man who could cry somewhere in his life. He had found one, two years earlier, his sleepy branch of coral, in a cramped office with blood on the ceiling.

Faced with what was clearly a suicide, Guérin was required to ask the parents the usual questions. If you couldn't do compassion, professionalism was usually appreciated by civilians in shock. He checked the things he had to: statements from the neighbors, timing, state of the apartment, make of pills, level of alcohol required to make them lethal, state of the body, and so on.

Standing there in the bedroom, he wondered distractedly what was wrong with his Easter Island theory. He sat down to think and after a moment slapped his forehead. Churchill had laughed when he saw the American anglers, too, and yet they were genuinely sad people . . . This wasn't his usual behavior. When the pathologist arrived to write the death certificate, he stood at some distance looking surprised and troubled. Guérin greeted him at first without thinking. He smiled, before realizing that he was sitting on the bed, alongside the corpse of the literature student who was holding a telephone out to him. A wave of shame swept over him, and he sprang up from the bed.

As the hot blood flooded out of his face, he felt a great chill all over his body, followed by an immense fatigue. It was the responsibility weighing down on him despite his shame. The intimate responsibility of having to explain underground forces, violent and hypocritically denied. Invisible forces that sometimes emerged—passing through parents whose innocence was doubtful and coming to the surface as a show of power—in the shape of the dead body of an unfortunate young woman. Guérin had realized, as he saw himself sitting on the bed occupied with distant theories, that he was becoming a habitual and willing plaything of these forces, a fragile rationality in a mur-muring flood. The young woman's stomach gave a grotesque gurgle. Her body was losing liquid substances that had nothing to do with the eternal flow of the soul.

The pathologist, sickened, stood back to let Guérin leave.

2

On the steps of the church, two slices of history were warming their bones in the sun. With their fading eyesight and bent backs, they stood gazing at the springtime leaves and the village facades, whose cracks they had watched expanding over the years. The view before them contained trees, flowerpots, the town hall, Mme. Bertrand's general store, the post office, Michaud's bakery, the Bar des Sports, and the main road cutting through the middle of the village.

Under his bronze helmet, the metallic eye of a World War II soldier leaning on his rifle seemed to cast doubt on the durability of the plasterwork on the houses.

The old men, cloth caps pulled down over their heads, their outlines as angular as the twisted arms of sundials, projected onto the steps shadows of a timeless rural existence. The church clock struck the half hour, a single dull note. Reminded of the passing of time, the old men shrank a little more inside themselves.

The stones were warming up, the wooden shutters made cracking sounds, and in the bar three glasses were saluting the sun by clinking. In the priory garden, under the gentle shade, a woodpecker was terrorizing a colony of insects with its beak. The village stood quite still, representing nothing but France, on a day like any other.

A little breeze sprang up from the west, fluttering the flag on the town hall, and the tender leaves on the trees, carrying all the sounds away with it. Silence fell on the square for a moment. The bronze eye projected its mute inquiry to the horizon, the village waited, and some of its reason for existing went into that wait.

A new sound, distant and raucous, came to rescue the two old men from boredom. They straightened up and listened, their rheumy eyes dilated with curiosity.

Up the little road from the valley—along which they had already witnessed the arrival of electricity, two or three wars, family-planning clinics, and the odd guitar-playing hippy—came the sound of a car with a faulty exhaust.

"Oh, ah. The American."

"Hadn't seen him for a bit, had we?"

They waited, eyes fixed at the place where the road entered the village, to see the car arrive. Their excitement mounted.

"Reminds me when the Yanks come marching in, in '44. Remember?"

"Do I! Fritzes going that way, Yanks coming this way. And their teeth! White as anything."

"Mme. Bertrand, she chucked her geraniums out the window."

"And old Michaud, he come out with his bugle an' all."

"Hadn't seen hide nor hair of him all the war, had we?"

The caps turned toward the bakery.

"Him and his rotten flour, six feet under now, and good riddance."

Two disapproving faces dispatched further disgust in the general direction of Michaud's tomb. The racket from the car grew louder as it passed the cemetery.

"Here he comes."

With a popping of its exhaust, the rusty little white Renault van passed in front of a billboard, braked, and rolled to a halt in front of the post office. The two old men immediately became absorbed in gazing up at the cloudless sky.

The American extracted himself from the van, carrying a shopping bag, and waved to them. They replied with an imperceptible nod from each cap, then, as the tall foreigner turned away, they riveted their eyes on him until he vanished inside the grocery. He closed the door behind him.

"Oh, ah, here comes André."

Attracted by fresh blood, another old man was approaching, leaning on a stick with a rubber tip, bringing the number of sentinels on duty to three.

André looked across at the Renault. The other two, with a tilt of their heads, indicated the grocery.

"He's on his own, just got here now."

Ten minutes later, the American emerged from the shop. He crossed the square on his long legs and entered the baker's. The sound of its bell tinkled across the square.

"André, remember old Michaud and his bugle in '44?"

André turned toward the church's Romanesque doorway and spat carefully, so as not to dislodge his dentures.

"The priest, he was holding up the music for him and all, his eyes as dry as the pope's balls, oh he was happy, no bother."

"We all had a good time with the Yanks."

"That's right, we all did."

"Washed our hands in wine an' all."

"Communion wine!"

From his granite plinth above the twenty or more engraved names, the bronze soldier from 1940 affected not to hear.

"Funny to see him here, though, the American."

Silence fell once more on the square.

A milk truck went slowly past. The three old men followed it with their eyes until it disappeared down the road from which the van had come.

André pushed at the gravel with the rubber tip of his walking stick.

"Eh, oh! Where's he gone now?"

The baker's shop was empty.

"Morning, *messieurs*!"

The American, appearing from an unexpected angle, came up to them with a smile. The three caps jumped, shuffled closer together, and tipped down toward the ground, mumbling inaudible greetings.

The American now went into the post office, emerging a couple of minutes later with a parcel under his arm, got back in the van, and drove off again back down the valley. As he disappeared, the sharp reports from the exhaust echoed through the streets.

The three sentinels redeployed in a straight line, each one seeking a place in the sun.

"Always in a rush he is. Never even stops for a chat."

"Matthieu said he saw him up the dam only yesterday, with his bow and arrow."

"He don't fish, he just shoots."

"But what does he shoot if he ain't fishing?"

"Matthieu didn't say he was fishing, he said he was walking."

"With a bow and arrow? And anyway I know what he said, seeing he said it to me, didn't he?"

"I was there, too, didn't say he was fishing."

"Well, tell you something, he don't buy much meat, that lad."

"Anyway, he don't say much either, the American, so you wonder what he's doing here."

"Yeah, it's like he was just coming back. But he never come here in the first place."

The church clock started striking eleven. The three old men took themselves off in different directions. André hobbled toward the post office, while the other two headed for the grocery and baker's respectively.

The square was empty. In the distance the sound of the faulty exhaust faded away.

●

He cut the engine, after running along the flat out of the village, and freewheeled downhill. He put a cassette into the old car stereo, and alongside the squeaks of the bodywork and the colors of springtime, Jimi Hendrix's guitar made his loudspeakers crackle. "Voodoo Child." The van gently gathered speed.

He braked as he reached the turnoff, then took the forest track. The suspension, completely shot to pieces, let the wheels do what they liked, and the van seemed to float along on the stones. From here in, to get to the end without the engine, he didn't even have to brake. The vehicle bounced along so loudly that he couldn't hear the music.

A turn of the wheel to the left, and up the little track. A slalom between the dried-out ruts left from the winter.

The van slowed and came to a stop at the end of the trail, just under the big oak tree. He celebrated his small victory by listening to the end of the track, hands still on the wheel, before he switched the cassette player off. Getting out of the car, he went down the steps made of logs. A quick glance at his universe. With the ambiguous satisfaction on his face of a man who owns nothing.

The winter had been long, but now spring was there, brushing away his doubts about the wisdom of his return. He rekindled the fire, then, with a few tools and the parcel newly arrived from Australia, he walked farther into the forest. He had been waiting two whole months for this spare part. It took him only a few minutes to replace the propeller of the little wind turbine installed at the end of the hydraulic system that he had set up: fifty meters of PVC tubing, running along the hill to transform the stream into enough energy for two electric bulbs, a very small fridge, a radio, and a Dremel power tool.

He walked back, started to prepare the perch he had shot the night before up at the dam, and put it on the embers. In the wood, above the sounds of insects and birds excited by the spring, he could hear the little Australian wind pump recharging the four twelve-volt batteries with its new propeller.

The fish tasted good, and he smiled, thinking of the three old men.

•

The four-by-four shook as it traveled over potholes and rocks. The cool morning air came in through the windows, and the woman at the wheel took off her cap, which wouldn't stay in position. The equipment, radio, shotguns, flashlights, spike strips, and radar rattled together, preventing any communication between the three gendarmes.

The vehicle, overladen already, gave up completely in the deep grooves of the uphill section. Grudgingly, the three of them embarked on the final stretch on foot. The officer with a gray mustache brought up the rear behind his colleague, Michèle, a fine-featured blonde with a Teutonic backside. Her gun bounced on her wide hips, which was a cheering sight. The third, leading the way, was a spotty, stiff-legged youth who took his career rather seriously.

They reached the camp out of breath. The beat-up Renault van, the hippy's tepee, the suspicious vegetable patch.

The youngest walked around the car, sniffing like a dog, and kicked one of the smooth tires. The blond, hands on hips, was looking closely at the tent, from which floated the last wisps of smoke from the night before. On a line, stretched between two trees, some clothes and undergarments were hung to dry. The officer had thrust his thumbs into his belt, as a way of registering his overall disapproval of the encampment.

"So where is he?"

The valley ran down from the tepee toward a stream shaded by trees. The other way was the north-facing slope, dark and steep. The woman went down a few steps made of logs. The uprights of the tent, made of chestnut stakes, were wide open. A little excited, she leaned inside. A camp bed, with blankets rolled up, a fireplace, a small fridge, some cooking pots, a wooden chest, and two rows of books stacked directly on the ground. The blonde pulled her head back out from this deserted intimate scene.

"Not here."

The youngster, having finished his inspection of the van, pushed his cap up on his forehead.

"What's that noise?"

His superior listened. In the forest, up above them, came the distant echo of an ax. *Chtock.*

The three gendarmes took a path leading toward the little wood.

They were sweating under their uniforms, and they masked their annoyance with serious official expressions. The path forked several ways, and the chopping sounds ricocheted between the trees. The thicket was dense, making it hard to see anything ahead. The officer muttered, and the blonde spotted a splash of color on the right. They pushed their way through the undergrowth. The youngest noticed a wad of straw attached to a tree, above what looked like an archery target.

"There!"

A threatening whistle made them duck. A flash, and *chtock*. The blond hid behind a tree, and the youngest, clutching his gun, put one knee to the ground. The senior officer had stayed standing. He wiped the sweat from his mustache.

"Hey you! Can't you see we're over here? What do you think you're doing?"

The arrow had hurtled past about two meters in front of them.

At the end of a natural clearing, about forty meters away, they could now see the tall American, who was holding up one hand in apology. He was smiling, but not moving from the spot. The gendarmes advanced down the clearing, readjusting their caps and belts. The American just went on standing there, at the end of the archery lane, with his Anglo-Saxon smile and his stupid bow. The officer thrust out his chest.

The Intelligence service had a few leads, but in truth they knew very little about him. A Franco-American, age thirty-three, who had been in his hippy camp for about six months. The land belonged to his mother—another dropout—and had been bought in the 1970s. At the time, it had been the site of some kind of lefty New Age commune. One of the men had died of an overdose, it had brought bad karma, and they had all left. Now here was this child of 1968, an intellectual and no doubt a smoker of illicit substances. He had had an education, quite a good one it seemed, but no details were known: registered unemployed and entitled to benefit. The nearer they got, the taller he looked. Not a spectacled nerd at all, that was for sure. One meter eighty-five, strong jaws used to churning chewing gum, and a fine set of teeth. It really got up the officer's mustache that this guy was half-French. Hell's bells, that smile was fake.

"Now then, you, for a start, you should be more careful with that bow and arrow!"

"Excuse me, I didn't see you."

The woman officer wriggled her bum, blushing deep red from neck to forehead and not just from the climb.

"John Nichols?"

"Yes."

"Tell me, are you hunting with this weapon?"

"Sorry, what did you say?"

The mustache muttered: "What did he say?"

"I think he asked what you said, *chef.*"

"So how do you say 'hunt' in English?"

The blonde tried not to smile, imitating the stern expression of her male colleagues.

"*Hunte*, I think, to *hunte.*"

"So, you *hunte* with your bow? *Kill* animals?"

"Oh? Hunting? No, I just practice shooting, for my concentration."

"Whattheheckhesaying now?"

"He said no, *chef.*"

All four voices fell silent in the middle of the woods. The officer started again, no one else being keen to step in. He spoke loudly, as if the foreigner was deaf.

"We have to take you to the gendarmerie. You. Come. With. Us."

"What?"

"Oh shit. Police! With us. Come along! To Saint-Céré."

"I don't understand."

The fur trapper lookalike was still smiling.

"You didn't have a telephone, we couldn't reach you. No phone!"

"No, I don't have a phone. You need to make a phone call?"

"*You come*, police, with us! To Saint-Céré!"

"What? Now?"

The three gendarmes looked at each other. Did he mean no?

"Obligatory!"

The blonde cleared her throat:

"You must to come with us please, Mister Nichols."

The other two stood open mouthed: why, Michèle was practically bilingual!

The American slipped the strap of his quiver onto his shoulder. After all, he didn't see many people, and certainly very few women.

"*Okay. Can I take my car?*"

"Michèle, what's he saying?"

"Should he take his car?"

"Tell him we'll take him there."

They moved off again toward the yellow-and-black target with its red bull's-eye. From a distance, it looked like some tropical bird that had strayed into the forest of the Lot, or from farther away still, like a furious eye at the end of an imaginary tunnel.

As he went down the path, the American wondered if it had been that old guy at the dam the day before who had tipped off the authorities. No fishing permit. That must be it.

From his seat in the back he tried to catch the eye of the blonde, who was driving. She swerved a bit too much on a sharp turn, and the chief had to grab a door handle.

The gendarmes exchanged no words, either with their passenger or among themselves, until they got to Saint-Céré.

At the gendarmerie, which was dozing in the sun, surrounded by railings, they left him cooling his heels in a waiting room. He went over to a poster: faces of kids and teenagers who had gone missing. From behind a counter, another gendarme was watching him, visibly put off by his long hair. The station commander came in person to fetch him and introduced himself courteously.

"Commandant Juliard. Could you follow me, please? Do you speak French?"

Nichols's face changed shape as he said carefully in French: "I understand a little."

Behind his desk, facing the American, Juliard tried to find a comfortable position on his chair. He emptied his lungs, rearranged a few papers on his impeccably ordered desk, and breathed in noisily.

"We got a call from Paris this morning. From the American Embassy. A call concerning you. That's why we came to fetch you, because you don't have a phone. You understand? I'm not speaking too quickly?"

The American uncrossed his legs. They were treating him with kid gloves. It couldn't be anything to do with the perch up at the dam.

"I understand. So what does the embassy want?"

Juliard raised an eyebrow in surprise. Nichols had spoken French with hardly a trace of an accent.

"I don't know. But don't be alarmed. They just want a word with you."

Looking awkward, Juliard dialed a number while squinting at a piece of paper.

"Commandant Juliard, Saint-Céré gendarmerie. I need to speak to Monsieur Hirsh, please. That's right."

There was a pause, during which the commandant looked hard at the American.

"Hunting good up there?"

Juliard smiled, a diversionary smile. Nichols smiled back.

The officer now concentrated on the call.

"Monsieur Hirsh? I've got Monsieur Nichols here. I'll pass you over to him."

The American took the telephone, suddenly numbed by the impression that every gesture, every word, since the police team had arrived at his tepee, had been rehearsed in advance.

"Monsieur Nichols?"

"Yes."

"Forgive me for disturbing you, but I had to get hold of you urgently. Frank Hirsh here, assistant secretary at the U.S. embassy in Paris. I'm sorry, perhaps you'd prefer to speak English?"

Hirsh had been speaking the kind of French you learn at an international school, in the refined accent of an American who loves French literature.

"No, it's okay, you can speak French. What's all this about?"

This time Juliard gritted his teeth. Nichols was looking him in the eye, and there was no longer the slightest trace of an American accent, nor of a smile on his face.

"I'm sorry to have to call you in circumstances like these. I'm afraid I have some bad news."

Juliard was looking at his hands and had a formal expression on his face. Juliard already knew, he was just avoiding having to deal with it himself.

"I believe you know Monsieur Mustgrave, Alan Mustgrave."

Hirsh had pronounced the name with some awkwardness.

"Yeah, he's a friend of mine."

"Monsieur Nichols, I'm very sorry to have to tell you that Monsieur Mustgrave is dead. We've been trying to reach you for two days. Monsieur Nichols . . . Are you still there?"

"Ye . . . *Oui*."

"We have a problem here. Monsieur Mustgrave's parents can't come to France . . . Monsieur Nichols?"

"What?"

"We need you to come to Paris." Hirsh cleared his throat. "To identify Alan Mustgrave's body. Monsieur Nichols?"

John had let go of the telephone and was walking out of the office.

This time the woman wasn't driving the police car. The two male gendarmes, the spotty youth and his mustached boss, dropped him off at the top of the track. John cut across the woods to his tepee, passing the target, into which his arrows were still stuck.

He stuffed some clothes into a backpack, loaded a few blankets and his bow and arrows into the van, without asking himself why he was taking a weapon to Paris. He threw away any leftover food and lifted the lid of the wooden chest where he kept important documents, looking for the car's papers, his passports, and his French driver's license. He stopped when he found his PhD thesis and a note from Alan, scribbled in ballpoint pen, alongside a bundle of letters in a rubber band. John pulled out the last-dated, received two weeks earlier, without knowing why he did so. Last words of a corpse.

A couple of minutes later, without a backward glance at his camp, he drove off, slaloming in reverse through the ruts on the path.

Once he reached the main road, he wound back the cassette and pressed "Play."

Voodoo Child . . .

Alan's stage name.

Al standing in front of a little tape recorder, Al smiling as he answered his questions.

"I started when I was twenty-one, when I came back."

Al, drunk, years later, in a bar in La Brea.

"Paris? Hey John, why Paris?"

Al, last autumn, in a bar in Paris.

"Will you come see me sometime, Wild Man of the Woods?"

3

Lambert shed fewer tears when it was a man. There were more of them, and they were less affecting.

His eyes still full of sleep, he looked at his watch and stretched his back. Through the window, which someone had very wisely opened, the sounds of the night came in, a constant, nervous background of traffic, accelerating and braking. Lambert asked himself what the hell they were doing there.

It was difficult, without shocking people, to explain that they had their own preferences where suicides were concerned. Lambert would have been in a better mood if it had been a woman. They fell less often, but harder. They must have had to put up with more grief before deciding to die. That was another reason why Lambert felt he was more useful when asked to witness a woman's corpse: as if by his presence he was paying homage to their efforts.

Men seemed to give up more easily, once their source of pride—work or marriage—had been lost, after some incident that had made them lose face in other people's eyes, whom they usually blamed. They tended to commit suicide in the name of their self-image. Women often killed themselves for the sake of an image, too, but theirs were of a different kind, and more moving: constructed images as well, but more important than male pride. Namely, illusions. When a woman committed suicide, a greater portion of the hope of a better world went with her. Women died in everyone's name.

Guérin's mother had not committed suicide: she hadn't needed to. She had lived with men's treachery so long that the cancer had caught up with her just as surely. For him, men's suicides contained a certain element of justice, or at any rate of fairness, but women's were the cancer of disillusion that was eating away at society. In his case, he felt not sadness, like Lambert, but anxiety. Guérin never wept for anyone in particular. He shed tears, when he did so, in the name of everyone. In this he recognized the generous influence of his mother, who had brought him up on her own.

If by chance the suicide resulted in the man's head being obliterated, Lambert was left completely cold. Especially if it was some thug with no family to comfort. Anybody else (they were not the only people in Paris who handled suicides) could have taken care of it. But when the central switchboard received a call in the middle of the night for a truly terrible suicide, it had become the traditional routine, for two years now, to wake up Guérin and his faithful dog. Lambert had jumped into his car and gone to pick up his boss at boulevard Voltaire before driving to the eighteenth arrondissement. Outside the apartment building, the flashing lights of police cars of every color were blazing, and the city police were there, along with neighbors in robes.

They should have given a medal to the patrolman who had found the body: he had excelled himself.

The shotgun pellets had redecorated the wall and peppered the plaster with little dents behind the body. Even if one imagined that the guy had been able to fire both barrels at one go, it was impossible for so many shots to have gone through his head. The detail might have escaped the notice of a novice, it was true. And the scene was certainly impressive, if all you ever did was stick parking tickets on cars. But if you looked more closely, and if you could stand the sight and the smell, you could easily see where the bullets had gone. There was a hole in the back of the skull the size of a grapefruit. On the wall, in the middle of the galaxy of shotgun pellets, was a larger impact made by the high-caliber bullet that had preceded the shotgun. A black hole in a bloody galaxy. And that wasn't all.

Lambert, arms folded, looked down at the victim. He was black, as you could see from his neck and hands, and the dreadlocks still around the face that had been blown away. He had been a small man, sitting on a chair with the gun wedged upright between his legs. Guérin's lanky junior, in a foul mood now, shook his head from right to left.

"Who the fuck do they think they're kidding?"

Although not particularly gifted in the analysis of a crime scene, Lambert had enough experience by now to feel disgruntled. He knew that Berlion and the others would be along presently, and that he and Guérin had been got out of bed for nothing. Sickened, he let Guérin walk around the body taking notes. Finally, thrusting his hands deep in the pocket of his tracksuit bottoms, he started looking at the CDs on a stand. Nothing but reggae. Lambert wasn't into reggae.

Guérin went on noting inconsistencies. This was a murder, possibly an execution. How else could you explain how this Rasta had managed to shoot himself in the mouth, then raise the shotgun to a horizontal position and, with his arms, which were too short, pull both triggers, and finally stand the gun upright again between his legs? You might argue at a stretch that he could have used his toes to pull the triggers, if he had been really agile. But the man was wearing sneakers. Apart from his having been dead sometime, they were asked to believe that he had previously ransacked the flat like a madman, no doubt looking for a book on accidental suicide for beginners.

Guérin took his cell from deep in a pocket and called HQ. He gave the address and asked for a homicide team. Closing the cell, he took a deep breath and went on walking around the chaos-filled apartment. Lambert watched him rubbing the top of his head nervously, a sign that the boss was starting seriously to think.

"The neighbors say they heard a noise, some banging, not for long, then nothing, then music. Judging by the mess here, there must have been more than one of them, two at least, I'd say, at a reasonable guess. No sign the man had been tied up. Someone must have been holding a gun on him. But I'd say three at most. And given the kind of victim and the area, it's ten to one this is a drugs case—check if he had a record. They were either looking for cash or a stash. But serious dealers don't keep the stuff at home, and they didn't do this for the three joints in the ashtray. So it must have been money. Which they didn't find. The music was to cover the fisticuffs. We'll have to get the pathologist to confirm, but they probably beat him up to try and find out where the money was. And they shot him because he wouldn't say. They simply lost it. It wasn't an execution. Just some small-time amateurs who didn't know that you get trigger-happy when you're nervous. And then they had to hurry to disguise it somehow and made a mess of it. The music would have covered the sound of the beating, but not the shots. The neighbors are saying they didn't see or hear anything like gunfire. If you ask me, they were too scared to come out."

Guérin was smiling now, working out the score at the speed he could scribble it down in his notebook. Lambert had woken up and was drinking some milk.

"It's a quiet neighborhood, not crime-free, but quiet. The Nigerians have got the Goutte d'Or sewn up. A well-established stamping ground with clear rules. The shotgun was already in the flat. It's not a city weapon. He wasn't expecting trouble; it was just to be able to say he was armed. Too trusting, the familiarity syndrome, Lambert. He opened the door to them because he knew them."

Lambert, warmed up by the effort of concentrating, unzipped his tracksuit top and looked to be on the point of arguing. Without looking at him, Guérin continued.

"See the door, Lambert, quite a solid one. Not forced, opened from the inside. Or perhaps he even arrived with them. They smoke a few joints, listen to some music. Guys he knew, Lambert, the kind of guys who go around in threes. Homicides may have to go through the antigang unit to find them. But it wasn't really a holdup, just a spontaneous bit of temptation. Some youngsters thinking of starting their own racket, on the lookout for funds. Or maybe they wanted to buy a car. They wouldn't be from immediately around here, but not from too far away. The Nigerians could probably take a guess. We'll find them in a local garbage can in a week or two, if we don't arrest them first. With ballistics and fingerprints—they left them everywhere, they didn't mean to end up killing him—it should be easy. Especially if the antigang brigade already have them on file—best to check with Young Offenders, too—and if the Drugs Squad is already operating here. Not complicated. But we'd need to move fast. They're probably half-dead with fright right now, waiting for something to happen. But the gang leaders aren't soft on kids like that, even if, when the going gets tough, the young ones think the old ones are past it. Dealing's a business like any other. It's getting gentrified, Lambert."

Guérin turned to the corpse and seemed to be addressing it directly.

"You move up in the world, you find a flat in a nice building, you get used to the good life. You even get to think you can make new friends."

Guérin had leaned toward the dead man, lecturing him as if he were talking to a child who had done something silly. He stood back up, paused a little then started walking around again.

"These hotheads must have figured by now, wherever they're lying low, that they've screwed up. The Nigerians won't let them get away with this. Otherwise they'd lose face. The law of rival empires, Lambert: they rise, they last as long as they can, then one fine day they collapse. The barbarians are always at the gates. The bosses have to show they know what's going on. They have to make a spectacle of it. Another way to find our three barbarians—but we don't have the manpower—would be to have half the neighborhood put under surveillance. The really big men, the ones who supply second-rank retailers like our client here—take a look at the apartment, Lambert, he was a cut above a street dealer—there aren't all that many of them in the Goutte d'Or. But they have plenty of people working for them, way too many. Now then, young Lambert, if someone *really* wants to find these guys . . ."

Savane and Roman burst into the room, followed by a cloud of aggressive smoke.

Their suits were crumpled, they smelled of Chinese takeaway, their skin was greasy, their eyes red, and their blood heated by beer and amphetamines. Two raging beasts, their nerves on edge, fresh from a long surveillance stint, champing at the bit in their closed van, and ready to fall with ferocious cries on the first sucker they came across. Lambert hesitated over whether to retreat, or to move toward Guérin. So he stayed where he was, and felt the air displaced by the two men brush his face. Like bloodhounds, they pounced on the boss, who was staring at the ground.

Guérin remained without moving, and in his head, calmly completed his demonstration. *If anyone wants to find these three guys it means going via the Cousins, the Drugs Squad.* He added, still for his own ears only: *but these two won't do that. They'll just barge in, like the macho types they are, and they'll end up looking through the dustbins.*

"Still here, Guérin. Nothing else to fucking occupy you?"

Savane was confronting him, without even bothering to look at the corpse. Lambert admired the boss, a little man, just a few kilos, who stared out the attacker without blinking. If Guérin had had enough hair, Savane's breath would have made it flutter. Guérin, still lost in his own thoughts, was looking at his huge colleague as if he were a baffling puzzle that had to be assembled, a series of chaotic events leading to no fixed certainty. And what happened every time, happened again. To Lambert's ever-repeated surprise. Savane fell silent.

As if inside Savane's entirely muscle-bound head, a red light went on when the little lieutenant looked him in the face. An alarm bell and a short circuit that stopped him going even a millimeter farther.

Roman, an officer of very little brain, put in his two cents' worth: "So, what the fuck are you waiting for?"

Guérin slipped his notebook back in his raincoat pocket. Savane, a glimpse of sadness in his eyes, watched the notebook disappear. Guérin walked slowly around him, and out of the door. His assistant trotted behind him, hearing a volley of insults as he went. Before he was quite outside the flat, he heard Roman's hoarse voice saying, "Savane! Are you going to get your ass in gear or what?"

•

Boulevard Voltaire was deserted.

"Goodnight, what's left of it."

"Goodnight, boss, see you tomorrow."

Lambert waited in the car, like a father dropping off his child at school, until Guérin had gone inside the apartment building before driving off.

The inner courtyard, with its little squares of grass surrounded by ten-story buildings, was silent. No light in the windows to show any sign of life. It was the hour when the city took time off, just a brief half hour when nothing moves. Four in the morning. Guérin savored the calm, the suspended moment when even death took a break. Suicides at this time of night were exceptional. Suicides at four in the morning were mostly people without any previous history who were suddenly faced with some frightening revelation they hadn't anticipated and that allowed no delay.

The only faint light came from his room on the first floor. Behind the curtain, Guérin could sense the hunched shadow of old Churchill, dozing with his head toward the courtyard. Waiting for him.

He walked past his balcony without looking up.

Guérin clenched his head between his shoulders, anticipating the end of the silence. He had hardly stepped inside his flat, before Churchill's raucous voice accused him:

"You're late! You're late!"

The old strident, aggressive cry made him breathe in sharply. He emptied his pockets onto the hallstand, took off his raincoat, and hung it up. Once the ghostly robe was on the wall, all that was left of Guérin was a tiny silhouette with a potbelly, in a woolen sweater and corduroy pants. On his slight shoulders sat his disproportionate head, smooth-topped with the last vestiges of a thin fringe of dark hair, like seaweed on a pebble. The stone seemed no more than precariously balanced on his neck, ready to fall to the ground. To someone seeing him stripped of his soft shell, Guérin looked like a living cup-and-ball toy.

His large head drooped as Churchill started up again:

"You're late! Hundred francs for a blow job! Hundred francs for a blow job!"

Guérin swiveled around and turned on the bird with a fierce pointing finger:

"Oh, shut up!"

The ancient and bedraggled parrot, claws firmly clutching his perch, squinted at the finger and swung over backward.

"Assassin! Assassin!"

Guérin looked at the upside-down bird, passed his hand over his bald head, and went into the kitchen. He filled a glass with water and drank it in small sips. In a murmur, he went on talking to the furniture.

"It was a mistake. A dealer. Made to look like suicide."

In the living room, Churchill was still imitating his mother's voice: "Ha, ha! Assassin!"

Troubled, and drinking a second glass of water, he muttered "Dead right, Churchill, spot on."

He switched on the television and sank into an armchair. Churchill hopped off his perch. His claws clattered on the wooden floor, and he jumped up onto the armrest. Hanging off the sleeve of the sweater, and using his beak, the bird hauled himself up to Guérin's shoulder, where there was just room for him to cling on. The parrot rubbed his old beak against his master's bald head and cried out again in his mother's voice:

"You're late! Sweetie-pie! Sweetie-pie!"

Without conviction, Guérin told him again to be quiet. He channel-hopped, using the remote. When some Formula One cars appeared racing around a circuit, Churchill started up again, this time in a man's voice Guérin did not recognize:

"Morons! Morons!"

And ended with a screech of feminine laughter.

Guérin decided to stay with the racing cars and tried to think what the link could be between a Nigerian drug-dealer in the Goutte d'Or neighborhood and a Formula One racetrack.

The ancient bird, this time imitating his master's voice, stared at the screen and squawked: "Why-eee-eye? Why-eee-eye?"

From the courtyard came another voice.

"Can't you shut that bloody bird up?"

Almost 5:00 a.m. Paris was waking up.

The link was the illusion shared by junkies and the public watching a race. They all think life is a little circuit going around and around, but that if you keep on consuming vast and ever-increasing quantities of fuel, you can get right away from it. Guérin thought of Savane, of the drivers, of the galaxy of little dents in the wall of the flat, of the dealers and their clients, and concluded that this night had been organized around the idea of the wall, and of the speed at which one thought one was going to hit it.

On the screen, a car left the track, after colliding with another and somersaulted several times in a cloud of dust. Churchill, digging his claws into Guérin's shoulder, gave a burst of cynical laughter, again imitating the voice of the unknown man.

Other images now mingled with the race. His eyes half-closed, Lieutenant Guérin was seeing in among the cars, plastered with advertisements for cigarettes, DIY stores, and motor oil, a naked man running with his arms up in a frenetic race. And he knew, now without hesitation, that the man on the ring road was also an element in the Big Theory.

As he dropped off to sleep, his arms falling to the sides of the chair, Churchill, with his clipped beak, gently rubbed the top of this overfull head.

4

The van had started overheating somewhere around Limoges. John stopped at a roadside café to drink a beer and eat a soapy-tasting ham sandwich while he waited for the engine to cool down. He started off again as darkness fell, drove some way, then left the main road, looking for a field to park for the night.

He opened the back of the van and rolled up in a blanket, letting his legs hang down outside. It took a long time to drop off to sleep. During the journey, he had been going back over the story of his acquaintance with Alan Mustgrave.

Twelve years. Alan's absence, even though it seemed unreal, was revealing a presence whose weight he had not yet measured.

Lying in the van, he had reached the end of the story, the last time he had seen him. Two months earlier, in midwinter, in the tepee. As usual, Alan had turned up without notice.

The real surprise was that he had made it that far. Al hated the countryside, any countryside, because he had grown up in one of the deadliest patches of it: the endless plains of Kansas. That winter morning, John had been coming out of the wood, holding his toolbox, after failing to fix the turbine. His breath steamed in front of him and the undergrowth crackled with frost. In his other hand, he carried the propeller that had been damaged by ice: his wind turbine didn't react well to cold weather, and he was wondering whether the Australian guarantee would cover it now. From the edge of the wood, he could see someone standing in front of the tepee. He had stopped still, then hidden behind a tree to observe the intruder.

Leather jacket, hands in pockets, the man was stamping his feet to warm himself up, as he looked at the north slope of the valley.

Even before he saw the tattoos on the shaved skull, and the face streaked with tribal markings and pierced with rings, John had recognized Alan, who looked as out of place in this rural scene as a ukulele on an ice floe. As he approached, he heard his friend shouting insults at the trees, at the muddy paths that messed up your shoes, and at the sons of bitches who lived in the forest. Alan Mustgrave had just kicked a basin where John's underpants and socks were soaking.

"Shit!"

"Hi, Al."

The lines and piercings turned toward him with a nervous smile.

"Hi, big J. What the heck is this shithouse you're living in?"

Turning up, just like that, without warning. His French was a bit approximate, but to the point.

Alan had felt the urge to see him. He had taken the night train, then a taxi from Saint-Céré to Lentillac, asked the way at the Bar des Sports, and completed the journey on foot. Three kilometers. A feat that still amazed John. Alan hadn't had anything special to say, he had just been happy ribbing John about his encampment, joking about his own life in Paris. Alan was essentially laughing at himself, from embarrassment and modesty, perhaps, or as a sort of constant confession of powerlessness. Powerlessness to change. It didn't take long for John to realize that Alan was back on the habit. In midsentence, Alan had stopped speaking and looked down. As he watched his hands trembling, he had simply said:

"I'm sorry, man, I'm sorry."

Then he looked up again and smiled.

"I've met this girl, John, you'd really like her. She's called Paty, what she does is she strips off and runs at walls."

The subject of dope was dropped and Alan had dismissed it with his famous smile, the earthly reflection of the last element of his soul, once dazzling and as yet not entirely eaten up with suffering and heroin. The smile that was the only thing that stopped him from being thrown out of the bars he hung out in, from making too many enemies, and that helped him survive his image when he passed in front of a mirror. He had lost a few more pounds in weight, if that were possible.

Alan adored talking about his female conquests—the result of the fascination he inspired and that disarming smile. A ravaged homosexual, whom strange women fought over before being sent packing with another smile and some devastating remark.

"Hell's bells, John. What do you do in this hole when you wanna get your rocks off? Rub up against the trees, or think of me while you jerk off?"

The cruder Alan's talk, the nearer you got to what he was thinking about.

They had spoken a bit about the past and the present, studiously avoiding the future. Then Alan had fallen silent, locked up somewhere with his demons. Just the same old Al as in LA, when he had shown up at John's place. This time, too, he had just sat there, watching as John hung up his socks to dry, chopped wood, lit the fire, and prepared dinner. He had watched him shooting with the bow, and his only comment had been: "Want me to stand in front of the target, then you might hit it?" He had followed him around all day, cracking jokes now and then, shivering in his hoodie jacket, with his tattoos from the South Sea Islands. John knew that there was nothing to be said. He was the person Alan opened up to more than anyone else, so he knew when it was possible or desirable. All day long, he'd let Alan follow him around, pierced lips closed, unable to say what he had come all this way to say.

They had eaten some fish and rice by the light of an oil lamp, and Alan had cursed the fish bones. After the meal, which he had hardly touched, the LA junkie rolled himself up, fully dressed, in an Indian blanket, and turning his face to the canvas wall of the tent had said:

"It's good to see you, John. *Goodnight and good luck, man.*"

He had seemed on the point of adding something, leaning up on one elbow, then had dropped back without saying it. John had watched him shivering inside the blanket as the withdrawal symptoms started to kick in. Alan was going to ask him, for the nth time, to help him get off drugs. He wouldn't hesitate. Even if the sight of his friend vomiting, biting, and screaming was the last thing he wanted to see again. Even if Alan had already broken hundreds of promises and dropped John in the shit more times than he cared to remember.

Because nobody, before Alan Mustgrave, had ever entrusted their soul to him with such confidence and hope.

The first night at least would be calm, despite the sleeplessness. John had just been wondering how you would stop a fakir coming off drugs from escaping from a tepee.

But in the morning, the problem was solved. Alan had vanished.

On the copy of John's PhD thesis, beside the fire, Alan had scribbled in English under the title.

"I borrowed money from the café in the village to pay the taxi. I said you'd be in to pay them. I'll make it up to you. Thanks, old man, and don't think about me too much!"

On the paper there was still an echo of Alan's smile where he had signed it: *Your best friend, Big A.*

By checking his most recent memories, John had reached the end of the story. A story that would end with a disappearance, one more, in Alan Mustgrave's life. Or was it the opposite, the last time Alan was turning up without notice? He gritted his teeth, and blinked back his tears, before falling asleep in the van.

An hour later, waking up drenched in sweat, facing a wall of amnesia, he leaped out of the van, walked in the darkness to the center of the field, and drew his bow horizontally with all his strength, before loosing an arrow straight up in the air over his head.

Breathing out slowly, he waited, looking up.

He heard the arrow lose height, then more and more clearly, the gentle whistling of its fall to earth.

He felt a slight breath on his face. He judged the impact to be a few meters behind him. Then he smiled as he heard the metal tip—it must have been one of his hunting arrows—pierce the van's bodywork.

When he woke again at dawn and opened his eyes, he saw directly above his head the arrow's vertical tip pointing downward, through the Renault's roof. The red feathers on the black-painted arrow were like a kind of medieval pennant on top of the van as it took off again toward Paris. He smiled as he imagined the arrow embedded over his head, moving across a map of time indicating the present. You are here. He told himself, as he left for his last meeting with Alan, that destiny might be no more than an idea of ourselves that never ages. Just an idea, following us, going ahead of us and surviving after us.

•

John had a good memory for places, not so good for the itineraries that connected them, let alone for the one-way streets that separated them. So he drove haphazardly around Paris—with the heat gauge of the Renault on the point of exploding—until he found a boulevard that seemed familiar. He thought it must be the boulevard Saint-Germain, his hunch confirmed when he arrived unexpectedly on the place Saint-Sulpice. After driving three times around the block, he finally parked his heap of rust on a delivery space on the rue de Tournon. The holey exhaust gave a few sharp burps and the engine died with a throaty rattle. His head was swimming. He pressed his nose to the windscreen and watched the passers-by on the pavement. Two months earlier, he had been hiding behind a tree and surprising a visitor to his camp. The close proximity of the crowds and the buildings rising far into the sky above him oppressed his chest. He felt as if he were diving deep underwater into a foreign and densely peopled environment. Half an hour's drive through the city's crazy traffic had left his nerves jangling. Five kilometers! Back home, he would have had time to go into Lentillac, do the shopping, shoot a couple of fish, start them off grilling, and still have had time for five minutes' relaxation in his hammock. Feeling breathless and sick, he got out of the car, his mouth tasting of exhaust fumes, his back and head aching, and his legs as wobbly as skittles. He stretched, breathed in deeply, and almost retched on the polluted city air.

He thought of locking the doors, then remembered what the farmer who had sold him the van had said: "Son, I don't use the keys no more. Round here, anyone takes your car it's when you've had too much to drink, say the opening of the hunting season, and they're taking you back home." So John swung his things onto his back and walked away. He turned around after a few yards, worrying that he might never find the van again, then decided he didn't care. If he had to, he'd leave the city by train, or hitching, or on foot. The arrow was still planted in the roof like a bait, making him believe he was still under its tip.

After walking for a few minutes, his legs came back to him and he remembered growing up in San Francisco. These streets too were full of women, and he too was a townie. Though to judge by the reactions of the Parisians, that wasn't the way he looked. They parted as he approached, like the Red Sea before Moses.

Glancing at a shop window, John Nichols viewed his reflection, with a creeping new anxiety. Alongside a suit priced at four hundred euros, he saw a Marlboro cowboy crossed with an Indian on the warpath and a Canadian fur trapper, all three of them influenced by the Beat generation. The bow was protruding from the rolled Indian blanket on his back. Heavy boots, patched combat pants, check flannel shirt, blond stubble, and a fringed bandana around his head. He wondered when he had developed the face of a hungry beast. How long did it take, and to what extent, he wondered, did your personality change if you didn't bother about your appearance. He trudged on, not daring to look at any of the women. What had Alan said, as he watched him peg out his underclothes on the line: "Man, soon you'll be losing the power of speech."

At a *bar-tabac*, he bought a pack of filter-tipped Gitanes, a phone card, and a map of Paris to make up for the gaps in his knowledge. The tobacconist had looked alarmed at his appearance. Oddly, though, John's resurfacing American accent had seemed to reassure him. In the street, he forced himself to think in French, as if it would show on the outside.

At a phone booth, he called inquiries for the number and address of the U.S. embassy. A secretary told him that Frank Hirsh wouldn't be in the office before 4:00 p.m. John gave his name and the voice said that Hirsh would see him as soon as he got back. The only person he would have wanted to see in Paris was waiting for him in the morgue, and the only one who could take him there was away somewhere.

He began seriously hoping that the van would be able to start again.

Consulting his map, John set off along the streets toward the Seine. Having managed to keep all his painful thoughts at bay as long as possible, now he began to imagine how Alan had died. At once, the image came into mind of a skeletal body collapsing in the lavatories in some café, with a syringe in his arm. It pursued him at every step he took, and he walked faster and faster to try to leave its stench behind him. Sometimes he managed to change the setting. Alan dead, lying on a bed with the shadow of a smile on his lips; Alan passing out while completely high (this image was ridiculous) on top of some tall building at sunset. But every time, Alan had a needle planted in an infected scab on his arm. Whatever scenario he imagined, his own dirty shirt, drenched with sweat, seemed to stick of piss and vomited beer. He thought of the stream below his camp and of the cool water he would have liked to dive into.

There had been a day once, when John had found Alan on Venice Boulevard, sitting in his own shit between two dumpsters; the fakir from Kansas had told him that dope would never kill him, because he had died long ago from an overdose of corn. John forgot what he had said in reply, something stupid about the will to live. He could remember only that he hadn't believed what he said, and that day, he hadn't had the heart to believe in it. Maybe it was his fault that Alan had given up the fight. When he had come down to the tepee in the winter, John had just let him go. Perhaps he had been slow to react, but he didn't really think that now. He knew what was going to happen. He couldn't have done much about it, but that didn't change anything. He walked even faster.

On the place du Carrousel, by the Louvre, he splashed some of the greasy water from a fountain over his face. Hundreds of tourists were taking pictures of the Louvre pyramid. Africans on short-stay visas were selling mechanical birds, winding up their tiny springs and throwing them in the air. The toys flapped about for a while, then ran out of steam and crashed pitifully to the ground. The Africans smiled at the tourists between anxious glances to see if there were any police about. It was a fine day, and the sky was light gray without any dark clouds.

John cut across the Tuileries Garden and felt better once he was among vegetation. Spring was further on here than in the Lot, boosted by the artificial warmth and the carbon monoxide cloaking the city. He sat down for a moment on a metal chair. At the far end of the gardens, but immobile at that time of day, the giant Ferris wheel reared up above the trees. Women pushed buggies along the dusty paths, and a one-legged pigeon perched on the head of a Henry Moore statue, a long curved shape. The pigeon skidded on the bronze and flapped its wings furiously trying not to fall off.

In the arcades along the rue de Rivoli, the luxury shop windows succeeded one another like the links in DNA. He had to cross the rue Saint-Florentin and the rue Royale before he saw the embassy building with its huge stars and stripes flapping on the facade. On the place de la Concorde, the cars seemed to choose where they went, traveling in all directions.

At the door to the embassy, a marine with a Texan accent hesitated to let him in, even after he had shown his U.S. passport.

"I have an appointment with Frank Hirsh."

The marine pressed an intercom button and asked for confirmation. John looked up at the huge flag drooping over his head. Where was the spring that was holding it horizontal?

The soldier, having checked, gave him the nod but vetoed the backpack and directed him to a café farther down the avenue Gabriel where he could leave it. John trudged off, wondering whether it was the same for everyone, or whether his bow was the problem. On the window of the sandwich bar, a notice said in English, *"Luggage deposit, 2 euros an hour."* So perhaps the rule applied to everyone. Once inside, before he could open his mouth, a waiter in a maroon apron and cap pointed toward a door. John left his pack in the middle of piles of drinks crates and an assortment of other suitcases and backpacks. A nice little business that cost nothing and must have brought in a tidy amount of cash for the owner. When he came out of the room, the waiter gave him a date-stamped ticket.

The Texan marine looked askance at his clothes once more, then reacted a little more warmly to his fur trapper identity. No doubt sensing that John was a fellow hunter, the youngster was nostalgic for road trips in an SUV with his buddies, drinking Budweisers and blasting antelopes with M16s.

"The visitors' entrance, sir, in back and on your left."

Going through the porch, John reached the inner courtyard. A line of about thirty people waiting for visas. Men and women of every origin, dressed in their Sunday best. John, looking like a backwoodsman, walked past them all with his U.S. passport. He found the visitors' entrance at the left. The three GIs at the door made him empty his pockets and pass through the security archway. They put his keys and Swiss army knife in a plastic bag, asked if he had a cell, and gave him a numbered badge. While a young woman was checking his appointment once more against a list, Hirsh came toward him, holding out his hand. He showed no hesitation or surprise on seeing this Franco-American lumberjack.

"Thank you for coming so quickly, Mr. Nichols. Forgive me for keeping you waiting, but I wasn't sure when you'd get here."

Hirsh had not let go of his hand and hardly moved his lips when speaking, keeping his sympathetic smile intact. John's first impression, formed from their telephone conversation, was confirmed. This immaculate young man of a good family, thirty to thirty-two, international haircut, with a well-moisturized and mildly tanned complexion, was not just in love with French literature. He was a fellow traveler of Alan's, of a different type.

John managed to construct a smile he had not used before, one combining gratitude, seriousness, and fellow-feeling, though unsure of the result. Frank Hirsh blinked, trying to find an adequate reaction. In the end he simply said.

"I understand."

Well, if so, hell, he was the only one.

"We've got a car waiting, if you could follow me, Mr. Nichols."

They retraced the way he had come in, and John collected the keys and knife before passing out in front of the marine on the door.

A big black SUV with diplomatic corps plates was standing under the flag. A blond crew-cut driver, about John's height, was at the wheel. The other two got into the back and the car started.

As they passed the sandwich bar, John turned around. "Wait, my bag."

"Stop the car, please."

He came back out a minute later, as the driver waited with the trunk open. John loaded his scruffy backpack and archery materials, and the blond giant slammed down the tailgate: his neck was oddly short, almost as wide as his shoulders. Readjusting his uniform and smiling slightly, he was estimating John's weight with an expert eye. John got back in, intrigued by the bodyguard's aggressive stance.

"Where are we going?"

"The Medico-Legal Institute. The, er, Mr. Mustgrave's body is under the authority of the French police until we can repatriate it to the States."

"So what's all this about his parents?"

"Umm." Hirsh shifted his athletic shoulders under the well-cut suit. "It seems they either don't want to make the trip, or they can't. To be honest, it's not all that clear, and I haven't spoken to them directly. They've gone through all the legal formalities, using a law-yer in Kansas City, and they decided to ask you to carry out any-thing required this end. It's not exactly regular, because it seems you weren't informed they'd chosen to do this, umm, nor were you told about Mr. Mustgrave's death. Have you any idea why they did it this way, Mr. Nichols?"

"Well, for one thing, it was me that got Alan to come to Paris."

"Any reason why they wouldn't want to come themselves?"

Hirsh was more ill at ease than he should have been. John was irritated by his hesitations, his careful precautions, and the tinted win-dows of the smooth-running car.

"Alan didn't get on with his folks. For a long time now, I've been the one who sent news of him home. But that doesn't mean they actually like me."

Hirsh was looking fixedly straight ahead.

"What's going on?"

By raising his voice, John had been hoping to surprise him. The driver glanced eagerly into the rearview mirror, but Hirsh didn't rise to the bait.

"We'll soon be there, Mr. Nichols."

"How did he die?"

Hirsh half choked, turning it into a diplomatic fit of coughing.

"You know the kind of work Mr. Mustgrave did, don't you?"

"Yes."

"It was a dangerous way of earning a living, one where, how shall I put this, accidents could happen."

"Can you just give it me straight," John said in French, using the familiar *"tu."* Hirsh tugged at the knot in his tie and no doubt put the *tutoiement* down to Nichols's imperfect French.

"Mr. Mustgrave died during his act, Mr. Nichols. He died onstage."

John felt a wave of heat go through him, and the stench of death that had been following him since he set out for Paris started to alert his nostrils. He pressed a button to lower his window. The inside of the car was suddenly lighter, and beads of sweat were visible on Frank Hirsh's tanned temples.

The driver parked the car outside a dusty brick building near the Seine. The four-story box was squeezed between the riverbank and the overhead *métro*. The rails swooped down from a metal bridge across the river and vanished underground after a large curve encircling the Institute. The building looked sad and gloomy, even if you didn't know it was full of corpses.

The sudden proximity of Alan's body made John feel off-balance as he got out of the vehicle. He could have done with a shot of alcohol before going inside.

Hirsh walked in front of him to the entrance, visibly shrinking. It was almost as if John were going to have to support him, rather than the other way around.

"You've already been here?"

"Correct, Mr. Nichols."

He could hardly be fond of morgues, after all. It must be a part of the job that a degree from Harvard or Yale didn't prepare you for. Not that John had ever seen a whole lot of corpses at UCLA.

Behind a small counter, a man with the complexion of some underground mollusk raised his head from a newspaper.

"Can I help you?"

The white-coated employee opened a metal door, and slid out a gurney. Without pausing, he pulled back the sheet to uncover the head.

John shut his eyes, opened them again for half a second, shut them again, passed his hands over his face, then took a proper look.

How often had he imagined this body as a corpse when Alan was still alive? When he had taken him into the hospital, when he'd found him collapsed on his couch, in the last stages of overdosing and semi-comatose? How many times had he dragged him under a cold shower to make him vomit and come slowly back to life? The son of a bitch always allowed himself the luxury of a big smile when he returned to earth and found John leaning over him, beside himself with fear and anger. The smile that was the only thing between him and death.

John could stare as long as he liked now, his knees giving way under him, but he would never see that smile again. It seemed impossible. Alan didn't do dying, Alan always recovered at the last moment.

Alan used to shave his head every day. It was a ritual of death, John had written somewhere, a habit from his army days. Now his hair was a millimeter long, dark and obscene on the retracted skin of the skull. Like a parasitical plant living on the dead. The inertia of life. Absurdly, John thought of his car freewheeling with the engine cut to the end of the road.

Alan's earrings and piercings had all been removed, leaving only their holes in the flesh. In his hollow cheeks, larger holes were visible, into which he used to insert kebab skewers for his act; around them ran deep and dry wrinkles. The mauve eyelids were closed over his huge eyes, now disproportionately large in the face that had shrunk like that of a mummy. The gray lips were clenched over the teeth, the nostrils looked pinched, and the skin was crisscrossed with lines.

He looked like nothing so much as a shrunken head of the Jivaro Indians, a skull with bulging eyes and Maori tattoos, as dead as old graffiti on a ruin.

In John's mind, the image of a little gray dried-up rodent gathering dust behind an old sofa imposed itself over the face of the corpse. Then his sight became blurred, and his eyes felt too dry from trying not to blink.

Hirsh, after a quick glance at the body, had moved away to give Nichols time to compose himself. A uniformed policeman approached John sympathetically, holding a form in his outstretched arm. John nodded. The policeman put a checkmark in a box and handed him some papers. He signed the bottom of the page, and the official disappeared from the cold store.

The white coat wanted to cover Alan up again, but John stopped him. He pulled back the sheet and uncovered the rest of the body.

"Fucking hell!"

The stretched skin either side of the two slashes across the chest hung loose like the flabby breasts of an old woman. The ribs were exposed. Alan had lost weight yet again. A deep cut on his right forearm bisected the tattoo of a double crescent. It had not had time to form a scar. His whole body was covered with unhealed punctures, both from his act and from his needles, mostly on his arms and feet. The tattoos were just on his face and arms. Alan had only used ink on the visible parts of his body. His retracted penis and testicles were black.

John replaced the sheet and watched as the gurney slid back into the refrigerated compartment. Hirsh approached. Nichols was staring at the door of the locker as if he still needed to see, to be certain, and leave no room for any surrealist doubts. The embassy official put a hand on his shoulder.

"Are you okay?"

John moved his head slightly

"Where did it happen?"

"At the cabaret where Mr. Mustgrave was performing: sixth arrondissement, a place called Le Caveau de la Bolée, if I remember rightly."

John had no doubt whatever that Hirsh's recollection was perfectly accurate.

"Did you sleep with Alan?"

Hirsh withdrew his hand from John's shoulder as if he had been scalded. John turned toward him, but Hirsh was looking at the entrance. Standing by the door, under strip lights that flattened his boxer's face, leaving no shadows, the embassy driver was observing them. Hirsh left the room quickly, and his chaperone followed him out. John stood for a moment before going back to the locker. He touched the stainless steel handle with his fingertips, then walked out himself.

The light had changed, and despite the precocious spring, the late afternoon was quickly turning into evening. The driver was at the wheel. Hirsh stood alongside the open car door, his former aplomb in shreds. The young diplomat was clearly being watched; a shadow of scandal was probably hovering over his head. Alan, even when alive, was hardly the kind of person embassy staff should be hobnobbing with. Having died while suspended from hooks didn't help. John wondered how they could ever have met.

"Can we drop you off somewhere, Mr. Nichols? Do you need a hotel room?"

"When will Alan be sent back to the States?"

"It'll take a couple of days, no more. Would you like us to keep you informed?"

"I'll telephone. Just now I'm going to walk. I don't need a lift."

As they approached the back of the car, Hirsh pushed in front of John, opened the tailgate, and grabbed his bag before the driver, who was also moving quickly, could get there. The driver gave a kind of grunt, which Hirsh ignored, turning instead to look Nichols straight

in the eye, with a particular kind of smile: a mixture of thanks, sympathy, fear, and sadness. Plus a reply to John's unanswered question.

When he set out to seduce someone, Alan could be a monster.
This diplomat had been there, and was still smarting from it. John
replied to his pathetic grin with a short "Thanks." Then he directed
at the driver what he had been waiting for from the start: a ferocious
look that the giant repaid in kind.

John shook hands with Hirsh, the official's film star looks now
crestfallen, and watched the car with smoked windows slide away.
When it had disappeared into the traffic, he opened his hand to read
Hirsh's card.

5

The night porter had opened the service entrance at 8:30 p.m. About twenty staff, waiting and chatting outside, had stubbed out their cigarettes and filed in silently. After greeting the janitor as he went off duty, they had headed for the cloakrooms, where men and women separated. Once they had their uniforms on, they had taken up position. Cash tills, security, information, cafeteria, cleaning, and maintenance. By five to nine, everyone was ready and the lights had gone on. At nine, the glass doors had been unlocked and the first visitors had been admitted. They had each received a ticket with a photograph of a creature—monkey, frog, or bird—and passed through the revolving doors to the Great Gallery of the Natural History Museum, where they gasped as they looked up to the ceiling. Children began at once to shout and run about, with their parents chasing after them. By half past ten, about a hundred visitors were scattered throughout the different levels. By midday there were twice as many. By midafternoon, as well as its thousands of dead animals, the Great Gallery contained two hundred and forty-eight visitors, including three school parties. On the first floor, on a bridge, a group of seven-year-olds had stopped, with their teachers and two parents acting as helpers. As they looked at the skeleton of a whale suspended on cables, the teacher was asking if anyone had heard of *Moby-Dick*. A little girl, her finger pointing up in the air, had interrupted him.

"Please, sir! What's that man doing?"

The whole class looked up.

•

Lambert parked the car in the rue Geoffroy-Saint-Hilaire, opposite the mosque, and close to the entrance of the Jardin des Plantes, the site of the Natural History Museum, with the Great Gallery of Evolution at its center. He got out of the car and stretched. He was wearing a jacket in the colors of the French soccer team.

"Brilliant! I've always wanted to see the museum!"

Guérin was gazing skeptically at the obvious lump the Beretta 92 made under the tricolor jacket. Even Lambert was armed . . . He had always found it inappropriate that a man who found speaking quite a challenge should be carrying a weapon capable of firing off fifteen rounds in a few seconds. It was a totally absurd object, quite incompatible with the personality of his assistant. But the contradiction too was a logical link in a logical chain. Under Guérin's raincoat, nobody could see whether he was armed or not. He could have been carrying a heavy submachine gun.

Guérin took the time to look at the street, hesitating in front of the mosque, assailed by an unpleasant impression, as the scent of mint tea stirred his memory. The anxiety that had engulfed his Moroccan trip returned with a blow to his solar plexus. A luminous flash of vertigo made him wince.

Lambert, trotting along ahead of the boss, went in first, holding up his badge.

A policeman from the *quartier* showed him the way.

Impressed by the hall's huge dimensions and the exhibits on show, grandiose and morbid, Guérin felt his legs twitching with a mixture of unease and excitement.

Around the pool of blood a large crowd had gathered. Several men in suits—probably museum staff—four or five policemen, some paramedics, a perplexed-looking man—most likely a pathologist—and three firemen who were fixing ladders. Everyone was looking up, following the progress of two other firemen, who were rappelling down from the upper levels. Between the two men on ropes, and the pool of blood, floated the skeleton of a whale. In its thoracic cavity, impaled on a rib the thickness of a telegraph pole, was the naked body of a man whose blood was still dripping. Shrill excited voices echoed around the gallery.

A uniformed policeman greeted Guérin.

"They're going to try and get him down, lieutenant. But it's not going to be easy and the curator—that gentleman over there," he pointed to a suit, "keeps going on that we've got to mind out for the skeleton and not damage it."

"Any witnesses?"

"About thirty school kids, lieutenant, and three teachers, plus a dozen other visitors. They all saw him take his clothes off and jump from the balcony on the fifth level."

"Is that the racket I can hear?"

"They're in the café on the third floor; people are trying to calm them down. The cashier is asking for receipts for all the drinks and ice creams."

Lambert had joined the group standing under the skeleton, fascinated by the bloodstain. which functioned in the opposite way from the one in the office. Guérin had lost interest in the firemen and the technical problems. He left the scene and went up to the second floor, where he walked through a procession of giraffes, buffalo, gazelles, lions, and other animals that seemed to be fleeing from a forest fire. Stopping in the middle of the large platform, he breathed in the atmosphere. Amazed and on edge, he murmured to himself:

"Weirder and weirder."

With small, quick steps, he walked around the rim of the gallery looking for the best vantage point to view the whale. He passed a glass case of birds and winced as he noticed a couple of stuffed parrots, much older, but actually in better condition than Churchill. The idea that they could live in couples depressed him for a moment as he thought sadly of Churchill, a bitter fifty-year-old bachelor, alone on his perch. But the image was quickly swept away by the pregnant intuition that had taken hold of him as soon as he had entered the

Great Gallery. A final leap, in full view of the public and of dozens of extinct or endangered species! What a way to go!

As he was on his way up to the fourth level, he heard a shout: "Look out!" Then the thud of something soft hitting the ground, followed by a metallic clang, probably the ladder falling over. On the balcony of the fourth level, he found what he was looking for, the ideal vantage point. From here he could see all over the gallery, with a perfect view of the fifth-floor balcony, and down to the skeleton hanging below him. He went to the guardrail, looked searchingly at the wooden banister, then leaned over, taking care not to touch it: a pitiless sheer drop.

Under the whale, confusion was apparent. The rib had finally given way, to the audible despair of the curator, and the dead man had ended up reunited with his blood along with a piece of whalebone two meters long. The pathologist was standing with his arms crossed and his head bowed, while the firemen were at a loss.

Guérin ran back down toward the café. He went up to a policeman who seemed completely out of his depth, surrounded as he was by hysterical children who had started jabbering even more wildly on seeing the corpse fall to the floor.

"Lieutenant Guérin from Police HQ. I want you to cordon off the whole of the balcony from the fourth level up."

He pointed it out to the uniform, who was laden with sandwiches.

"Just close all this off, and I'll send you a lab team. I want the fingerprints from ten meters of the banister, either side of the column, see what I mean?"

He was still pointing his finger at the place. "Understand?"

"Yessir."

"Are there surveillance cameras here?"

"I don't know sir, we'll have to ask the museum security people."

"Get working on that balcony right away."

The policeman put down the sandwiches, radioed his colleagues, and hurried off, only too glad to get away from the schoolchildren.

The security guard, whom he ran to earth at the information desk holding animated discussions with the staff, told him that no, there weren't any cameras inside the museum, only at the entrance.

Ten minutes later, Guérin was coming out of the video room, a hard disk under his arm and in a high state of excitement. His big eyes darted here and there looking for a fixed point.

"Where's Lambert?"

The policeman the question was addressed to took a step backward.

"Who?"

"My deputy. Fair hair, soccer jacket, mouth hanging open."

"Oh, right, him. He went over there."

Guérin found Lambert in a corner of the ground floor admiring a badly lit creature: a small member of the whale family about three meters in length with a long, twisted horn sticking out of its forehead.

"Boss, did you know a thing like this existed? A . . . what's it say . . . ? Narwhal?"

"They won't exist much longer. Come on, Lambert, we've got work to do."

"It says here it's a tooth. But what use would it be?"

"That's why they're dying out: it's like you, Lambert. Get a move on, we're going."

Lambert hurried along behind the boss as they walked out.

In the car, driving with one hand and scratching his fair curls with the other, he went on.

"Yeah, but really, what use is that, a tooth in the middle of your forehead? Awesome, though! If I could choose, I'd spike myself on a narwhal tooth, not a sperm whale."

Guérin paid no attention to his deputy's ramblings. He was looking, as if it were the Holy Grail, at the little box full of ones and zeros sitting on his knees, as if he feared to lose a single drop of Christ's blood. He was ecstatic, on the point of shouting with joy, tapping his head as if sending a message in code.

"Don't you agree, boss?"

"What?"

"I said they'd do well to keep quiet about this, the museum people. Because a place like that, once it gets around, everyone will want to come there to do themselves in. What about the report, boss?

We didn't speak to the pathologist, we don't know the suicide's ID, nothing."

It was getting dark now, and Lambert was quite right. Suicides went in waves of fashion even if it meant breaking their own rules. Rebellion by suicide!

Guérin took out his notebook and started to scribble furiously.

Lambert failed to follow up his intuition, which was just a passing thought, and went on to something else.

"The brigadier-*chef* in the sixth arrondissement, remember him, Roger, he's called? The one who had to deal with the man who jumped in the river at New Year's? He was there just now. He remembered me, he said he got his death of cold after going in the water that time. And he said this guy, well a witness told him, anyway, this guy shouted something when he jumped."

Guérin was covering his notebook with signs Lambert could make neither head nor tail of, shorthand presumably, arrows, circles, little men, and death's heads. Lambert turned at the lights and said gently.

"Boss, are you okay?"

"What did you say?"

Guérin, hallucinating, was scratching the skin on his bald head until the blood started to run down his cheek.

"Nothing . . ." Lambert's voice died away. "Just that the guy shouted 'Thanks!' when he jumped."

"To the office, young Lambert. To the office."

"Boss, stop it."

Lambert had never been able to find any scientific words for what went on inside Guérin's head. When a crisis struck, he just put it to himself in his own way: the boss's brain was boiling over. He never mentioned this to anyone else, although he would have liked to understand, in order to feel reassured. But better not to let anyone else hear about his boss's funny turns. Of that he had no doubt at all. The only way he would settle down, as Lambert well knew, was to follow his own logic until the carriages got back on the track again. Hoping that the boss would find his way home. He speeded up. Their car had no siren, so he just lowered the sun visor, which had a black-and-white sign reading *"Police."*

He parked in front of the little side entrance to No. 36, praying that the encroaching night would be dark enough to cover their arrival. He glanced along the quai des Orfèvres in the dusk. Nobody. Guérin was already getting out of the car, clutching his hard disk. He had stopped mutilating himself but was still very hyper. Stifling a curse, Lambert reached into the glove compartment and grabbed a woolly bundle. Then he followed the boss, who was wandering about in the middle of the road. In his yellow raincoat, he reminded Lambert of that musical comedy with people dancing in the rain. Except that when Guérin went loco, he—Lambert—was the umbrella protecting him from the showers of shit. As further precaution, he jammed the crumpled wool cap advertising Berettas on Guérin's head.

"Where are we, Lambert? What are you doing?"

"Nothing, boss, nothing, er, let's go and look at the videos. We'll go up the side stairs."

Guérin brandished his hard disk and looked triumphantly at his assistant. A cup-and-ball toy with a spinning top perched on it, advertising a make of guns. The blood, by now soaking the last few strands of black hair that formed a wispy crown around his head, was reaching the corner of his mouth and trickling onto his neck.

"Right, young Lambert, let's get to work!"

Lambert took out the keys, unlocked the door, and they went past the row of stinking dustbins. Their entrance was through the garbage area outside the office kitchens. The heavy-handed humor of Police HQ. He put his arm on Guérin's to steer him up the steps. The little man was losing his surge of energy and starting to collapse, out of breath.

They reached the office safely without meeting anyone. Lambert breathed again as he closed the door. The ghostly glare from the strip lights drew a little cry of hope from the small room, which never saw daylight: after the first flash, it settled to its usual pale twilight.

Guérin pulled the woolly hat off and sat down at the desk. Still chasing his ghosts, he was shaking all over and his large, wounded head bobbed dangerously.

"Call Forensics, and tell them to send a team to the Natural History Museum. Fingerprints and anything else on the handrail of the fourth floor. I've had it cordoned off."

Lambert, filled with pity, watched as his boss tried, with clumsy gestures, to connect the hard disk to his computer. The light made him blink hard. Soon he would be seeing the dangerous moment once more.

"Boss, shouldn't you clean up a bit first?"

"What are you talking about?"

With his chin, Lambert gestured to his bald cranium. Guérin peered at him inquiringly, then felt it with his hand and contemplated his fingers, now smeared with blood. Slowly he looked up at his tall fair deputy. Deep in Guérin's eyes, two little men in yellow raincoats stood terrified and frantic, calling for his help to get them out of there.

A muscle twitched on Guérin's cheek and his gaze faltered. Lambert had the impression of hearing a windscreen splinter.

"It was . . . er, Churchill, he pecked me this morning . . . the old parrot . . ."

"Yeah, okay, boss, but still better clean it up."

Guérin wiped his bloodstained hand on his raincoat.

"I'm going to watch these videos . . . get me a paper towel, it's nothing, it's not serious, just a scratch."

Half his head was scored with bleeding grooves.

Guérin is completely nuts. As Lambert grabbed a paper roll from the coffee machine room, the sentence hammered over and over in his head. *Guérin is completely nuts.* When he opened the office door again, the room was empty. He went into the archive section, called out, then looked for the boss between the shelves. Gone. Back in the office he saw that the hard disk was still sitting there, but the cap had disappeared. He put out the light and went downstairs. Lambert searched his conscience, where he found an overwhelming desire to have a beer. Could a dog get his master certified?

6

John walked along the Seine, protected by the night, which gradually hid his tall silhouette against the background.

So Alan has sex with an embassy official. Then he dies during a stage act, hanging from butcher's hooks. The embassy official turns up in the morgue, because he has to see to the repatriation of the body of his lover. The embassy keeps a close eye on this deviant staff member, whose nerves are rather too fragile. That's all. But there seem to be too many things going on here. The persistent impression that everything had been rehearsed in advance, ever since the moment the gendarmes had turned up at the tepee, was giving him a migraine. Alan was free to sleep with whoever he liked, yeah, but to pick a man from the embassy was unlikely, stupid, and dangerous. Perhaps he had actually fallen in love? A sort of delicious swan song, like falling for a priest. Doing something stupid and dangerous was more likely, coming from Alan. But if he had learned one thing, it was not to die onstage. Piercing his skin made him happy. John had had to admit that in the end. But wait, he'd started doing drugs again. He must have gone onstage when he was stoned. End of story. OD onstage, hanging in the air. The fakir's apotheosis. Perhaps, after all, it was better than a backstreet, or a stinking latrine. The audience would certainly have a hangover from it. Would it have changed anything if John had been there? He had picked Alan up twenty times, but he couldn't be there around the clock. Pointless to speculate. End of, again. Should he wait for the ceremonial send-off of the coffin? That sort of farewell wasn't his thing. He should just get back home, away from this whole scene. John felt as if he were holding his breath all the time in Paris, and that he could really only start to grieve once he was back in his camp in the sticks.

But the headache wouldn't go away; there was something his brain couldn't let go of.

He lit a Gitane and started coughing at once. He hadn't smoked for months. The migraine got worse, the half-smoked cigarette ended up in the gutter. He stopped at a telephone booth, hesitating to take this feeling of unfinished business seriously, then called Information.

Was it the same girl on duty as that morning? He made up some improbable story on the spur of the moment. His loneliness was not about to be relieved yet. All he got was an address.

He crossed the river at the Pont de Sully and walked along the left bank, past the locked booksellers' kiosks. He went up the rue de la Harpe, declining the offers of waiters from the many restaurants. There were only a few tourists around, so they were competing for them. The photographs of Greek dishes, despite their horrible technicolor, made him feel hungry. At the St. Michel Fountain, the archangel, stabbing in the back a Satan who was forever in his death throes, conveyed a warning message to the handful of tourists wandering in front of it. John consulted his map. The Caveau club was very near, almost on his way. So he had time, before he left town, to do one last thing. To settle his mind.

He turned into the rue de l'Hirondelle, a quiet street. Only the French would name a narrow and dark street, where the sky was barely visible, after a bird, and a swallow moreover. The sign for the Caveau de la Bolée piled on the air of mystery: it was hardly lit at all, and painted in old-fashioned colors. The face of a diabolical magus, a sort of Uncle Sam with green skin, slanted over an upturned top hat from which a cone of light emerged. The association would not have escaped Alan, who was well acquainted with good ol' Uncle Sam. The club's name was written in creepy Gothic-Celtic script.

John knocked at the door, which had no handle, just a huge bronze knocker. A thin, dark man, unshaven and long haired, with a greasy apron around his waist, half-opened the ancient door.

"No show tonight," he said in French, then repeated it in English with a French accent you could cut with a knife and whistling through a gap in his teeth.

"No show tonigh-eet!"

The Left Bank equivalent of a gorgon, with a filter-tipped Gauloise between two yellowed fingers.

"I don't want to see a show, I'm a friend of Alan's."

"Ah." He looked at John, raised a black unkempt eyebrow, and opened the door wider. "Okay, you can come in."

There were only three customers inside. Two long-haired men were playing drafts, with beers at their sides, and a third, with bloodshot eyes and wearing a tailcoat, was shuffling a deck of cards. The furniture was varnished rustic wood, and it looked rather unconvincing as an underground scene. Not enough metal around. But there was a stage of sorts at the back, hidden by long black drapes. His eyes swept over them. Without realizing it, John held a hand to his heart. The room was arched, and the stone walls were blackened with time and the tar of millions of cigarettes. The walls were hung with old posters advertising magic shows.

"I'll get the boss."

The cook disappeared behind a curtain. To the left of it, a little opening, perhaps the remains of an old bread oven, acted as a tiny counter. A head poked out. The boss was a woman, but she met the requirements.

"Want something?"

"I'm a friend of Alan's. Voodoo Child?"

"Yeah, didn't think you were selling brushes. You do a number with the bow and arrow? But you can't shoot at yourself, can you?"

"No, I don't do any number, my name's John. I just wanted to come here to see what happened."

She hesitated, then came out from behind the stone counter. Her head came up to a point between his navel and his chest.

"It wasn't good for business, Alan dying like that. I don't really want to talk about it." She looked gloomily around the near-deserted room.

Short hair, about forty, round cheeks and smooth skin. Leather pants, reminding him of the blonde gendarme at the camp. She had almost as many piercings and tattoos as Alan, but there was more flesh on her arms. Under the fabric of her tank top, two studs prolonged the nipples of her ample breasts. Bait and hooks to fish for women.

John put his backpack on the tiled floor.

"Doesn't look like the places he usually worked. He must have thought this one a funny kind of dive, didn't he?"

The woman fingered a diamond in her nostril.

"Oh, he used to call it Long John Silver's Tavern. Before us, they used to put on magic shows, rabbits out of hats, all that stuff. And before that again, it was a Breton cider bar . . . that's what the name means. And before that, no idea. But I don't think anyone's had the cash to redecorate since the Bretons left. We only started six months ago, and I haven't got enough money yet to do it up. But we put on good shows, we're often sold out. There was always a full house for Alan."

The cook brought a plate of steak and chips out from behind the curtain and put it in front of the anemic conjuror.

"I wouldn't mind a steak like that."

"We only serve them bloody."

She no longer smiled at her well-worn joke.

"Only kidding. How do you want it?"

"Bloody will do."

"Chef. One rare steak."

"Coming up, boss."

She rolled her eyes to indicate that the décor wasn't the only thing that needed changing. Nodding toward the kitchen, she went on:

"He worked here with the Bretons or before, he doesn't remember. He comes with the furniture. But don't worry, he cooks steaks okay." She held out her hand. "So you're his pal who lives in the woods? Alan used to say you were a genius. What happened to you?"

●

"Alan had decided to stop, or at any rate he wasn't going to work for me any longer. I think he was talking of going back to the States."

John stopped chewing.

"Going back?"

"That's what he said. Anyway, that night was supposed to be his last show here. He decided to make it his farewell number. Shit, when I think of it, it gives me the creeps. Chef! Bring me a cognac."

"Coming up, boss."

"*Good-bye Mother Fakir*—that's what he called his last show, *Good-bye* . . ."

Ariel, the boss, sat opposite him as he ate. Short nails and plump hands, she was chain-smoking in her own club and didn't care who knew it.

"Nobody realized in time what was happening. When the audience reacted, some people in the front row got up onstage and tried to bring him down, but it was too late. He was rolled up inside his cape and at first you couldn't see any blood. But I have to say, because I was watching too, I think he had already lost a lot of blood before the hooks."

"Nobody saw anything?"

"Alan fooled us."

"He *what*?"

"He fooled us. He did his show so you couldn't see. He wiped his body down and he wore this cape. I found three of them afterward backstage, all soaked through."

Ariel drank half her glass of cognac; on her arm, a sexy mermaid folded in two, then straightened.

"But really, he did it so cunningly that nobody saw a thing. There wasn't a sound in the room, everyone was hypnotized. He had even stopped the music. It gives me goose bumps just to think of it. He got a girl to come up onstage, gave her a saw, and held out his arm. He was smiling so convincingly that she started to saw without taking her eyes off his face. She stopped just before she fainted. I've never seen the audience in such a state. At the end, when he hoisted himself up on ropes for the hook trick, he must already have lost half his blood, but nobody could see."

Ariel looked at John uneasily.

"Or perhaps nobody wanted to see."

She drained her glass, turning toward the stage, embarrassed by this last idea. Perhaps in the end, people who were fans of this kind of act, the ones who were going to pay for her to redecorate her club, were really waiting for something like this to happen. She had sold them Alan's death, and people hadn't complained. John, who was a specialist in how low humans could sink, followed her thoughts. But he had no wish to twist the knife, nor, to be honest, to console her. He pushed away his plate without finishing the meat.

"Was he already high when he went onstage?"

After a final hesitation, Ariel probably decided to trust him and lowered her voice.

"As a kite. But no different from usual."

The club owner had more to tell. John waited for her to go on. After pulling nervously on half her piercings, including the one in her tongue, she stretched her neck like a boxer.

"He knew what he was doing. That's what I think. He wanted to kill himself in front of everyone. He hung himself up there with the pulleys, he pulled up the ropes and he made a knot. They couldn't get him down. When I asked, the police told me it was a hemorrhage. But that would be too crazy, a fakir who was a hemophiliac."

John smiled. Alan had made a joke like that one day. The steak and chips stirred in his stomach. He swallowed and clenched his teeth as an acid liquid filled his mouth.

"Heroin might do it, if he was already weak."

"It wasn't that bad. He knew; he wasn't stupid. And then he didn't stop. *Bye-Bye, Mother Fakir.* He wanted to go. I won't believe any different, and that's not just to cover my back. Alan killed himself. If you want my opinion, I think he had taken something else beforehand to make the blood flow."

John put down his knife and fork. The idea that Alan had committed suicide was a tempting idea for everyone. And to some extent for him, too. Shit, he needed some sympathy and Ariel wasn't more to blame than anyone else. She had obviously liked Alan, you could tell; no reason to treat her as the enemy.

"I think so too. And I'll tell you something: it fits."

A short silence followed, punctuated only by the bleary-eyed magician, who waved as he left the club.

"Had you known him a long time?"

"Twelve years. We met in Los Angeles. We were both young. But he was already piercing himself with skewers and needles. It was three years after Iraq."

"Iraq?" Ariel let the question hang in the air a moment. The idea was hard to assimilate. "You mean Alan had been in the war?"

"Alan had been in *a* war. The First Gulf War."

She dropped back on her chair.

"Fuck, I can't really see him in camouflage, *yes sir, no sir,* all that shit." John gave a bitter smile.

"He went off there when he was nineteen. He wasn't so thin then, and he didn't have the tattoos."

Ariel tugged too hard at her eyebrow; a little metal ball rolled onto the table and a brittle steel stem remained in her fingers. She made a little grimace and started to put the pieces back together. Apart from the large tattooed arms and the eyebrows, she had the coquettish gestures of a woman adjusting her earring. It made John see her for the first time as a woman. His look made her smile, an amused warning. John laughed and Ariel shrugged.

"I didn't think he was that old. Some days he looked twenty-five, others nearly forty. Days when things were going badly, he was . . . unbearable, you know." She gave a little embarrassed grin.

"Alan could be a perfect bastard half the time. I won't argue with you about that."

"Alan as a savior of democracy. Well, he never said so."

"It didn't do him much good. Alan had already died a lot of deaths. The first time was out there in the desert. The last time was here."

Ariel turned toward the curtain masking the kitchen, chin in the air and arms outstretched.

"Chef! Two cognacs!"

She was making a big effort not to seem feminine, despite a bosom ample enough to feed a tribe.

"Coming up, boss."

Either the cook got the message or thought he was still talking to the previous, male boss.

John picked up his bag and started feeling in his pocket.

"No worries, the food's on me."

"Thanks. Just one more thing. In the audience that night, was there a guy who looked well heeled, thirtyish, blond, smart suit, and edgy. A guy who already knew Alan. I guess you wouldn't have many people looking like him here."

"More than you might think. That night, there were about fifteen people from the smart set in, men and women. Alan had this reputation, you know. They were the first to head for the door when the panic started."

"Okay."

"But not your blond guy. He was in the front row and he was the first up on the stage to try and get Alan down. He vanished when the police got here."

John smiled. So Alan *had* found himself a lover to be witness to his final farewell. Someone who was his opposite. Now he had succeeded in placing Hirsh: a representative of the U.S. government weeping tears of love.

"There was a girl, too, a friend of his, an artist, called Paty?"

"Now you're asking too much. There were lots of people in—the place was full to bursting."

"Okay."

John gave her a hug and she let him.

"You're like your pal; you act like a couple of gay Boy Scouts."

"*Thank you.* I needed to know all this."

As he closed the door, she called out:

"Johnny! Take a shower next time you get close up and personal with a girl!"

He lit another Gitane, and this time he savored the taste of tobacco. The headache had gone. Alan Mustgrave killed himself. Finally. He had chosen his own way to go: well, it was better than collapsing in the gents. It offered him a path to follow for grieving.

There remained only one thing to think about once he got back to his tepee. How did he feel about being the only person not to be invited? Perhaps Alan wouldn't have dared do it in his presence? He wondered how many times he had stopped his fakir friend from killing himself, and whether in the end that had been any use.

Two hooded silhouettes emerged from the corner of the rue Saint-André des Arts and the rue de l'Hirondelle.

"Got a light, bro?"

The "bro" sounded all wrong, and not just because of the accent.

The first blow caught him on the temple like a sledgehammer. The second made him vomit up the steak he had bravely kept down at the Caveau, and he sank to his knees. A kick sent him sprawling on all fours, then two knees in his back forced him face down on the tarmac.

"Your pal, the fakir. He owes us five thousand. And he's not here now, so you get to pay, Davy Crockett. You were his backup, he said. We know your name. Nichols. You've got twenty-four hours. Five thou. Tomorrow, same place, by the fountain. Where you looked at the map. You don't turn up, we'll get you. You're *dead*. Understand?"

A high-sided trainer kicked him in the ribs and he heard the two men run off. Spitting blood, John laughed and cried with his remaining breath:

"Aren't you ever gonna die, motherfucker?"

●

After wondering for a moment if he should return to the Caveau, he dragged himself, limping, toward Saint-Sulpice. It was hard to have a clear idea of the damage. His temple throbbed, and he could feel a lump there, but the pain was passing. It was Ariel's steak that hurt the most. The guy had hit him in the stomach, but the liver and spleen seemed to be untouched. He might have a couple of cracked ribs, which he'd know about when he woke up next day. If he managed to sleep in the van. He couldn't get back on the road in this state.

Once on his feet, his first thought had been: I can take down the tent in an hour, and they'll never find me. Then he had felt a surge of anger, after the adrenalin and fear. Fucking drugs. He had met some of Alan's dealers before, and sometimes paid his bills, but it was the first time he had been beaten up. The headache had come back, to the power of a thousand.

The nearer he got to Saint-Sulpice, the better his brain started to work. What kind of idiot would ever believe the word of an Alan Mustgrave, a man who lied through his teeth from dawn to dusk, when he said his backup was some hippy who lived in the sticks in the southwest of France? Who in the world, once they took a look at him, would think he could ever lay hands on that much money? And who, for such a relatively small sum, would make such forceful death threats? This wasn't Colombia, for God's sake. Human life was a little more valuable in Paris, surely?

In the rue de Tournon, he leaned on the wall by the delivery space. Apart from idiots, who else? The answer, as he looked at where his van had been parked, made him laugh once more. Someone, on the contrary, who wanted him out of there as soon as possible.

Well, destiny had taken a hand,

Arrow and van, the whole shebang had gone.

"*Fuck.*"

John skirted around the Luxembourg Palace on the pavement opposite the gardens, in the shadows of the Senate colonnade. He passed the official meter measure in the wall on the rue Vaugirard, and felt pleased that human beings had agreed about one thing at any rate: the distance separating them. Whether you used meters or feet and inches, a kick in the teeth was the degree zero of intimacy, at least people could agree about that.

He limped across the street, then followed the Luxembourg Gardens railings. Between two streetlamps, he waited for a car to go past, glanced around to see that no one was in sight, and gripped the bars. He managed to haul himself over the metal spikes at the top, tearing his combat pants, and let himself down the other side, stifling a groan of pain. As quickly as he could, he made for the cover of the first trees and hid behind a trunk. Nothing moved. He went deeper into the park.

His eyes grew accustomed to the orange twilight, that absence of total darkness common to all big cities. From the fountains, wisps of mist rose into the air. It was a cold night: winter had not quite loosened its grip.

He passed a fast-food kiosk made of varnished wood, its shutters closed, and moved on, then collapsed under what he thought must be a plane tree. Leaning his pack against its trunk, he lay down, trying to get his breath back. Once his heart had stopped pounding and he had grown used to the sounds of the park at night, he unfolded his blanket and rolled up in it. Someone had just given him a warning to get out of town. It didn't seem like bad advice. Train, hitchhiking or even on foot, John would simply wait for daylight to get going.

As long as he didn't move, his ribs were painless enough to let him doze off. The presence of the trees reminded him that the essentials were somewhere else, far from here. His last thoughts, before slipping into the sleep of a guilty sentry, were about Alan Mustgrave. In fact, Alan's debts were small beer compared to what was owed him. His last debtor, John Nichols, unfrocked PhD in behavioral psychology, was wiping the slate clean once and for all. The logical end for a friendship with a hemophiliac fakir.

He didn't know how long he had been sleeping when he woke up with a start, as the beam of a flashlight flashed in his eyes. It was still dark at any rate. The voice was low, and came to him hazily as his ears began to function.

"You ain't got no right to be here. You listening? Get lost."

John felt something cold and damp on his cheek and someone's breath on his face. He tried to get up, but the pain in his stomach paralyzed him. The light twirled around then disappeared.

7

Guérin, arriving early at the quai des Orfèvres, went in at the main entrance and walked through the building. He was wearing a tartan cap and a dark overcoat. Nobody in the early-morning office paid him any attention. He surprised himself by looking at his feet, usually hidden by the long raincoat, as if they belonged to a stranger.

He pushed open the door to the archive room and went in.

Lowering his head and imagining he had blinkers, he went through the rows of shelves, stopping only at the last, at the very back of the room. He picked up the box file, carried it as fast as he could down the old staircase, and, when he reached the bottom, lifted the lid of a big dustbin. Sweating heavily, Guérin felt the weight of the files for a moment in his arms.

Forty-eight suicides. Forty-eight suspect pieces of his delirium. Collected over two years, according to criteria established only by himself. That was the problem.

The oldest ones went back to 2004: they had been unearthed in the archives, by searching day and night for unexpected connections. Before 2004, his criteria had not matched any case; the thread was invisible, even if it had been woven earlier and had been in preparation for some time. Since 2006 and Kowalski, particular cases had emerged out of his everyday work, like the man on the ring road the week before.

Forty-eight files. But the thread connecting them was just an idea in his sick brain. It was his own psyche and nothing else that he'd been studying and researching in the archives. 2004, the year when, for the first time, he had looked in the mirror and failed to recognize himself. The year he had started to lose his footing. *It runs in the family, sweetie, better watch out.* The year his mother, from her hospital bed, had given him the warning. 2004. Death of his mother and the birth of the Big Theory.

He had to cut the thread, even if it was an umbilical cord or an artery. The Big Theory only existed inside his head. Guérin had been up all night convincing himself of that. His final doubts fell into the dustbin with the box. If he didn't do this now, then one day, and soon perhaps, he would find it impossible to return from the world of ideas, and the thread would wind itself tightly around his neck. The box hit the bottom of the empty dustbin. Going back upstairs, he began to feel almost at home in the new coat.

The office door was open and now all he had to do was apologize to Lambert.

He stopped dead.

Savane was sitting on the chair, hollow eyed, with dark rings marking his face like bruises. A smell of sweat and alcohol invaded the room.

The big policeman rose to his feet, though he could hardly stand, and moved toward Guérin, pushing aside a table as he came. He looked as if he had come out of a rubbish dump after looking for his keys all night. In his enormous hand, with its swollen and grazed joints, he was holding some crumpled sheets of paper. Guérin tried to look him in the eye.

The mastodon was at his wits' end, finished, defeated.

Savane stopped at the lights, a pace away from Guérin when their eyes finally locked. He held out the papers. Guérin took them without lowering his eyes and asked what they were, in the gentle didactic tone he used for Lambert. Savane dropped his gaze, more dead than alive.

"The preliminary autopsies."

His voice was broken, and he was rubbing the joints of his right hand with his left.

"Last night, I demolished these three guys from the Goutte d'Or. One of them probably won't make it. Barnier's suspended me, the committee will send me straight to the disciplinary panel, and this time they won't let me get away with it. It's the end, I'm finished, they won't even send me to Suicides."

"What about Roman?"

Savane grimaced in disgust; then his shoulders drooped with fatigue.

"He's saved his skin."

Guérin was about to rub his head, but his hand met the cap and stopped, uncertainly.

"You found the kids on the run, then?"

Savane looked at his swollen hands, as if he were amazed to find them empty.

"Two of them, in a cellar in the rue Blanche. The Drugs Squad are pulling out all the stops to find the other one. The gang bosses got in twelve hours ahead of us. But I don't regret it, at least those three gang leaders didn't get away with it. But the one in intensive care, if he doesn't pull through . . ."

Savane's lips trembled. His jacket was filthy and stained with dried blood.

"Fuck it, Guérin, I don't want to go in front of the panel with the press and all the rest of it. Nine years, for God's sake, nine years I've been eating shit."

He raised his head.

"*You'd* have got to them first; you could have done it. What the hell have you done, Guérin? Why did you have to mess everything up? Roman and me, we just went charging in like idiots, made a complete mess of it."

Savane wanted to shout, but he choked on his words. Saliva filled his mouth and he struggled to speak.

"Shit, if you'd been there, we'd have found them like in the old days. What happened, what did you do, what the *fuck* did you do, Guérin? You're not crazy, but what game are you playing, for fuck's sake?"

If Guérin had put his hand on Savane's shoulder, a hundred kilos of policeman would have fallen into his arms and started to cry like a raw recruit in the arms of a psychiatrist. All that was left of Lieutenant Savane was an empty husk of a man. Guérin would have been glad to do him that service, to open the door that generations of his colleagues had learned to keep shut. But Savane didn't move and Guérin himself was paralyzed, stuck somewhere two years earlier, standing outside a house in flames. Guérin tried to believe that Savane was telling the truth: he had spent the previous night trying to convince himself that he wasn't going mad.

They stared at each other, two lovers terrified on a day of conflagration.

Alerted by the shouting, Lambert burst into the room, with a sporting newspaper under his arm. Savane, surprised in a state of total collapse, swallowed his anxiety and charged head down, sending Lambert flying against the wall and throwing him a friendly, "Get lost, Forrest Gump!" before escaping down the corridor.

Guérin had taken off his cap and was rubbing at the dressings on his head, gradually tearing them away.

Lambert brushed down his tracksuit and wondered if the whole of the quai des Orfèvres was falling apart, or whether, on the contrary, things were settling down. He sat down at his desk, keeping a wary eye on the boss. Guérin looked odd, even allowing for everything else and the dressings. He looked at the dark overcoat in puzzlement: the absence of the yellow raincoat was simply inconceivable. He laid down the newspaper, but decided to wait before turning to the soccer reports. After a few paces around the room, the boss had sat down and started to read the crumpled papers. Things looked as if they had returned to normal. Guérin had made Savane go away, the telephone would soon be ringing, he would have to tear another page off the desk calendar. Lambert relaxed on his chair.

"Know what? I met Chassin this morning. He's in Homicides. The oldest guy in No. 36, never promoted, holds the record. Remember him? Retiring soon. Anyway, he was telling me about Padovani, the detective who disappeared. About the time you got to Suicides . . . well, here. Big fat guy, worked in Vice Squad. Chassin was saying they've stopped searching for him now, after two years. Officially missing, presumed dead. Did you know him? Still. Thirty years on the force, and nobody knew anything about him. They only started to talk about him when he went missing. Well, they were talking."

Lambert cleared his throat.

"What did Savane want? Chassin told me he's been suspended; it's serious. Want my opinion, no great loss. Well, let's say I wouldn't lose any sleep over it."

Lambert looked up at the ceiling and observed the stain. It had shrunk a little since the last rainfall. Nose in the air and neck out-stretched, he went on: "Lots of news today, eh, boss? Boss?"

Lambert still looking up into the pink circles, heard Guérin move a little and took it as a sign he was listening.

"I called the lab when I got in last night. I got Ménard, know him? The guy who worked on the double suicide at Bastille in the summer, husband and wife? I had a drink with him. Not that he's a bundle of laughs, I tell you. So, Ménard called me back late at night. He's a workaholic, that guy, he's sick. Anyway, he said he had twenty-three different sets of prints, just from half the railing, and he'll be back on the job this morning. Ask me, he's already back there, sniffing the dust, no wonder he's always got a cold. He'll bring all the results over here."

Lambert looked down, timidly but proudly. After half a dozen beers last night he had taken a decision: instead of calling a doctor he'd called Ménard in Forensics. The boss was still deep in the paper.

"I thought you might be interested."

Guérin wasn't listening. His fingers shook as he held the prelimi-nary autopsy reports.

Savane was totally finished. It would be the last case he ever worked on. Even if he managed to escape from the administration—which was doubtful—he wouldn't be back. A sad end to his career. Pigheaded as ever, he was probably sitting at his desk that very minute writing his last report, completely drunk, before chucking his chair out of the window and leaving, cursing everyone. A bad exit.

The Nigerians had decided to make an example of the killers. Two examples. Eyes, tongues and genitals cut out, limbs slashed and crushed, probably with large hammers. One of them was dead on arrival at the emergency room; the other one's heart was still beating when they loaded him into the ambulance. A fantastic day's work.

Eighteen and twenty years old. Two kids from Gennevilliers, petty criminals, small-time dealers. The third would turn up at a police station any minute and stretch out his own hands for the handcuffs. Unless he was already on his way to Spain or on the ferry to Algeria. The accuracy of the scenario he had imagined frightened him. These autopsies obliged him to have confidence in his judgment once more.

Guérin felt a moment's concern for Savane, wondering just how far Roman, his big buddy, would be pushing his pal in deeper in order to get out himself; then the impression that something was hanging in the office atmosphere brought him out of his thought.

"What did you say, young Lambert?"

The telephone began to ring with an arrogant sense of timing. Guérin let it ring a few times. For the first time in two years, he didn't want to pick it up.

Slowly and deliberately, he put the receiver to his ear. He listened with an intense expression, then stood up. Lambert pointed like a gun dog.

"Boss, your coat."

At the foot of the staircase, while Lambert was describing Ménard's phone call a second time, he saw the boss lift the lid of a dustbin. He thought the boss looked pretty smart in the new overcoat, even when he was half swallowed up inside a dustbin. Guérin brought out a large box file without any label and tucked it under his arm.

When Lambert heard the boss muttering that he wasn't mad, he rubbed his hands and savored the cool morning air.

Guérin put the box on the backseat. A smell of rotting vegetables filled the car and escaped through the window, which Lambert opened, whistling his favorite tune.

"Where to, boss?"

"Well, young Lambert, it wasn't clear. But I'd say between avenue Churchill and the esplanade of the Invalides."

"Off we go then." Lambert thought for a moment and frowned.

"But, boss, between the avenue Churchill and the Invalides it's the Seine."

"Precisely."

Lambert shrugged and moved off into the traffic, pulling down the sun visor.

Guérin got out his cell and punched in a number. Voice mail.

"Savane, look here, kid, if you need to talk, give me a call."

His assistant did a spectacular U-turn, saluted by a chorus of hooting.

Between the Invalides and the avenue Churchill there was a bridge: the Pont Alexandre III.

They arrived via the Right Bank, pushing through the chaotic traffic. The bridge was sealed off, and at each end drivers had been transformed into a furious audience.

Sometimes they didn't know whether it was a joke being played on them by their colleagues, or a mistake by the switchboard, but they were sent to a suicide that hadn't quite ended. Someone vomiting in an ambulance, a clerk locked inside a toilet at work, having cut his veins, a drunk in his living room with a gun in his mouth, shouting at his wife. At any rate, the two psychiatrists attached to the police were overstretched and rarely got there in time. They might just as well have sent anyone, for a joke or by mistake. The most frequent cases were people jumping out of high windows. Looking down gave you more time to think than a bullet, and was more frightening than pills. It was a surprising paradox: would-be suicides, who suddenly realized they were scared of heights.

The two policemen plunged into the crowd, waving their badges over their heads.

The firemen, who were probably also victims of misinformation, or of some bad joke, were standing around looking stupid with an inflatable mattress. The man hadn't jumped yet, true, but when he did it would be into the water.

Alone, in the middle of the widest bridge in Paris, a man was clinging on to the column of a gilded lamppost. He looked grotesque, ashamed and terrified, and no one in the crowd around him seemed to be taking his wish to die seriously. A burst of laughter might be enough to make him jump.

They made their way toward the center of the police cordon, a group of about ten men: uniformed city police, lacking any sort of coordination. The information had certainly been misleading. Guérin approached a portly constable.

"Have they contacted the River Brigade?"

"They're sending a crew, and they also have to stop the boat traffic. But it seems they're still dealing with an accident at Joinville. It'll take them half an hour to get here."

"The psychiatric service?"

"I think they're trying to get hold of them. But it's chaos over there; we were called for a road accident and the firemen were told it was someone jumping from a window."

Lambert added calmly, "And we were told to come pick up a corpse."

Guérin ignored the policeman's laughter.

"Has he said anything?"

A puzzled look: "Just that he wants to jump."

"Who's the senior officer here?"

The man pointed to a young man in uniform in the middle of the light-blue tunics. He looked less cheerful than the others and, unlike everyone else, did not seem to be waiting eagerly for the guy to jump. Auburn-haired with a mustache and a square jaw, he gave an impression of wrestling with a tide of entropic stupidity.

"I'm from HQ. Lieutenant Guérin. I'll take over, if you don't object."

The young officer nodded, relieved to have found someone who was keeping calm.

"You'll have to get all these people to move back. Can you do that?"

Guérin was watching the man on the bridge all the time as he spoke.

"Yeah, we'll manage, I've radioed for a traffic patrol to come back us up. But this lot is going to make it even more difficult."

The officer frowned as he saw the first TV vans start to arrive. He had a voice like a foghorn, booming from his flat muscular stomach.

"If the River Brigade is late, try the firemen. They have divers, too, and they might be able to act quickly. If need be, requisition a pleasure boat and pump up the mattress on it."

The young man raised his eyebrows before he realized that Lieutenant Guérin was serious.

"Yes, sir."

"What's your name?"

"Gittard, Brigadier-Major, eighth arrondissement."

The 8th was well-known for its *savoir-vivre*—probably because it was in an elegant district, and had a splendid set of offices in a wing of the Grand Palais. The officer looked at Guérin as if he had suddenly made a connection between a face and an idea, and added in a confidential tone:

"The Kowalski affair, that was you, wasn't it? Not everybody went for the official version, lieutenant. I worked with Kowalski once, good at his job, but my God, what a pervert. He was completely insane. And I'm not the only one who thinks that."

Completely insane. Guérin had a sudden internal vertigo, a rush of different thoughts, and felt a surge of warmth shoot though his body, making the scratches on his head itch under his cap. He gave a grateful smile to the policeman, embarrassed by this show of solidarity. The last thing he wanted was to become the pretext for clan warfare. But Gittard was sincere, so he was not about to reject a little support.

"Thanks. But let's get on with this business."

Lambert, hands on hips, was looking doubtfully at the candidate for the high jump. The man hadn't let go of the column and kept turning his head one way then the other, toward the crowd and toward the choppy waters of the Seine. He was on the downstream side of the parapet, and still clinging to the lamppost, which was being lit up by a ray of sunshine.

"Lambert, go and help Brigadier-Major Gittard and his men to keep the crowd back. And take care of the journalists first. Hey, kid, wake up."

Lambert shook himself and approached. He shook Gittard by the hand, gave a big smile and unzipped his jacket (Brazil national colors today). The Beretta, in its ill-fitting holster, looked enormous on his narrow chest.

"I'm Lambert, I'm the junior at Suicides."

Gittard looked anxious, then smiled as if out of bravado at something unaccustomed. Guérin had turned toward the bridge with its sole occupant.

"I'm going to talk to him. Try and keep the others calm, Gittard. Who's at the other end?"

"Leduc, he's my colleague, a safe pair of hands."

Gittard was indeed a clansman.

"Well, tell him the same thing. And contact the River Brigade, tell them or anyone else who comes up by boat not to make themselves too conspicuous."

"Are you really going to talk to him?"

"Is there any other solution? As long as he doesn't get too stressed, he shouldn't jump."

Guérin looked at his watch.

"At this time of day nobody jumps into the Seine. If a boat starts approaching, make a sign like this"—Guérin made a wavy motion with his hand. "And wait till I give a signal before you make any move." He tapped his cap. "Just a few men in plain clothes. Even better if you've got a woman you can use. The gentle approach. Get it, Gittard? Thanks."

Guérin had dictated his orders in the tones of one making his will. Gittard had taken it all in, though he looked puzzled at the reference to the time of day.

Guérin went forward on to the bridge, between the newly regilded Pegasus statues on the Right Bank, representing Commerce and

Industry. With his dark overcoat and tartan cap, he looked like a character out of a Le Carré novel, about to cross over from one side to the other, betraying himself and carrying the secrets that would bring about his downfall. His small, dark silhouette, with its drooping shoulders, attracted the attention of the crowd.

As he walked on, the silence spread. The sounds of the city fell away, the rumble of voices stopped, and the sound of the rushing current under his feet sounded louder. Now he could see the other two Pegasus statues, Arts and Sciences. Framing the Invalides esplanade like a set of gates.

The man had seen him approach and was fidgeting nervously. He swayed away from the edge, then back to the balustrade, but kept hold of the lamppost. Finally, he let go with one arm and pointed it at the little man in the woolen cap.

"Stop! Stay where you are! Stop!"

He was beside himself with loneliness, but refusing to admit it. Guérin, standing twenty meters away, had to call out loudly to be heard.

"I just want to talk to you. I promise not to touch you."

Guérin looked toward the Right Bank. The security cordon had moved back a dozen meters, further accentuating the impression of solitude on the bridge. Gittard had not yet made the sign like a fish in water.

"This is the thing, I've got a parrot called Churchill, like the avenue over there. Churchill hates all human beings."

Guérin could make out the man's features now. About forty, about one meter eighty, short thick hair, graying a little at the temples. He was dressed like a cell phone salesman, in casual business clothes. He had something perhaps of an Armenian about him, or a Kabyle: of mixed race perhaps? His arm was still stretched out toward Guérin, and his lips were moving silently, searching for an impossible reply. Guérin moved about ten paces closer. The man was pale and trembling with fear. He had freckles and Guérin decided he was probably a Kabyle.

"He's about your age. And a bachelor. He used to belong to my mother, and I grew up with him. He was the man of the house. Well, the only one who was there all the time. Churchill was her favorite politician, because after the war he said the time of great men had passed and now it was the age of dwarfs. My mother was a prostitute, and she agreed with him. Churchill was a kind of guard dog. He's not really dangerous, but he has a lot of character. I was too small. Do you know what my parrot thinks? He's never said so, but it's obvious: he thinks the only species on earth you could wipe out without creating problems is the human race. If earthworms became extinct, life would disappear from the face of the earth. But without us, everything would be better. What do *you* think?"

The man stuttered, blinking.

"Why, why you talking about a bird? I'm in trouble, monsieur. I'm going to chuck myself in the water. Can't you see? I'm in trouble!"

He was becoming hysterical, but still clutching the column with all his might.

"It's not any old bird, it's a macaw. A big parrot. From Mexico. In the old days, before we had antibiotics, parrots used to live longer than humans. He thinks the same as you just now, that's why I'm talking about him."

"How do you know what I'm thinking! I don't know you! You don't know anything about me!"

"Shh. I know everything. No need to shout."

The man remained openmouthed. Guérin moved to within five meters, sure now that he wouldn't jump.

"Stop there!"

Unless he had a sudden reflex, that was . . . The man had suddenly let go of the column and flung himself against the balustrade. Guérin wondered, curiously, whether death might be a reflex.

But the man's knees were buckling. He bent almost in half, twining his arms around the steel guardrail.

"Talk to me, then . . . What do you know?"

Guérin put his hands in his pockets and started speaking slowly, using the manner of a lawyer talking to a family about the last will and testament of the deceased.

"For starters, I know that this bridge is named after Alexander III of Russia, and it was inaugurated in May 1900 for the World's Fair.

The president was there, Loubet his name was, and plenty of ministers. The Third Republic liked this kind of big show. The bridge is a good example of the kind of over-the-top ugly stuff they built then. I wouldn't have picked this one, in case you're interested. It was designed at the same time as the Grand and Petit Palais, but they're much better buildings. Do you know what these three monuments have in common?"

Guérin stopped. "What's your name, by the way?"

"Alex. Alex Monkachi. What are you on about? Oh God, what are you talking about? I'm not well; I'm going to be sick. What am I up here for? Why are you telling me all this?"

"My name's Guérin, Richard Guérin. I work at Police HQ, and for two years now, I've been handling all the suicides in Paris. Before that I was in murder and homicide."

At the word "suicide," Monkachi had given a start before collapsing even further.

"Well, I'll tell you. What these three monuments have in common is that they're built on alluvial soil. In other words, it's unstable soil; it's moving all the time and wants to get back into the bed of the Seine. So all three of them are sinking into the ground. They have to be propped up continually: it's a gigantic task. The bridge is the easiest to deal with. But they had to strengthen the banks when they built it, because it pressed down much too hard on them. See the four statues of horses up there? They're part of the weight needed to hold it down; they're utilitarian, although at the same time they're a bit over the top. The bridge is trying to push the banks apart—rather an interesting reversal of symbols, don't you think? And the Grand Palais, now, they've been pouring concrete into the foundations ever since World War II, millions of cubic meters of concrete. They're trying to keep it up in the air, but it keeps trying to sink in deeper. It's permanently on the move. It's a problem for a lot of these buildings near the river. Can't you hear them, day after day, gradually sinking? I think it's in the early morning, at dawn, that you can hear it best. They get older overnight. We keep doing them up; we want them to keep looking young and beautiful. So what do you think, Alex, because you're looking for an answer, too, aren't you? Don't you think all that's a bit artificial?"

Guérin was now about three meters away from Monkachi. He calmly sat down on the pavement and breathed out, feeling tired. At the same time, he shot a glance across at Gittard. The policeman was making a sign of a fish swimming in water.

"Suicide, Alex, is a very delicate moment. It's a difficult truth to swallow for the people left behind, even if they don't know you. Because it makes them doubt their own foundations. They can feel the ground shifting under their feet. It's an important move, Alex, because of what it reveals. The hypocrisy of people who just accept it as your personal fate, instead of asking questions about the building they live in with you, that's not worth dying for."

Alex Monkachi slipped to the ground, his mouth, now dribbling saliva, against the paintwork.

"Who the hell are you? Who are you? You're supposed to be cheering me up, telling me a lot of stupid stuff, making me feel better."

"Can't do that, Alex, sorry. Do you know what the connection is between you, my parrot Churchill, and the Grand Palais?"

The unhappy candidate fluffed his answer. Guérin could hear a few muffled words. *Work. My life. Need someone to listen to me.*

"Give in? I'll tell you. Probably nothing at all. Except the kind you might make up. You're all of you alone, perched on some high rail, or on some shifting sands. And all of them, the parrot, the steel girders of that building, and a man, in spite of a few different features, I grant you that, are incapable of expressing what they think about their state. And so they let themselves die, because they think they're less significant than an earthworm. I'm your friend, Alex, please believe that, I mean it. Stay with us."

Guérin took off his cap and waved it at the police cordon. He turned his back on Monkachi, who stared at the dressings on the policeman's head. "Tell me, Alex, have you recently met people who seemed full of good intentions, on the surface at least, and who might have persuaded you to kill yourself? People who, now you come to think of it, seemed to be friendly toward you, but really they just wanted you to die? Insidious friendships, you might say."

Guérin looked at the banks, scrutinizing the crowd at either end of the bridge. From the avenue Churchill, a group of three people, one of them a woman, was moving discreetly toward the parapet. Lambert was with them.

"Tell me, Alex. Think back for me. Did you meet anyone who encouraged you to come here today?"

Alex wiped his nose with his fingers. He had let go of the balustrade and was leaning his back against it now.

"Every day, just about. Everyone, just about. Is it true the city's sinking into the ground?"

"I reckon so, Alex. I'm glad to have met you before you died."

"You're crazy!"

"That's fair comment."

●

Lambert dropped him off at his flat. The boss, now exhausted, had retrieved his box file and stood on the pavement with the car door open.

"Lambert, my boy, I'm sorry about yesterday. It won't happen again. Thanks for your help . . . and for calling Ménard. Have a rest this afternoon. They'll find someone else if they have to."

He was about to shut the door when Lambert leaned across.

"Boss, don't thank me, I mean, I'm just doing like normal. Boss? About . . ."

"Savane used to be my second-in-command. He worked with me until . . ."

". . . Kowalski!" Lambert was swift to add: "Boss, you did a really good job out there today." He blushed. "Boss, I won't let you down."

This was too much for both of them. Lambert straightened up inside the car, and Guérin slammed the door shut. He watched the car disappear, thinking again of Monkachi, of the nurse who had smiled at him, and how in the end he had been able to throw up into the gutter.

He put the box down in the hall and was greeted by Churchill in the voice of his mother.

"Late back *agaaaain*! Late back *agaaaain*!"

"It's only one o'clock, Churchill, I'm early today."

The parrot raised its feathers into a red crest and adopted a new voice.

"Just a quickie, my angel. A quickie!"

Twenty years on a perch overlooking a bed as busy as a railway station.

"You're being rude? *Maman* didn't like you to be rude."

Mention of his former mistress threw the bird into a frenzy. It spat out a string of insults, interspersed by tongue clicks and squawks. Guérin smiled briefly, enjoying the old bird's rage.

He opened the washing machine, took out the yellow raincoat, and put it on a hanger. The bloodstains had gone. Crossing the room, he hung it from a clothesline on the balcony. The raincoat, like a yellow quarantine flag, began to sway gently in the breeze. Churchill had stopped squawking and was hiding his head under his wing. Guérin shut the French window and pulled the box file to the middle of the room.

Churchill jumped down from the perch and, walking carefully crabwise, came to peer over the files, pecking at the edges of the box. Guérin put the tape in the machine and sat down on an armchair. The parrot went around in circles, making a scratching sound on the parquet floor, in a ritual submission. He went around the room three times.

"So just stop being rude and making such a din. I'm tired."

The parrot moved toward the armchair.

Once on his master's shoulder, he started pecking the dressings, while saying quietly, "*Come* on, sweetie," in the warm voice his mistress had used when encouraging a less than virile client. Churchill could mimic the intonations perfectly, though Guérin didn't suppose he had any idea what it was about. Still. The only thing the parrot had not inherited from anyone else was its anger.

Guérin had always needed, somewhere in his life, a man who could get angry.

He pressed "Play."

As soon as the naked young man started running between the cars, Churchill began to laugh.

When John P. Nichols had woken the first time, he had felt only pain as shadows danced before his eyes. Muffled sounds, smells, and a roof over his head. He had closed his eyes and gone back to sleep. The second time, he concentrated and saw a woman looming over him. A peroxide blonde, like a Dutch advertisement for peanut butter. She was brandishing an orange chainsaw in a plastic forest: her little breasts were naked and perky, and she was wearing tiny denim shorts. She was holding the machine as if it were a precious object, charged with horsepower, her lips were parted, and she was flashing her come-and-get-me eyes. Before he lapsed back into sleep, John stammered his apologies to this woman who was impatiently waiting for a brawny lumberjack to get the saw started for her with his big hands. He apologized for not feeling up for it and slipped away into the plastic forest, with the feeling that the pain was subsiding.

Once the chainsaw had started spitting out sparks, and the blonde had slipped out of her shorts, while John used his teeth on a ring piercing her navel, a hooded man appeared and started licking his face. He woke up, and found a dog's black snout up against his nose.

A barrel-chested voice filled the air.

"Down, boy!"

The dog, panting, rested its head on John's chest.

A Husqvarna power tools calendar from the 1980s was pinned to the wall in front of him. On the page for April, the blonde, as faded as her photograph, had her shorts back on again. The surroundings briefly swam before his eyes; then he felt he had come down to earth again. Under the calendar, leaning up against an unlit wood-burning stove, were his backpack and his bow. He was on a low camp bed in a wooden cabin. From his lying position, he could see a shelf with a few books, a dark cap hanging on a hook, some rough plank flooring, and two legs of a metal table. Between the metal legs appeared the bottoms of a pair of pants ending in two heavy leather boots.

"Here, boy!"

The dog, a mongrel with graying fur, wriggled to the foot of the bed.

The voice made the air in the cabin move and John felt it vibrate through his ribs. He raised himself on one elbow. His neck was stiff and his head heavy. His first immediate thought was "how clean it is here." The hut was immaculate. He tried to turn on his side, but his stomach wouldn't let him.

"Ah! Shit."

The boots moved on the floor. His second, more developed, thought was to his impression of the face of the man who was leaning over him. He was the spitting image of Edward Bunker.

"Where the fuck am I?"

"You speak French? Yes or no? Where do you come from?"

"The USA."

"Can you get up?"

He really was Bunker: green eyes, hair not quite so white, but the resemblance went further than his features. It was the face of a wild beast who had worn his teeth down on the bars of a cage.

"Am I in prison?"

Bunker raised his eyebrows, stopping a smile.

"You catch on quick, beat up or not."

"I'm a psychologist."

"A psychologist! Shit, Mesrine, get a load of that."

The black dog sprang up.

"Down, boy!"

On Bunker's hand, a cross tattooed with ink surrounded with little lines, no doubt symbolizing the divine light of window in a prison high-security wing. Maybe he didn't look all that much like the famous ex-con and crime writer from Los Angeles after all, but he was from the same stable. John was sure of it.

The dog poked its head through Bunker's legs and looked at him as if it were meeting a shrink for the first time.

"Yanks come in bigger sizes of everything, eh? Shrinks don't look like you round here. Not so bloody stupid either."

"It's not a prison . . . ?"

"Way off. Public garden."

"But you *were* in prison, right?"

The grizzled bear tensed. The dog shrank back at the same time, fur ruffled, looking fiercer than at first.

"Now tell me, what the fuck you were doin' in my park?"

John groped for an honest answer.

"Someone stole my car. And I got beat up because of somebody else. And I like trees."

The dog relaxed its ears and sat down. On the keeper's face, which had all the expression of a breeze block, loneliness was fighting a battle with distrust. John managed to twist himself to a sitting position on the bed, clutching his belly.

"I live in a hut, too. Were you in for long?"

The old keeper put his hand behind his back and pulled out a small weighted club. It just fitted in his hand, dark, polished, and in theory unthreatening, as harmless as the dog. John followed it with his eyes, one hand on the back of his neck. It landed on the table. Crash.

"Long enough to know a dropout when I see one. You been in the shit long?"

He was still trying to give an honest answer, because Bunker clearly had a nose for the truth. A talent that years in jail must beat into you. But the big American couldn't speak and just looked at him without saying a word.

"Yeah, I can see it wasn't yesterday."

John stood up slowly. The cabin was only about three meters by five, and between them they almost filled it. He didn't find it hard to look unthreatening, but Bunker was still in a defensive position, legs apart. The old convict had the hard-boiled grin of a cock of the walk. His park keeper's costume fitted him about as well as a theory would a wardrobe.

The American bent down to look at the dog.

"What does 'Mesrine' mean? Sounds like a chemical or protein or something."

Bunker's thin lips parted and he ended up smiling. Between his incisors was a gap, oddly like a little boy's. But the smile made him even more dangerous. An uncontrollable libertarian madness. The smile and the eyes were fueled by some kind of nuclear reactor, which he must have been carrying around since his childhood. Logically enough, it had taken him to prison.

"Bloody hell, don't they teach you anything at shrink school? Mesrine's not a chemical! He was an enemy of the system! And how come you sometimes talk with an American accent, but not all the time?"

Bunker's confidence in strangers was not that well developed.

"My mother's French."

Bunker looked serious and consulted an old clock with a scarred glass face.

"Ten a.m., kid. Let's have a quick shot of red."

The idea of a glass of red wine made John's stomach rise in revolt.

"Yeah, sure."

The cabin was an improved garden shed, furnished by the joint efforts of the Red Cross and the ex-convict. A cell, clean and tidy. Three books, the unlit stove, a shelf for clothes, a naked bulb swinging from the ceiling, two chairs, a table, the camp bed, and a mat for Mesrine. In one corner stood a small wooden chest, repainted God knew how many times, a hot plate, and three bowls. The light entered through two windows with small panes, and behind one of them in a plastic pot some red geraniums were swaying in the wind. If it had had four wheels it would have been a gypsy caravan; made of canvas it would

be a tepee; of corrugated iron, a shack in a shantytown, except that
the floor wasn't beaten earth. While Bunker was feeling around in
his kitchen corner, John went over to his pack and checked that the
bow was still in one piece. The confused memory of the latest events
dragged a grimace out of him. At least he was on his feet, and although
he didn't have much experience of being beaten up, it didn't feel as
if anything serious was broken. He scrutinized more carefully the
photograph for April 1983 on the wall. A blonde pinup, something
between *Playboy* and Pierre et Gilles, a madonna for prison cells, faded
but forever young, like a memory. He lifted the page and glanced at
May. A weed trimmer this time. And more generous breasts. Twelve
women for Bunker. John smiled at the thought of these girls, dreaming of an artistic career by posing nude and then ending up as fantasies
for long-term prisoners. It was charity work. You had to give them
that. Bunker put two Duralex glasses on the table, with an unlabeled
liter of wine.

"Right then, Miss April, better put some clothes on, we got
company."

Bunker didn't smile at his own joke. His absence of humor was
profound. His soul was worn to a thread. When he wanted to laugh,
Bunker probably had to hide in a cellar. Perhaps he even hammered
his own fingers. Or maybe he was smiling inside. Like John and the
fur trapper in the shop window, his prison identity had taken him
over. You couldn't see what lay underneath, unless you could penetrate the gap in his teeth. Which he took care to show as little as
possible.

The first mouthful of wine practically took the skin off John's throat.

"This is the better stuff. Watch out, after this it's just the cheap
stuff."

No irony, but the serious tones of someone who has experienced
the rationing of essentials. Bunker smacked his lips, savoring the acid
richness of freedom, then looked John straight in the eyes. Apparently it was for the first time, since John had not noticed before the
scar running from his forehead across half his right cheek, taking in

the eyelid. A thin white line that slightly distorted the wrinkles on his face.

"Kid, in prison, you can wait five years before a buddy tells you anything personal. What's good about life outside, you can make up time, instead of wasting it. Don't get me wrong, you don't have to tell me your life story, but thing is, I'd like to know how this American shrink ends up at my place, in a state like that. 'Cause maybe you didn't notice, but you fell down just behind my shack. Even Mesrine heard you."

Violence, fear, sincerity, and solitude were all strangely combined in the pale green of his eyes. That gaze reminded John of Alan's: more cunning, but perhaps a bit less wild. Using AJJA 17, extra-strong tobacco, the old man was rolling a cigarette between his huge fingers. Precious gestures. John lit a Gitane and put the packet on the table.

"I came to Paris because this friend of mine died. He owed money to some dealers. They want me to pay his bills for him. So they beat me up."

Bunker tipped the glass up and drained it, then looked at John again with his weary eyes.

"Your turn."

"What?"

"You get a question now."

The wine was doing him good, even if it burned. He thought for a few seconds and rubbed his bruised temple.

"Was 1983 when you came out of prison for the last time?"

"No, last time I went *in*. Came out in '91. Since then I've stuck to my promise. Calendar's the only thing I kept. When I see it, it reminds me what I kept telling myself for eight years. Next time, stay out."

Mesrine rubbed his haunch against his master's. Bunker patted his head. The enemy of the system accepted some masculine caresses. John took another swig and the tissues of his trachea seemed to adjust a bit better. The green eyes narrowed, hooded by the wrinkled eyelids.

"That bow, that's gonna be for some kind of vengeance, is it, for your friend?"

Vengeance? For Alan? The idea made him smile, sending a stab of pain through his jaw.

"Vengeance isn't really the right word. He did it himself. He committed suicide."

Bunker refilled the glasses, and before drinking rubbed the cross on the back of his hand. He drank the wine off in one long gulp and banged the glass on the table.

"Next question, I know what's coming. No, I never killed nobody. Maybe I came close once or twice. Armed robbery, that's what I went down for. Always worked alone, except two or three times. That was a bad idea, too. Two years, five years, eight years—fifteen years inside."

He rubbed his hand again.

"First time, I nearly died of being lonely. Last time, the joint was heaving, lot of trouble."

His big fingers touched the scar.

"This place now, courtesy of city hall, charity for an ex-con. Don't get any more pay than if I was sewing mailbags, but at least I get a bit of peace."

Bunker dropped his head and looked down into the glass. John guessed the older man was about twice his age, sixty-five or so, but still sturdy with it. The toughest thing about Bunker was the way he spoke: every word like a nail being hammered into a plank. His words were backed up by reality, they had the solidity of objects.

"So, kid, this friend who killed himself, who was he?"

The question was transparent: tell me who your friends are, I'll tell you who you are. But you couldn't do better than Alan as far as Bunker was concerned: the kind of friend you get beaten up for is as good as a reference. John sat up and drank some more. He felt he needed to nail down reality with words as well, nails in Alan's coffin.

"My name's John." He held out his hand and Bunker shook it in his square paw. The old man did not give his own name but accepted a formal introduction.

"It's a long story."

"Plenty of wine here, son."

John took another swig of rotgut.

"I met Alan about thirteen years ago, in '95. I was twenty, he was twenty-three. I lived in Los Angeles, Venice Beach, and I'd left my mother in San Francisco. I'd started college, but I didn't want to live on campus. I found a room near the shore. In the evenings, I used to go along the boardwalk by the sea, drink a beer, eat something, watch the world go by. Venice Beach, you see a side of America on show that's not always nice, but it's always interesting. Always something going on. Music, street theater, girls rollerblading in bikinis, families, preachers pushing supermarket trolleys, veterans, old folk, shops, artists, fortune tellers. One evening, I was on a terrace eating a sandwich and looking out at the ocean. On the other side of the Walk, this guy spread out a blanket and took off his T-shirt. He started with fire eating; then he put needles in his arms and legs. When too many people had stopped to watch, I got up. This fakir looked sad, but he smiled all the time, so people didn't notice. I don't know if it was because I'm tall, or because I was looking fascinated, but he hauled me out of the audience and gave me this empty Jim Beam bottle and told me to break it on his head. Just a gag, he was doing the show, pretending to be in rehab. He was trying to stop drinking, so this was therapy. Everyone was laughing. I just stood still. I couldn't do it. The people started laughing more than ever. Alan looked at me, and I was the sad one. Then he insulted everyone, and went on doing that till they all left."

John stopped. Overcome by his memories, he had forgotten Bunker and the cabin. But the keeper was still patiently listening, as if he expected the shrink's story would last hours. Without changing expression, Bunker said.

"Have to start on the ordinary stuff now."

Another bottle appeared; the glasses were refilled.

"After that, he took me to a bar, saying I'd really made him laugh, standing there with the bottle in my hand. But in fact he seemed depressed. It was then that I realized the most important thing about Alan. It was only when he was joking that he told the truth. His trick with the bottle was funny. He really was an alcoholic. When I hadn't been able to hit him, for reasons I later realized, he was possibly on the point of killing himself right there, in front of all those people.

"He used to come almost every evening after that, to do his street act in Venice. Sometimes we went for a drink. I paid. After listening to all his jokes and nonsense, I understood that with his system of reverse truths, he was on heroin. It took longer before he started making cracks about gays. And I picked up on that, too. Well, for another couple of years that's how it was, we'd see each other now and then. He would sometimes vanish for a bit, then come back with a new tattoo and a new act, more violent. I finished my first degree and wanted to specialize in behavioral psychology. I began a master's. I was doing this research on post-traumatic disorders associated with war, because we've got a lot of those back home, and people don't want to talk about them. We built the country on them, and organized it around them, but they don't exist. Alan had been gone a few months. One day he came knocking at my door. He was having withdrawal symptoms, but he wanted to stop. He stayed with me, and he was clean for a few weeks. One evening I was reading through my notes, and he said with a laugh that I could do some research on him. He said he'd been in Iraq in the First Gulf War. A homosexual fakir who's seen combat— there weren't a lot of those. But if they were anywhere, Venice Beach was the most likely spot. Perhaps I'd already suspected that, and I was already making choices because I'd met him. I don't know. But his story became a part of my life. Before it became my work.

"You can really only understand Alan's life if you go back to the beginning. He grew up gay, on a farm in Kansas, with parents who were Methodists. They went to church every day, and all day Sundays! All the rest was a logical consequence of that, and of his personality. Alan was 90 percent rage. The day after he told me he'd been in Iraq, he vanished again. With my TV, my stereo, and my records. He came back of course, not long after. He'd started to use my place as a refuge. He never propositioned me, and he never brought any partners home. That was an unwritten rule he seemed to have decided on. And that went on for another two years. He would come, he would steal from me, he'd feel better, he'd go off again and come back in a worse state. There were always problems when he was around: steal-ing, dealers, fights in bars, tantrums. I was carrying on with my life, and he kept bringing chaos into it. Every time it got a bit worse. He had gangrene under his skin. I was working on plenty of other cases like his, but he was a friend; I wasn't his shrink. Then in '99, I began my PhD, still on the same subject. I know now it was because of him that I wanted to go on with the research. Anyway, about that time he asked me straight out; did I want to know what he had been doing in Iraq. I finished my thesis in 2006, and in the end the subject wasn't what I had expected it to be.

"After 'homosexual,' the second word that explains Alan's story is 'torture.' It was a long business, very long, because the subject was him, and it was a kind of therapy. We were both beginners, and he kept disappearing without a word, for weeks or months. We stayed friends, but it was difficult. So two years ago, when I'd finished the research, he was at the end of his tether. He'd been through the worst. When I wanted to submit my thesis, it got hard for both of us. Amer-ica wouldn't leave him alone; it was killing him as much as the drugs were. I said, 'Look, you should go away, go abroad.' And I thought Paris might be a good idea. He listened to me and he went. A year later, I couldn't stay at home either, and I came to France, too. My mother had bought this bit of land in the Lot in the 1970s before she went to San Francisco. And she still owned it. That's where I live now. Alan Mustgrave died four days ago, during his last show, in the rue de l'Hirondelle. In front of an audience."

The bottle of *vin ordinaire* was empty, When he had finished speak-ing, John was almost paralytic. The old gangster's eyelids were heavy, and he was looking strained.

"So what you going to do about your friend's debts, then?"

John leaned forward a little.

"Don't know . . . I thought maybe the best thing is to go back home."

John looked around at the cabin that reminded him of his tepee.

"Where I live, Bunker, it's . . ."

"Bunker, who are you calling Bunker?"

"Edward Bunker: He's this guy back in the States, he was in and out of prison a lot. And one day he came out with a book; he'd written, a novel, and after that he stayed out of jail. He's dead now, but he died outside."

Bunker accepted this introduction of his double without flinching, except for a slight twitch of his eyelids.

"So, I was saying, where I live, it's no bigger than this, only the walls are canvas. I don't like the city anymore. Walls scare me."

Bunker shook out the bottle to catch the last drop.

"Yeah, well, keep clear of them, kid."

Mesrine was dozing at their feet. John was persuading himself that he should get out of Paris. But the clarity that alcohol can bring before it knocks you out was troubled by the sense of unfinished business. The warning he had received was anything but an answer, and he still had questions.

"Bunk, is there anywhere I can get a shower?"

"Yeah, son, behind this cabin there's a little shed. And let's hope a bit of cold water'll open your eyes for you. 'Cause you look to me like someone that's going to do something stupid."

John got up, and flexed his muscles to try and regain his balance.

"All I want is to understand. That's all."

Bunker blinked slowly again.

"Stupid bloody shrink."

The cold water and a shave did him good but failed to clear his eyes. Bunker had put on his park warden's cap and had Mesrine on a leash.

"I can't stop you, son, but I think you're headed for trouble. Christ Almighty, I don't know if it's because it's your job, but I haven't had anyone talk to me that long for ages. Your story of meeting your pal, that reminds me of another one, just tonight. I don't believe in luck, I believe you get what you ask for. If you've fallen in with an old geezer like me, it was to give you a message. This guy who stabs himself and all, you've done as much as anyone could for him, you should save your own skin now. Joke intended, because the truth is going to cost you. So now, it's up to you."

"I'll watch out. But I've got debts, too, Alan wasn't the only one."
John held out his hand again.

"So what's your name really?"

"Just call me Bunker, that's fine. In Paris, this is your home. Your stuff's safe here."

He gave John a key, explaining which gate to use after eight at night. Mesrine barked as John walked off and Bunker was left standing in front of the pot of geraniums, feeling certain he'd got his arm caught in a very bad machine. As he looked up at the sky, he pronounced with the air of a final judgment:

"Mesrine, something's going to hit us."

Around him, a green wire fence half a meter high marked out his little territory in the middle of the Luxembourg Gardens, a little plot among the trees, at the end of a lawn. And a white notice: *"Closed to the public."*

9

Boulevard Voltaire, Métro Saint-Ambroise. Delivery vans unloading clothes made in China, triple-parked, hazard lights blinking, Asian warehousemen going to and fro, cigarettes in mouths. Guérin was standing on the pavement, holding a box under his arm, like everyone else.

The boss got into the car without a greeting. The reappearance of the yellow raincoat worried Lambert. The cap was still in place, but not sufficiently firmly to reassure him. The boss was looking like a conspirator again, and Lambert could see from his fidgeting hands that he wanted to scratch his head.

"Where are we going?"

"*Périphérique*, Porte Maillot."

"The kamikaze?"

Guérin nodded, with a bob of the hat. The box of files, now once more on the backseat, gave off a smell that did not augur well.

"Don't worry, I know what I'm doing."

His perplexed deputy started the car, still preoccupied by the subject that had been worrying him all night. Savane. He couldn't understand how anyone could call Savane "kid." Something wrong there, something that got you in the gut. He was still formulating a question as they reached the place de la République, when Guérin started to answer him. It was always amazing to Lambert to discover that he was so transparent.

"The thing is, Barnier thought Savane was promising. But he was too unpredictable and violent. The Service needs a few pit bulls, but it's got to keep them under control. He'd been blocked for three years, still only a brigadier-major. Never made it to lieutenant. He wasn't put in for the competition, and his promotion would upset too many people. Barnier told me that and asked me to try and make something of him. He wanted a dog handler for Savane, and I tried to turn him into a bloodhound. He got promotion a year later. A good lad, but easily led. For better or for worse, Savane was thick with Kowalski and those other two, Berlion and Roman. The Fatal Four, Tough Guys, Inc. After Kowalski's death, he took against me. But he knows what he owes me, and that I still believe in him, in spite of everything. That's what makes him so aggressive. He couldn't take sides, so he just fell in with the rat pack. And the rat pack is eating him alive."

Guérin paused and turned to his junior. "Lambert, kid, watch out for the future. I don't want the same to happen to you."

Lambert stopped at a traffic light, dazed by this information rattled out at him machine-gun style. The lights changed without his noticing. From the whirlwind of words, something emerged, like a sprig of parsley on top of mashed potato. The boss thought he was capable of something! Trainee officer suddenly sounded in his ears as if it might actually lead to something else.

"Lambert . . . Green light."

He pulled away, feeling on top of the world.

"Boss, why are we going back there?"

"Because of the dog, Lambert. A dog in the grass."

●

Lambert parked the car on the hard shoulder and got out. He puffed out his chest, clad today in the colors of A.C. Milan, and put out his hand in authoritarian mode to stop the traffic. He walked to the middle of the road, keeping the vehicles at bay for Guérin to cross in his own time.

They stepped over the guardrail and walked on to the waste patch. A dusty flat piece of ground. Above them was the Palais des

Congrès. On one side, the exit to the Porte Maillot and the *péri-phérique*, on the other, the exit to the outer ring road. A Boeing 747 took off above them.

In a supermarket cart, a headless doll shared the space with an electric toaster, a deflated bicycle tire, and an office lamp with trailing wires. Two floral garden chairs stood on an eastern carpet, with several board games, a sewing machine in pieces, a radio, and some books: thrillers, special air service stories, literary bestsellers of yesteryear, and cheap romances. In front of the carpet was a TV set, its screen replaced by a piece of cardboard on which someone had written in felt pen: *"Paco's Junk Yard."*

Guérin looked up at the bridge, searching for the CCTV camera and the angle from which one would be hidden from it. The plot of land was not in its range: all you could see was a bit of grass to the right of the rail. On the final image of the heavy truck skidding, after he had watched the video twenty times with Churchill screeching in his ear, Guérin had seen something in the grass. The head of a dog and two paws, merging into the fuzzy black and white of the security film. A dog, lying in the grass at the edge of the *périphérique*. And a hunch. The dog must have an owner. Possibly even a witness, right beside the point of impact.

Leaning against one of the bridge's supports, sitting on a stained mattress, holding a liter bottle in his hand, Paco was eyeing them. At his feet, the dog was asleep.

When they had arrived the other day at the scene of the "accident," there had been nobody on this triangular patch of polluted ground. Paco and his dog had made themselves scarce before the police arrived. They had come back afterward. The hawker of junk didn't seem surprised to see them, and his expression showed that he could tell the difference between a couple of antiques hunters and two detectives from police HQ.

The dog didn't even twitch an ear until Lambert planted himself in front of the mattress, badge in hand. When the dog did wake up, it fixed one yellow eye on the young trainee; the other was blank, a black hole surrounded by bristles. A one-eyed dog then, probably deaf too, and smelling of old age. Paco, under the dirt, was unhealthily pale. Guérin could already feel his throat itching and his lungs on the verge of caving in. It was a lethal place to spend even a short spell of time.

Under the bridge, the noise drowned out their voices. Paco stood up, slid the bottle into a large pocket in his overcoat and signaled to them to follow him. They stopped at the point of the triangle with cars shooting past them on two sides, driving around Paris in both directions. The dog stretched out among the straggly weeds, near the rail, in the same place as on the video. He watched the cars with his one eye, remembering perhaps how he used to chase them when he was a pup. Guérin was hoping that this half-blind and deaf creature wasn't the only eyewitness.

Paco looked sharp in a depressing sort of way. His intelligence hadn't saved him from ending up here. The thin face, originally dark-skinned, now yellowish, was deep under layers of dirt. His filthy and ill-fitting clothes were in absurdly bright colors, like his junk, at the meeting point of dilapidation and hope. He choked when he started to speak, and cleared his throat by spitting out a gob of phlegm. It was impossible to guess his age: anywhere between thirty and fifty.

"I know you cops come back."

His voice had adjusted perfectly to the noise level, loud and clear. Guérin had to force his own to make himself heard.

"Why did you run away after the accident?"

Pure rhetoric, of course. Paco, if that was his real name, would have worries about his residence permit and ID papers, even if he had made a good choice of this no-man's-land. Just bad luck. Some rich kid had decided to kill himself just in front of him, and his dog had been caught on camera.

"No trouble. Plizz! You give me work, I work! Now here I am, I sell junk stuff. I don't want no problems."

A volcanic fit of coughing that produced black sputum was evidence enough that he already had serious problems. His red-rimmed eyes bulged out of their sockets.

"Where are you from?"

"España."

Guérin's round eyes looked deep into the feverish eyes of this illegal immigrant.

"And before that?"

"Tunis . . ."

Paco was trembling and his panic described in a second many difficult border crossings. Perhaps he had found something a bit better here than over there. But it was a toss-up.

"Don't worry, we're not here to give you trouble. We want to know what you saw."

The tubercular junk vendor scrutinized them for several seconds. The little man with his flat cap didn't look too threatening. The big fair guy, with his tracksuit and curly hair, was yawning.

"I say what I see, you help me? Human right, yes, political refugee?"

"Political?"

"Immigration people, say I have no danger back home. Two years' prison, *Inspecteur*! All because I don't sell my land to policeman in my village. They don't believe! My family back there, *Inspecteur*. Four years now I am in France. I don't want trouble!"

"Tell us first, and then we'll see if we can do something."

"Promise?"

"Yeah."

Paco scratched his pants and frowned. He looked as if he were remembering other poor devils like him who had tried to do the right thing and ended up being guillotined because nobody believed them.

"Not much I see. This mister, he come running, the black car go one way, then the truck hit him. Nothing else, and I run away."

The little guy with the cap didn't look satisfied. The big one, grinning like a kid, unzipped his jacket. Paco jumped as he glimpsed the Beretta.

"No, Mister, plizz! That's all I see! Three people in the car, dead man, truck!"

Guérin raised his hand theatrically at Lambert to restrain his deputy, who was bursting with lethargy.

"*What* did you say about the car? Who was in it?"

Paco coughed up a bit more of his lung. The traffic went on roaring past. He tried to overcome his fear.

"No problems!"

"You're fine, no problems, just tell me!"

"Shit. I know it. Now I'm going to have big trouble!"

"If you need papers, I'll see what I can do. And we'll get you to a doctor. Okay?"

Paco scratched at his clothes again, and at the colony of fleas at home inside them.

"A doctor?"

"Yes, promise."

"So this mister, he's running, no clothes, big smile, arms out like this!"

Paco stretched out his arms, which made him cough some more.

"In the black car, Allah be my witness, these three, they don't look surprised, like they don't worry or nothing. The car, it just goes past, and then boom! The truck."

Guérin was holding his cap with one hand, and his raincoat trembled as he began to shake. The sound of the *périphérique* was invading the racket inside his head.

"Who was in the car?"

Paco put his hands together and looked up at the sky.

"Allah help me, why am I so stupid? In the car, two men, one lady. Blonde lady. All I see, see with my eyes."

He waved toward the traffic.

"Nothing else. *Makach*!"

"What were they like? Clothes, age?"

"Mister Commissaire, it was very, very fast. The lady behind, the men in front. Rich guys. Good clothes. Like you, not young, not old. Driver, he's got a beard. Lady, she looks back when the truck squash man. Then I'm off. Allah's my witness, I never come back here no more."

Lambert had stopped the traffic again, to spare Guérin the humiliation of being run over absentmindedly. In the car, the boss had almost had another crisis. He had taken off the cap and scratched the scabs on his scalp, and written in his notebook signs that luckily this time looked like letters. Then he had fallen silent, a block of congested ideas, completely prostrate. Lambert shifted from one foot to the other. The boss's Big Theory interested him about as much as a chess match on TV He had some inkling of what he was after—one or more people who got their kicks out of following suicides—a bit like themselves in a way—but he didn't take it very seriously. Just another peculiar tic of his boss. This Paco guy said he had seen someone. The boss ought to have been happy to know he wasn't alone in his crazy ideas. Obviously his joy at not thinking himself mad had lasted about ten minutes. He was back in the black hole again.

Lambert had driven them home, whistling to himself to keep his spirits up . . . Spring had decided to pack it in, too. The sky weighed down on them like an upside-down privy, waiting to pour its dark contents over their heads.

•

On the office door, someone had taped up two newspaper cuttings. When other colleagues made the trip to their outpost, it was never good news.

On the larger cutting was a photo of a little man in a cloth cap walking on a bridge toward another who was clinging to a post. *Rescue on the Pont Alexandre III!*

A news item of a few lines followed, describing the courageous feat of Lieutenant Guérin from the prefecture of police. Scrawled furiously across the photo: "So you rescue some people, do you, Guérin?" signed "K." Lambert read through the article—his own name was not mentioned—but Guérin showed no interest in it. The other cutting was just a news-in-brief item:

Last night, Sunday April 13, at the Caveau de la Bolée in the 6th arrondissement, a performing fakir died during his show. Alan Mustgrave (36) a U.S. citizen, died of bleeding caused by the wounds sustained during his act.

The anonymous scribbler had been there too: "Too late for this one then!"

Guérin leaned his head to one side, then took down the small cutting. Lambert, holding the still-malodorous box on his shoulder, pulled the other piece of paper off and looked down the deserted corridor.

"The bastards! You shouldn't let them get away with it, boss. Bloody disgusting."

Guérin calmly put the scrap of paper on the table.

"Lambert, kid, we've got work to do. You take the videos. They didn't arrive together. A blonde woman, middling sort of age. Two men, similar. One with a beard. Well dressed. The suicide in the museum was at twenty past three. So look at that moment, check just afterward, people leaving, and then go back and see who came in earlier. Probably a couple plus a man on his own. If you don't find anything during the hour before, check the video back to opening time."

"Boss, you believe that tramp's story? I mean it was a bit off beam, wasn't it?"

Shit! In his head and in his mouth, the sentence came out differently: "Do you believe your story? I mean you're a bit off beam, aren't you?" But Guérin wasn't listening. He had picked up the box and was disappearing into the archive room. Lambert threw the larger cutting into the wastepaper basket, promising himself to find some copies without the graffiti: one for the wall alongside the calendar, the other for the bookshelf in his own one-room apartment, next to the soccer jersey signed by Zidane and the cup from the rifle competition.

•

The forty-eight dossiers were piled up, opened, and scattered around on the big table for consultation. Richard Guérin had made notes on them:

—Male, 45, G. Del Pappas. Jumped from window in front of a demo by civil servants, rue de Marseille, June 2006, dossier no. 21. Concierge statement: "A couple not from this building had come out just before that," blonde woman about forty, no clear description of the man.

—Male, 58, M. Attia. Pistol, one bullet to the heart, at market, boulevard d'Algerie, August 2006, dossier no. 26. Street vendor statement: "There were even people taking photos. A couple of tourists." Woman in a hat. Man about forty-five. Both well dressed.

—Female, 27, L. Biberfeld. Heroin overdose, January 2007, rue de Solferino, dossier no. 32. Doctor, chance passerby, gave statement: "Tried to revive her, but she'd taken a massive dose, right there in the street, she was on her knees. There was a car parked nearby, but it pulled away when I asked for help. An expensive car, black or dark blue."

—Female, 47, S. Granotier, cut her wrists, from the circle in the Odéon theater, September 2007, dossier no. 39. Spectator in the stalls gave a statement: "This blood started to drip on me and a man next to me, he went off covered in blood, middle-aged, unshaven."

—Male, 32, J.-B.-F. Pouy du Terrebasse. Knocked down by truck. Porte Maillot, April 12, 2008, dossier no. 48. Homeless man, Paco, statement: "two men, one with a beard, and a blonde woman," in a black sedan. (Cf. video, Renault Vel Satis, car number plate incomplete, but registered in Paris.)

That was all he had found in three hours, from four years' worth of archives, gone through, forty-eight files, to try to back up his thesis, encouraged by Paco's witness statement. But even if there had been four people in the car, all with red hair, he would probably have found some kind of supporting evidence in this garbage. Before 2006, he hadn't been compiling files or following cases: the interrogations were all botched and useless. He could have called the witnesses again, and perhaps consulted the files on other suicides in the city, the ones he hadn't handled. But his reputation would complicate life, not to mention the hundreds of hours that it would take.

He added at the end of his notes: "Dossier no. 49, whale skeleton, Natural History Museum, Great Gallery of Evolution, CCTV and prints awaited. Dossier no. 50. Fakir in 6th arrondissement?"

Six cases. The thread was so thin that he could only see it by straining his eyes. But Guérin was prepared to donate one of his organs to keep it alive. Because it was there, somewhere in the papers, the only possible and necessary link. A certainty, and he would pursue it at the cost of his reason.

Paco's statement was a point of no return that he had passed calmly, in the crazily lucid fashion . . . that of a man preparing his own suicide.

The shelves gave off a cynical little whistle as he went by, an infuriating refrain that his parrot would not have disavowed.

In the office, Lambert was snoring, slumped in his chair with his head thrown back. The CCTV film was running silently on the screen, as the gray silhouettes passed through the glass doors at the museum. Probably he had looked up at the stain on the ceiling and not managed to wake up after that. The amethyst was quite busy today. The center was darker, a sign that it had been raining outside their windowless walls for at least an hour. The stain, Guérin realized, had become a little lighter lately. No reason to think that crime had changed its habits. More likely their colleagues were fed up with traipsing up to the attic to dump the clothes there.

"Lambert?"

His deputy grabbed at his holster, without opening his eyes,

"Wha . . . What?"

Someone knocked at the door. Surprised, Lambert pulled the gun out and leveled it.

"Lambert! Put the gun away!"

Ménard opened the door. He had time to see the automatic going back in its holster and stood stock-still, his hand on the door handle.

"Am I interrupting?"

"No, come in Ménard, everything's fine."

Guérin murdered his blond assistant with a look. Lambert rubbed his face.

"Sorry, boss, I was having this dream . . ."

"Got any results, Ménard?"

The technician came into the room cautiously.

"Thirty-seven identifiable sets of prints. I don't know what you're going to do with all this, but that's not my problem."

His nose was red, and his neck was muffled in a thick woolen scarf. He put a packet of papers on the table.

"I picked up dozens of samples on the floor too, mostly hairs, but it's going to take me days to classify and analyze them. Is this some big inquiry, lieutenant? Because if you want quick results, you'll need more people on the job, I can't do any more for now. I'm not well again, what with the change in the weather. Is there an inquiry going on? I haven't heard of anything; nobody in Homicides seems to know. Lambert told me it was serious . . ."

Ménard was a rubbish collector both in his job and in the corridors of the quai des Orfèvres. He'd been asking questions ru;mors must have started in the offices. *Guérin's at it again.* The cuttings on the door were just the beginning.

"The suicide in the Natural History Museum had taken out a big life insurance. The family and the insurance company are going to court, over the insanity clause. There's no rush, the prints will do. If I need any more, but I don't think it likely, I'll contact you."

Ménard listened, lackadaisically, unconvinced.

"Well, it's your call."

Lambert stood up.

"Want to go for a coffee, Ménard?"

"Sure, an herbal tea perhaps."

Guérin placed a hand firmly on Lambert's shoulder.

"You're staying right where you are, Lambert."

No more Mr. Nice Guy, the metaphysics of his new future seemed to carry responsibilities and work. Lambert affected not to be bothered.

"Another time, okay?"

Ménard looked at them and sniffed.

"Yeah, right, see you."

Guérin gave a cold smile.

"Thank you. Very efficient work."

Ménard backed out of the room.

Moment of discretion over. The whipping Lambert had been expecting for some time fell on his shoulders with all the weight of Guérin's accumulated anger.

10

John had left the Luxembourg Gardens by way of the rue de l'Observatoire, passed in front of the Val-de-Grâce, and crossed the boulevard Port-Royal. Then he walked along under the wall of La Santé Prison without knowing what lay behind it, but imagining the worst: the biggest pile of blackened stone he had seen for a while. When he went past the main gates, Bunker's warning took on a new meaning. There are some walls you don't ever escape from.

His bruised stomach was feeling better for the walk. His black eye added to the distrustful glances he attracted. He was a bit fresher after the cold shower, though. In his shirt pocket, folded up, was Alan's last letter, which he had read one last time on a park bench before setting off.

Hey Doc!

What's new out in the sticks? Guess I'll come down and see you one day, find the time. Unless you want to come up here? Haven't you got some call to come to Paris? Find a girl, come see your old pal? I'm working quite a bit, the Parisians like a bit of S&M, they're romantics basically. Weird audiences here though, they don't let themselves go like we do. You got to shake them up a bit, these European types.

Must be your fault. I'm starting to think about the future, settling down. I'm still at Paty's, but I need something more permanent. A place

of my own, what do you think?! I've got money, don't need any more,
John, no need to get your wallet out. I'm clean these days, my head's clear
for once, and that's your fault too. In fact, let me tell you, you're the one
worries me now. You lead too healthy a life, you need a change. You're
still like in that photo in Venice Beach, a college boy hiding in your mom's
skirts. I do my best, but let's face it, it's not easy with a guy like you!

Well, you're the one who's good with words, not me. Try reading between
the lines here if you get bored, Doc. Then it'll be like my letter's longer.

Remember in Venice, when I told you about the desert? I think I'm
getting it all out of me now. For good. I think I'm going to be able to talk
about it to other people soon. Is that a good sign, Doc? Man, it's crazy
how much stuff is your fault.

Watch your ass, Big J., without me around, it'll rust up.

Big A.

Nothing there. Nothing about planning to die. Nothing about
Hirsh. Nothing like a good-bye. Just the usual bullshit: I'm clean
now, I'm thinking about the future, maybe I'll be able to talk about
it . . . Nothing, except for some words that took on a new meaning
after the visit to the morgue. *A place of my own, something more perma-*
nent, my head's clear for once. Come see your old pal. It was a letter like
plenty of others he'd received, a mixture of optimistic lies and good
intentions, a smile covering a pile of rubbish, and some well-disguised
friendship and strong feeling. And always that sense of guilt that Alan
tried to transfer to him. This time it did hurt. But apart from that,
what was there to read between the lines? Not a lot. The stuff about
his ass wasn't out of the ordinary, that was the way Alan always went
on. The letter hadn't affected him as much he'd expected. But he had
not failed to note Paty's address on the back of the envelope. That
was perhaps the only surprising thing about it since Alan didn't usually give an address. *Still at Paty's, find yourself a girl.* He had already
mentioned Paty back in the winter. He was playing matchmaker, and
again not for the first time. Even if it wasn't the same thing anymore. He thought again about the photograph. Alan, bare-chested,
tattooed, smiling, his arm around John's shoulder. And himself age

twenty-two, a big, blond, baby-faced boy with a crew cut. Behind them the beach, the ocean.

He went up the boulevard Blanqui toward the place d'Italie. A drumroll in the sky told him the weather was changing. A minute later, the sky disgorged a deluge. The pavements were quickly running with water, streams cascaded from above, the gutters were full. He ran toward 78A, and reached it soaked to the skin. Water ran down the names on the intercom.

Patricia Königsbauer replied after the second buzz. An impatient voice came from the little speaker in a crackle almost drowned by the sound of the rain. Over the door was a dark, cold security camera.

"What do you want?"

"This is John Nichols, I'm a friend of Alan's."

Cars went past, sending up waves of water.

"First left inside the courtyard."

The big metal door opened.

John found himself in a small courtyard, streaming with water, and ran across it. The left-hand door was another metal one, painted white. She opened it for him and he pushed past the woman to get out of the rain, without seeing her.

His shirt smelled of wet dog, an odor quite distinct from the fresh, sweet smell of the paint. A puddle of water was forming at his feet, on a concrete floor stained with colors. The darkness of the thunderstorm that had drowned the city was less oppressive in this large room, stretching the length of the house, with all the walls and furniture painted white. The canvases too were white, with a few minimalist, electric splashes of color. One color per canvas. Some of them had handprints and here and there what looked like the profile of a face. It was an artist's studio, a great empty space, needed for self-expression, he supposed. There was a small American-style kitchen and in the back wall were three doors, one of them half open. Through it John glimpsed a futon, a white quilt, and a pale carpet.

"Alan told me about you. What are you doing here?"

Patricia had a slight German accent and blonde curly hair. John, remembering the kind of women who were drawn to

Alan—intellectuals who took an aesthetic interest in him, or dropouts from the protest counterculture —wondered which she was.

She was barefoot, and wearing a white paint-stained smock. The top three buttons were undone and below her collarbone light skin showed through; no bra or underclothes. She was tall, taller than the average Frenchwoman, with a sturdy, upright bone structure. The Scandinavian type, athletic and fit. He had been living in the woods for six months. A prickling in his thighs made him take a few pointless steps forward. Above the tempting décolleté, her regular features were cold, her eyes hazel. and her expression suspicious. All in all, she looked arrogant.

"I went and asked some questions about Alan." John pointed to the bruises on his face. "Someone told me to get out of town. I was wondering if you knew anything."

"How did you find me?"

"Alan gave me your address."

"You thought you could just turn up like that, without notice?"

The blonde's default position was hostility. A nervous hostility that charm wouldn't disarm, and which he associated, he didn't know why, with a brunette. John realized he was facing a girl who would bite and scratch and make a scene in public: if I make love to you, there'll be tears, then I'll kick you out.

"So did Alan have problems, apart from drugs, I mean?"

She dragged a ten-liter tin of paint noisily into the center of the room.

"Not that I know of. He didn't say much."

"But he did tell you about me."

She looked him up and down scornfully, with blazing eyes.

"So?"

"I mean, were you close?"

"We screwed now and then. You got a problem with that?"

A second tin had now joined the first.

"As a rule, he didn't stay as much as a few months anywhere. But he stayed a long time with you. Did he ever mention a dealer, someone he owed money to?"

"Alan's dead. It doesn't matter now."

Third tin. She was taking the lids off, without waiting for his answer.

"It does to me."

She undid the rest of the buttons on the smock and slipped it off. Underneath she was naked. A German-manufactured, ready-made fantasy. A thirteenth calendar girl for Bunker: the house painter. John was blinded by her golden bush. Perhaps it had been worth having that shave earlier. She held the smock out to him.

"Take off your shoes and put this on. I don't know what you're talking about. I didn't know Alan's dealer. The only thing he said was that you'd used him for your research. It's a bit late to turn up here now, worrying about his problems."

She turned her back on him and walked over to the tins of paint. Her tight buttocks hardly shook as her heels hit the floor. John's mouth was dry, not a drop of saliva.

"I didn't use Alan, he was a friend. And what about you? What did you ever do for him?"

John didn't know why he was suddenly so furious. Fear, desire, the rain beating on the studio roof. Paty had frozen, then bent over the tins of paint with legs tensed. John stared at the inviting buttocks offered to him. Her voice was a growl.

"Just shut up."

She turned around, her nipples arrogantly thrusting up like brown pebbles. She was angry for sure. That was obvious from her voice, but she was more in control than he was.

"Alan was . . ."

"I never treated Alan like some experimental animal. I helped him for ten years. I didn't use my ass to do that."

She smiled, as if it were a hilarious remark. It was presumptuous certainly, to compare the respective pulling power of their buttocks. John wondered what was going on under that faultless skin. She looked like a woman more inclined to inflict wounds than to bandage them.

She pointed at the wall.

"Stand up against that canvas."

John moved back, without taking his eyes off her, toward a blank canvas. She was lying, from start to finish, but he couldn't shake himself free, or penetrate her defenses. Her nudity was like armor.

"What happened in his show that night?"

Patricia Königsbauer was concentrating on the tins of paint. She lifted up the middle one, tensing her muscles, and tipped it over her head. Her body was immediately covered in brilliant red liquid. Threads of viscous paint dripped from her fingers, the scarlet fluid making her shoulders, breasts, and belly glisten. She waited while the paint flowed down her legs, then came toward him. She stopped within arm's reach, standing with her feet slightly apart, letting him look at her as much as he wanted. The hazel eyes, their lashes now thick with paint, shone out of her glistening and expressionless face. The paint had flattened her blonde curls, covered her lips, and thickened her now indistinct features. Heavy drops fell from her crimson pubis, like some kind of monstrous menstruation, attracting him. A red plastic doll, melting. He could look, but there was nothing to see. John remembered Ariel's words, when she had described Alan losing his blood, wrapped up in a sticky cape. His eyes widened in shock. Paty flung herself at him.

His breath was taken away. By chance or instinct, she had aimed at his broken ribs and his stomach. The pain of it made him groan. Flinging her arms open, she repeated it three times. The apprehension of pain turned into anticipation of pleasure. Invisible strings tied him to the canvas. She didn't take her eyes off his as she drew back before launching herself at him, and she hit the canvas with her hands when their bodies touched. The fourth time, she stayed pressed up against him, moving her belly against his with short sharp blows. Her paint-drenched hair filled his mouth. He shivered with a thrill of pleasure, and put his arms around her scarlet torso.

It was impossible to grasp the cold and slippery body. She escaped his embrace, turned on her heel, and walked away across the studio. He stood, unable to move.

Patricia disappeared behind one of the doors, leaving red footprints on the floor.

He took off the smock, tried to wipe his face and threw the garment on the floor. He would have liked to fight a punchball for a few minutes, to stop the trembling in his hands.

He put his shoes on and walked around the studio, trying to compose his thoughts. Was she in love with Alan? They were both impermeable to normal feelings. Had this handicap brought them together, creating a bond between them, even a corrupt one? Did she really know anything? Alan never said much, that was true enough. An old hand at the game, he wouldn't gossip about his dealers over cocktails.

As he walked in front of the canvases, he wondered which one Paty had used to crush the Kansas fakir. This kind of game would have amused him. Not exactly John's cup of tea, though. After a winter in the tepee, something more straightforward would have been enough. But the result was the same. The urge had passed. His ribs were aching again, desire receding, and his bruised stomach was making him feel sick.

The rain had all but stopped. Behind the door he could hear a shower running. Either she was crazy, or she had managed royally to evade the issue.

Five minutes later, she emerged from the bathroom, wearing a bathrobe that offered no glimpses of flesh, a towel twisted around her head.

If this whirlwind of a woman was some kind of proxy gift from the lovelorn fakir—a final possibility after all—the casting was way off target. The hypothesis began to seem plausible. In his refrigerated locker, Alan was mocking him one last time.

In spite of his unease, John was recovering his confidence and the blonde, draped in her cheap disdain, felt it, too. Once clothed, she had lost her assured air.

"Were you at the Caveau that night?"

"You've no business staying here now."

"Alan killed himself; it wasn't an accident."

She poured herself a Scotch at the bar, and sipped it while looking at her latest work.

"You're too tall. You take up the whole canvas."

It was true, on his Paty-style portrait there was less paint than on the others. A few splashes of red, Patricia's handprints and traces of her feet. In the center of the canvas, a big empty space. A hollow left by vanished desire? The questioning of existence? Nothing without another person? A negative portrait. An absence where John P. Nichols had been. His sick feeling was turning to distress, and the urge to get away. The Königsbauer neurosis was catching.

"You know perfectly well it wasn't an accident."

No reply. A shiver. She was still looking at the new canvas. It must be annoying her that she had not managed to imprint more of herself around John.

"Just get out."

"Do you know Frank Hirsh? He works at the U.S. embassy here. Alan was sleeping with him."

An extra long swig of whiskey made her grimace.

"There's no point carrying on like this."

"Did Alan leave any of his stuff here?" John was remembering the photograph. "There is one thing I'd like to find again."

She was almost shouting now.

"I've chucked it all out! Alan didn't give a damn about that sort of thing."

Her German accent had become more pronounced.

He walked past her slowly, not looking at her, heading for the door.

"Yeah, I suppose you're right. I guess he left without any regrets."

As he put his hand out toward the door handle, the whiskey glass shattered against the white-painted metal.

"Fuck off!"

The translucent alcohol trickled down the door. She was certainly obsessed with leaving traces on walls: well, at least she left a mark on your mind. *She strips off and runs at walls.* Alan had not thought to mention that she stuck someone else up against the wall first.

He glanced up at the tiny control screen above the intercom, and went out, crushing the fragments of glass underfoot.

Rain: colorless water. The air between the drops lets ideas circulate.

A girl waiting for him, naked under her smock, when he had turned up without warning. Two closed doors, and the bedroom door ajar when he got there. Three doors shut when he left. Perhaps it was not only for *his* benefit that she had taken her clothes off. Sad but realistic.

•

He took up position in the place Saint-Michel at 9:00 p.m. The rain had stopped, but his clothes, and the city, were still dripping wet. He stood at the back of a newspaper kiosk, holding a copy of *Le Canard enchaîné* and smoking Gitanes to keep himself warm. His face, discolored with bruises, was lit by the rosy tip of his cigarette. A fugitive specter in the dark.

He kept his eyes fixed on the square in front of the fountain, a favorite rendezvous point for Parisians. Men and women, mostly young, came and stood, looking around, cell phones to their ears. Smiles of greeting, handshakes, lovers' embraces. Couples formed and disappeared, to be replaced by single figures waiting their turn.

By 9:30 p.m. John was shivering with cold. He left his windswept corner for a covered café terrace, where there was a gas heater. He drank a coffee, sitting well back in his chair to keep his blond head out of sight. The warmth was welcome, even if his feet were still frozen.

By 10:00 p.m. he had only five cigarettes left and his upper garments at least were dry. He ordered one more coffee and stirred sugar in to it. He was watching a black car that had been double-parked for several minutes in the rue Saint-André des Arts. A long car, glistening with rain. The light reflected off the windows made it impossible to see inside.

Two traffic wardens on motorbikes and wearing fluorescent jackets stopped at the driver's door. The window was lowered, but now the driver was hidden from him by the jackets. They went away after exchanging a few words, and the car moved off. John waited another half hour. The car did not return. He paid and left the café at a quarter to eleven.

No hoodies. No obvious watchers, and nobody turning up for the supposed meeting. Their absence worried him more than it would have done to meet his attackers. He was spoiling for a fight. Being the bait on a fishing line was not an alternative. Did the dealers think he had really been scared off and was far away? The beating the night before had left little room for doubt. They should have been there.

He kept close to the walls as he walked away, keeping his eyes peeled. The city, dark and damp, had become a huge stone forest. The hunt was on and he was the quarry. Nothing to do with five thousand euros. The more questions there were, the surer he was about that. Speeding up, he turned a corner, sprinted about fifty meters, and ducked into a doorway. Five minutes. Nobody following. He tried it again, and in the end, feeling ridiculous, he headed back to the Luxembourg Gardens.

After one final glance around in the rue Vaugirard, he opened the gate, closed it quickly, and plunged into the park. The light was on in Bunker's hut, a relief at first, then it worried him. The isolated light amidst the trees was like an enchanted lantern. The previous evening at this time, the cabin had been dark. The wait at Saint-Michel and his walk back had made him paranoid.

He approached cautiously from one side, going around in a curve, weaving between the tree trunks and shrubs, and then kneeled down under the geraniums. Mesrine hadn't barked. John stood up slowly to peer inside, and Bunker appeared at the window, a roll-up crushed in the corner of his mouth.

"Looking for something, son?"

The American stood up and dusted off his fatigues.

"Aren't you asleep at this time of night?"

The old man had been waiting up for him, but wouldn't admit that he had been worrying. An open bottle of red wine was keeping him company; by the look of his eyelids, not the first. The feeble light-bulb and the alcohol combined to etch deep lines around his eyes and mouth. He filled two glasses, switched on the hot plate, and put a saucepan on it.

"Mesrine, he won't bark at night, case you're thinking of playing cowboys and Indians. Find what you were after?"

"*No.* This afternoon I called the embassy. My friend was sleeping with some guy who works there, Frank Hirsh his name is. He was the one who took me to the morgue. And now Hirsh seems to be off someplace. I called his home address, no answer. He was at Alan's last show at the club. I really need to see him. I got this other guy in the embassy, and he told me the body's being flown out tomorrow. He didn't sound too friendly. Alan must really have caused a lot of trouble there. This guy didn't want to discuss it. He said it was nothing to do with them anymore, and not to call them again. Nobody wants to know, nobody will tell me anything. Even the girl he was staying with."

"You saw a girl today?"

Bunker put the saucepan in front of John, a fork standing up in a magma of ravioli.

"I did, and she got undressed in five minutes flat."

The old man smiled, showing his gappy teeth like those of a kid.

John wedged the piece of paper in a crack in the pine tree bark, and moved thirty paces back. The little white square was quite visible in the orange glow of Paris by night. He strung his bow and the wood creaked as it bent. Once the string was knotted, he twanged it to make it vibrate, checking by ear that the tension was right. Bunker was sitting on a bench, Mesrine at his feet. It was one in the morning. John needed to think. He fitted the first arrow.

The improvised target was pretty close, but he wasn't really trying for points, just exercising. His ribs were sore as he drew the bow. His whole body ached, and he had trouble controlling his breath. The arrow whistled off and he breathed out. The tip went into the bark, *thwack*, just to the left of the paper.

Mesrine flinched. The sound of the arrow had made him jumpy.

Paty had cracked twice. The first time was when he mentioned Hirsh.

"Then what happened?"

"What? What are you talking about?"

"This woman. When she got undressed."

"She poured paint all over herself and then got dressed again. There was someone else hiding in the studio."

Bunker was disappointed.

"Nothing else?"

"She's beautiful."

"Ah."

"And she's not telling the truth."

"That figures."

John fitted a second arrow. *Thwack!* Centered, but above the paper. Mesrine's ears went up again. Bunker patted his head. "Quiet, boy."

The second time was when she had started shouting . . . when he asked if Alan had left any of his stuff with her? No. When he had mentioned the photograph? Wrong, he hadn't mentioned the photograph. All he had said was that he would like to get something back.

"Hey, son, I didn't think your bow and arrow were that good."

"It's a hunting bow."

Bunker was holding a big army flashlight.

"Yeah, I can see. Because you go hunting with it?"

"Sometimes."

So what had there been in Alan's stuff?

John prepared a third arrow and aimed, his eye fixed on the little white square of paper, over the arrowhead in front of him. He was getting used to the half-light now. The arrow whistled off. *Thwack!* Spot on. In the center, where two diagonals met bang in the middle of the paper.

"Bull's-eye!" Bunker switched on the flashlight and played the circle of light on the target. "On the button!"

Mesrine was on edge now.

Was it drugs, perhaps? Alan hadn't been improvising; he had been preparing this for a long time. Perhaps there were more clues in the letter than he had realized. *"Between the lines."* But why mention the photograph? Photographs. Blackmail? Was the studio used for something else besides painting? Whose portraits did Patricia paint? Did she press her breasts and belly up against . . . diplomats? Rich men,

men like Hirsh, unearthed by Alan at the Caveau de la Bolée? *I've got money, don't need any.* That was unusual. Someone—Alan?—might have taken photos in the studio from a hiding place. Or maybe Alan was taking part. Perhaps someone else was there, a third party, the one who was there today, the photographer perhaps? Were there some photos now of him, John? Did the blonde have some other tricks up her sleeve that he hadn't been allowed to experience?

An antisocial fakir and a perverse bourgeoise. Their preferred prey: high-flying victims.

He pulled the cord tight. The target was in his head now, he had no need to look at it. He concentrated, his eyes half-closed. Then he sensed two movements to his left. Mesrine had sprung up, and Bunker had turned toward him. The flashlight was exploring the park, sliding over the tree trunks. Bunker spoke in a low voice.

"Over here, son."

Mesrine's hackles were up, his teeth bared.

"Stay right there, Davy Crockett! And you stay put, too, old man." This voice was familiar.

A dark silhouette, hooded, slipped behind the old park keeper. I was followed, John thought. So much for trying to dodge about like a secret agent. He still had an arrow engaged, and his arms started to tremble. The man was sheltering behind Bunker; he couldn't shoot. Then he heard a sound behind him. This was it. Trapped.

"Drop the flashlight!"

Bunker did as he was told. The man had a gun aimed at his white hair. At the same time, John felt a cold steel barrel on the back of his neck.

"Drop the bow! Move." He was being pushed toward the bench.

Two guns, two men; against them, a bow and arrow, a dog, a shrink 1 meter 80 tall, and an ex-con made of solid brick. Result: these two hoodlums weren't sure they had the upper hand. And in fact they didn't. That explained the nervousness in their voices. They had chanced on bigger game than expected.

John was calm. Bunker was imperturbable and even the dog was concentrating. In terms of nerves they had the advantage. John lowered the bow and took a step forward. The beam of the flashlight, pointing to the ground, moved imperceptibly. Mesrine crouched, ready to spring.

Thwack!

A scream.

John had let fly his arrow, which he had still held poised, taut and pointing downward in his left hand. Blind, aiming behind him, as he walked forward. The gun was no longer at his neck, and the guy was howling with pain.

Mesrine, without barking, had already fastened his jaws on a leg. Another scream. The flashlight was now shining into the mouth of the hoodie. A stupid face, its expression between pain from the bite and stupefaction. The cosh crashed into his jaw, and sent teeth flying. John had turned around. His own attacker was squirming in pain, his foot pinned to the ground by the arrow, which had gone right through it. Dropping the bow, he brought his hands together and whacked the man on the temple. Out for the count. John turned toward Bunker, who was calmly replacing the cosh in his belt.

The cabin was now crammed full of people.

Hoodie woke up first, finding himself tied to the stove. He probably wanted to speak, but things were against him. His jaw for a start, dislocated by about two centimeters; add to that the gaps in his teeth. Then there was the dog sitting opposite him, silently, but with a mouthful of sharp white fangs. And finally the sight of his fellow conspirator laid out on the bed unconscious, his foot pierced with an arrow and dripping into a basin.

John broke the arrow, and took advantage of the man's being unconscious to pull the tip out. The wood came out of the foot with a wet sucking sound. Better than a bucket of water over the head. The guy sat up with a howl. Bunker brandished the cosh above him, and he lay back down, shrinking against the wall. John tied a piece of cloth around the trainer, the same top-of-the-range model he had glimpsed the day before running away from him on the pavement of the rue de l'Hirondelle. This man, since his injury was to foot, rather than mouth, was the first to speak.

Two young Arabs, someone's sidekicks, still wet behind the ears. Once their guns were gone, they lived in a world of total fear. John had no need to insist. At the first question, Pierced-Foot confirmed they were working for Alan's dealer.

"We just do what we're told."

"And what's his name?"

Pierced-Foot turned to Hoodie.

"Fouad, from the Quatre Mille housing project."

"Fouad *what*?"

". . . Boukrissi. Man, we're just doing what we're told, that's all, we never worked for him before. He usually gets these other people to do it."

"And what did he tell you to do?"

"Get the cash. Wait at the café and ask for the money."

"How did you know who I was?"

"The picture, man, he gave us a photo."

"What's your name?"

"Kamal."

"You've got the photo?"

Pierced-Foot twisted around with a grimace of pain. The cloth was drenched with blood already and dripping into the basin again. From his jeans pocket, he pulled out a folded print. Alan and John. Venice Beach. Sunshine. Ten years back. John's head was ringed with felt pen and above it someone had written in capitals JOHN P. NICHOLS. He clutched the photograph tightly.

"How did Boukrissi get hold of this?"

"Shit, man, I don't know. He told us to pick it up from this mailbox in an apartment building, that's all. So we did. We didn't want to . . . He just told us to wait at the café, give you a scare, and get hold of the five thou, and if we got it, to contact him and we'd get one thou for us. Then he told us you were in here, and we had to start again. Look, we gotta go to the *hospital;* you can't leave us like this."

From the stove came a groan of agreement, stopped in its tracks by a growl from Mesrine.

About twenty-five years old, not-so-tough tough guys. A thousand euros and perhaps, if they were successful, jobs as a gangster's errand boys. They'd already had it. Their career as hard men was over before it had started. As if John, still less even less than Bunker, could give a damn about their future.

"How did he know I was here?"

"Don't know."

"You weren't at Saint-Michel this evening."

"No, he said to wait, not to go there. He sent us a text, told us you were here, that's all. That's how he contacts us. We don't get to meet him. Two days, Fouad's been sending us these messages. A bit of cash, that's all we were in it for. For fuck's sake, man! I'm in pain! I need a doctor."

"I'm going to call the police."

Kamal turned to his pal, his panic meter at red. Two useless sidekicks. All they were supposed to do was scare him off. First with fists. But the second time, they'd come with guns. Higher stakes.

Bunker moved toward the door and signaled to John to follow.

"Son, you really want to call the police?"

"No, it was just to frighten them."

"Well, glad to hear it. But these two? They're already scared to death. They won't say no more, they know fuck all about anything. Your dealer there, he's not stupid; he's covering himself, sending these two clowns. It's clear enough. They're just working for a dealer who wants his money, no more to it. What you want to do is, you just go away, don't get mixed up in this, or someone else is going to get themselves killed."

"All this just for the money? That can't be it."

"Hell, son, when you get an idea in your head, it's hard to shift it."

"What?"

"You're so damn stubborn. What the fuck else do you want to do?"

"Talk to the dealer, talk to Hirsh, ask that girl some more questions."

"Talk to the dealer? Are you off your head? Set foot in the Quatre Mille, you won't get out alive. These two, they got nothing to do with your pal's death. Come on, son, he done himself in. He'd had enough . . . you're just stirring up trouble for nothing."

"Alan mentioned this photo in his last letter to me. Why? And who followed me here, if it wasn't them?"

"Search me, but that's not going to bring him back."

"No, I know."

"I wonder what you *do* know. You're holding out on me, aren't you, not telling me everything?"

"I've just got this hunch, Bunk. I can't tell you yet."

Bunker ran his hand through his white hair.

"Son, way I see it, eggheads like you, they shit their pants when someone pulls a gun on them, right. So why do I get this idea that you're not a fucking shrink after all?"

John smiled

"'Cause I am a fucking shrink."

The old convict rubbed his scar, which reacted painfully to trouble, like rheumatism to rain.

"That's what you say. I've met blokes like you, think they know it all. Well, you're not running fast enough, cowboy, let me tell you." He thought for a moment, still rubbing at the white line running across his wrinkled face.

"These two losers, right, we chuck 'em back on the street, and they'll just have to take their chances; there's a hospital not so far away."

"That's all?"

"We get the dealer's address off 'em first, if that's what you want. One more thing, I'm helping you, son, okay, but if I land back in jail because of you and your pal, the fakir guy, there's another promise I'll keep. You've had it. No exceptions."

Bunker looked genuinely sorry to have made this point.

"Bunk, what accent do these kids have, where are they from?"

"They're from some housing project in the suburbs, son, it's not a country."

Back inside the cabin, the blood was still silently seeping into the basin. Bunker played with his cosh, swinging it to signify a more relaxed atmosphere. He had taken charge now.

"You, the cripple, where does this Fouad hang out?"

Kamal tried to summon up some saliva in his mouth; his lips were dry, and he was sweating and shivering.

"He's got lots of addresses, pal. We never know where he is. That's the truth."

"Respect! Like for my big friend here. I'm *not* your pal. So how do you get in touch with him, then?"

"Just by phone. But Fouad, you don't call him, if he doesn't call you."

"You give us the number, and we'll do you a little favor, right. No police."

Hesitation.

Hoodie, with his dislocated shuddering jaw and eyes wide open, was trying to find a convincing expression.

"Oh! Oh Oh-ee!"

Kamal seemed to understand.

"No police." He pulled a cell from his pocket, and Bunker snatched it.

"Not on. What's the code?"

He gave them the code.

"Take us to the hospital?"

"You get yourselves there; one of you can walk and the other can talk. What name on the phone?"

"François."

"Fantastic. And your names?"

"Kamal Aouch, and he's Nourdine. Nourdine Aouch: he's my kid brother."

Bunker smiled, without joy.

"Unemployment, brother, is the mother of vice."

John stationed himself at the south gate. 4:00 a.m. He waited a moment, then gave them a sign. Shoved from behind by the keeper and his dog, the two injured brothers dragged themselves to the exit. Bunker had put on his cap to look official. He unlocked the gate and let John have the last word.

"We hear another peep out of you, we call the cops. You find some excuse at the hospital . . . *don't talk*, don't mention us at all. *What do you* (Oh, fucking French! I'm too tired to speak it. Shit!), what do you do to contact Boukrissi?"

"A text saying *okay*, and the money in the mailbox if we had it. *GONE*, if we didn't find you. *P.B.* if there was a problem, and . . ."

Kamal stopped. He was meeting some resistance at the level of his conscience.

"What else?"

"*OVER*, if there was a different problem."

Over. A little text message, in case by any chance one of these two motherfuckers had put a bullet in his brain. The idea amused him. Bunker took hold of the Aouch brothers, Kamal the legless and Nourdine the speechless, and pushed them into the street. They collapsed in a heap, then got back up and, stifling their moans, made their way up the road, a three-legged pair.

Risky to let these two go free. But they didn't have a whole lot of choice, and the last thing they would do was go to the police. If they reported to Boukrissi, he didn't mind if they said "over."

"Son, I'm going to bury the guns. After that, not a peep out of you either. I'm going to sleep. And I get the bed."

John emptied the basin of blood at the foot of a tree and went back in. He pushed the table against the wall and spread his blanket on it. He lay down slowly, lowering his ribs one by one onto the wooden boards.

Bunker came in without a word, his hands stained with earth. He hung his cap on a nail, took off his shoes and lay down fully dressed. Mesrine stretched out with a snort, burying his muzzle in one of his master's shoes.

"Listen, son, it took me fifteen years to find this place. There's nothing in the world to beat a one-room cell. And if I heard right, you've got one like this down in the Lot. Well, you better get back there. The guns are under the tree where I found you. And the day you use them, you won't never come back here."

The bed squeaked. Bunker was snoring within minutes. He had left the light on, a prison habit that didn't stop him sleeping. But for John it was his first night in prison, and he slept not a wink.

11

A telephone call at eight in the morning. Guérin answered it and made a note. A hanging in the twelfth arrondissement. An eighty-year-old widower, one of the most common statistics in suicide. He had sent Lambert. His deputy, still smarting from the dressing-down of the day before, had slunk off, his tail between his legs.

The videos had been no help. Possibly doctored, more probably just nothing. Guérin had called the witnesses named in his six files. He had managed to contact the concierge, the doctor, and the theater-goer. They could all remember the suicides, but they had forgotten the details. A blonde woman and two men, one with a beard: vanished into the arbitrary meandering of memory. The street vendor couldn't be traced. Next he called the refuge for the homeless to question Paco again. Guérin had kept his word, finding him a place at the center, so that he could be examined and offered treatment, at least for a few days. But Paco had decamped overnight. Guérin spoke to the doctor who had seen him. He diagnosed double pneumonia, plus secondary infections, the kind of thing people pick up living rough: skin disease, parasites, early stages of cirrhosis. According to the doctor, Paco was not long for this world. A few months at most: as well as everything else, there were tumors everywhere, as big as fists, from the stomach to the lungs. The city had punched holes throughout the organism of the little Tunisian of uncertain age. He had slunk off to die alone in a hole somewhere, like sick animals do, without making a fuss or attracting an audience.

Guérin couldn't get hold of the fingerprint files from his office. He had called the lab. Ménard was a rotten apple, but better not to talk to anyone else. And the technician was off sick for three days.

Everything was falling apart, the elements were becoming atomized. The yellow raincoat had got bigger, or else Guérin had shrunk. Churchill was sulking as he slipped into depression. The apartment had become a mausoleum to the memory of his mother, watched over by a neurotic parrot. There were no more temper tantrums or cackles, only silence. Guérin had lost the thread. He simply saw a parallel between his own condition and that of the world: they were both chaotic, no need to imagine any conspiracy, just a complex mass alternating between hazardous free will and anarchic disintegration. In that steaming cauldron, anything might make sense. Believing gave a shape to your illusions. But faith had to be shared. Out there somewhere, it *might* be that three insane people were methodically killing others. Nobody was going to help him find them. All he had was one newspaper cutting and a bloodstain on the ceiling. And the Kowalski affair was bound to resurface: the Kowalski nightmare, rather. Absence of proof and lingering doubt. Doubt about Kowalski.

Guérin slipped the cutting into his pocket. In the corridor, he turned his back on the service stairs and walked resolutely toward the inner reaches of No. 36, wedging his cap down over his eyes.

Today he needed to see them face-to-face, the colleagues who had chosen him as a scapegoat for their own sickness—the delusion, stupid or hypocritical, that you could live in a cesspit without picking up its stink.

Guérin walked through the offices, outstaring his colleagues. The stigmata of their constant lies had punched holes in their skin. The ones who worked in Criminal Investigation wore themselves out as they aged. As young policemen, newly married, they were keen on justice, eager to go, and excited at carrying a gun. Once they reached forty, Guérin could read on their weary faces the divorces and the bitter awareness of the pointlessness of their task.

The ones over fifty clung in disgust to the cause of all their fail-
ures and disappointments: their work. They had no choice. They
handled their guns with anxiety, knowing that the bottle, night-
mares, and psychotherapy lay ahead. The prefecture of police was
marinated in society's turbid depths, registering, with every day
that passed, more damage from mutually inflicted decomposition.
Behind the hostile or evasive glances, Guérin found the evidence
he was looking for: the shame that drove his colleagues. Shame over
Kowalski—because that was the name that had become attached
to it—now converted, out of cowardice, into hate for Guérin. He
felt no satisfaction, rather a vague sense of pity, as he realized how
much he scared them.

In the stairwell, he met Roman and Berlion. The two lieuten-
ants gave off an aura of hunted beasts ready to bite. They reeked
of musk and hostility, scents of the night from which they were
emerging. Roman, on a lower step, but with his eyes on the same
level, snarled at him.

"You got a problem, Guérin? Lost your way?"

Shame, splitting open the hatred and seeping from infected internal wounds. Guérin looked from one to the other. Two fugitives.

"Kowalski was guilty. It'll come out one day, there's no way it
won't, and you know it. You're in it up to your necks. But there's no
justice in this world, so it'll only be on your consciences. If I were
you, Roman, I'd keep away from Savane for a while."

Roman grabbed Guérin by the collar and pulled him down a step.
Berlion intervened.

"Give over . . . he can't do anything."

Roman's huge hand was pressing on his throat. Guérin smiled,
standing on tiptoe, and managed to croak:

"What's the police coming to, when you can't count on your pals?"

Roman let him go. Guérin pulled his crumpled raincoat around
him and went on down.

On the way, he tried to find the connection between this world
where no revenge was possible, and a fakir who had died of a hemorrhage. Obvious. The connection was a perfect parallel. The world of

men, a bed of nails, on which they were balancing clumsily as they tried to run away from one another.

●

The sign creaked as it swung in the wind: ridiculous in broad daylight. A fairy-tale wizard, painted in a naive, realistic style, peering over a top hat. The Caveau de la Bolée.

A cutting from the *Parisien* and someone at police HQ with a weird sense of humor had sent him here. Chance, the fantastic double of his rapidly disappearing rationality, had drawn Guérin to the club.

The sheer stone wall had no opening except the huge door without a handle. He lifted the bronze knocker and let it fall. He knocked again twice and stepped back. A bolt squeaked and a small, plump woman covered in tattoos opened the door.

"What do you want?"

She looked as if she had just got out of bed; her lips and eyelids were puffy with sleep. Guérin checked his watch. Eleven a.m. How could anyone be so late getting up? He introduced himself politely. She replied in a husky voice:

"We shut down the music at one in the morning. I'm not responsible for anything that happens in the street after that."

"I'm here about the man who died."

A ray of sunshine lit up the silver stud in her eyebrow. Ariel blinked the light away as if it were an insect.

"I've already had the police around. Just get off my back about this business."

"I'm investigating a series of suicides."

She started to close the door.

"So what? This was an accident. I can't tell you anymore."

Guérin took his cap off and put his head to one side. His eyes rolled.

"I don't believe in accidents. Or suicides. I'm looking into murders."

The woman's pale cheeks were freckled. She slid her thumb into a strap of her tank top, adjusting one of the cups of her bra. Guérin bit his tongue as he saw the curve of her breast.

Ariel leaned toward him. Guérin had gone red, then white. He put his hand up against the stone wall.

"Are you okay?"

The little policeman stuttered.

"I . . . I'm not sure."

A cognac and a strong coffee. A lesbian and a detective sitting together, a cigarette consuming itself in an ashtray. Three overhead bulbs and in the half-light the smell of absent bodies, as if a packed house had only just left.

"Feeling better?"

"Thanks, but I don't drink."

"On duty?"

"No, I don't drink, period."

Ariel tipped the cognac into her own coffee.

"Cyclist's breakfast."

Guérin looked at his watch again.

"*Mademoiselle*, I'm sorry to bother you, but I need to ask you some questions. Monsieur Mustgrave, that was his name, yes? He died in circumstances . . . well, I'm not quite sure how to put this, but in circumstances that may be connected to my inquiry."

Ariel swallowed her hot and alcoholic drink and was probably wondering when she had last been addressed as *mademoiselle*.

"Why did you say 'murder'?"

"I can't tell you that. Are you prepared to answer my questions?"

The coffee cup rattled on the saucer.

"What are you frightened of?"

Guérin's head sloped several degrees to the side.

"Of your answers, *mademoiselle*. I'm afraid of coincidence . . ."

Ariel's mouth formed an O, in a tender pout revealing plenty of chrome and steel. She pulled up the straps of her tank top. The studs on her nipples stood out through the fabric. Guérin's head was almost on his shoulder.

"Are you afraid I might want to give you a spanking?"

"*I beg your pardon?*"

"Only joking," she said cheerfully. "It's my motherly instinct being aroused. What do you want to know?"

"It wasn't an accident?"

Coffee cognac. Her leather pants squeaked on the chair. She leaned forward.

"Will you want me to say this in court?"

"No, this is just for me."

Ariel chewed a metal piercing in her pink tongue.

"Well. I'd call it a pre-prepared accident."

"I'm looking for three people who might have been in the audience that night. A blonde woman, middle-aged, and two men, about the same; one of them had a beard or stubble. Does that ring a bell?"

"No, absolutely not."

Her breasts were resting on the table. Guérin tried to assemble his ideas out of the twilight.

"These people were, well, let's say rather more la-di-da than your usual clientele."

"It was full to bursting that night; I didn't spend all evening looking at their faces. Anyway, heck, don't you tell me the rich snobs don't come here. Take a look at the drinks prices, and tell me if the workers can afford a bottle of champagne here." She was sitting up straight, gripping the table.

"I'm sorry, I didn't mean to offend you."

"Offend me? What planet are you on? I'm not offended, I'm bloody angry."

"Please, please calm down."

"You're going to get your punishment, little boy."

"*What?*"

"Oh my God, it's test your IQ night, is it?"

"Do I gather someone has already been around asking you this?"

"No."

"Are you lying?"

"Yes. Does that worry you?"

"Yes."

"Incredible. Why should I trust you?"

"I'm looking for murderers."

"You think that's going to make me feel better? You could have told me I was pretty."

"But you *are* pretty."

Ariel gave a grin and slapped her leather-clad buttocks with both hands.

Guérin gave a start.

"I'm going to have another. Not tempted?"

"Yes."

●

Le Bourget Airport. Northwest freight hangar, 2:30 p.m.

The hearse is gray, with scrolled leaves on the smoked windows.

A representative from the funeral directors signs the paper handed to him by an embassy official; a customs officer stamps the pages of the form and checks the seals on the coffin. The Stars and Stripes are draped over the shining black wooden box, which carries a sticker saying "Proudly made in America."

The American observes from a safe distance, arms folded.

An airport vehicle draws up alongside the hearse, pulling a luggage trailer. Three airport staff load the casket onto it. The American hasn't budged. The convoy leaves the hangar and slips under the wing of a 747 cargo plane, close to where a loading ramp has been lowered.

John P. Nichols vanishes into the stairwell.

It's a day of sunny periods and passing clouds that bring the temperature down sharply. The wind ruffles his long hair. On his face the bruises are turning yellow and fading. He puts his hands on the rail and looks down at the Boeing. A Gitane is burning between his fingers. Various vehicles are busy around the aircraft. Like insects dashing around. The baggage ramp is hauled up, closing like the vagina of a sea monster. A tractor is hitched to the 747's nose, lights flashing, and a man is waving his fluorescent batons. The plane reverses off the stand; the pilots adjust their headphones and turn their attention to the instrument panel.

First stop Detroit, to unload top-of-the-range German cars, then on to Kansas City, where the coffin will be deposited on American soil, along with spare parts for agricultural machines. The import-export transit of machines and veterans' corpses.

There's another man on the terrace. John turns his head quickly. A tall man, with curly blond hair, gazing at the runways, hands in pockets. Just watching planes take off and land.

The Boeing swivels; the tractor detaches itself. A roar from the engines, and the plane begins to taxi. The engines roar again, then subside as it rolls over the tarmac. An Airbus without windows lands with a scream and a puff of smoke from the landing gear. The U.S. plane moves toward its take-off position. The engines now open up properly, thrusting their tons of steel and fuel forward. John grips the handrail. The plane's nose lifts; the roar of its engine fills the air. The Boeing starts its ascent into the sky. Alan's coffin is leaving the ground, disappearing.

John imagines Alan's parents, in jeans, on the other side of the Atlantic, waiting to welcome their son home. They haven't seen him for ten years. He smiles. He's thinking of an embalmer in Kansas City, working hard to put makeup on the tattoos. Alan's dead; he won't give a damn what he looks like in church. John turns his back on the runways of this gloomy airport with no travelers and walks away.

One plane lands; another starts to take off. The tall, curly-headed man is watching wide eyed like a little kid.

Bye-bye, mother fakir. Back to the wide-open spaces of your childhood.

Curly-hair takes his hands out of his pockets and confronts John. He's saying something, but the plane taking off drowns out his voice. He shouts louder.

"John Nichols?"

The sound fades. John looks at this young guy with the aquiline nose, who now shows him a police badge.

"Yes."

"Follow me, please."

The policeman is smiling. A real kid's grin, but a bit sad. John follows him. On the young man's back is the name and number of a soccer player he doesn't recognize. The jacket is in the Spanish national team's colors.

They go down several flights of stairs, leave the airport building, and cross a parking lot to where a small white car is parked. A man gets out, dressed in a ridiculous yellow raincoat: on his large round head is a deerstalker. He holds out his hand.

John shakes it. Why is the little man looking at him as if he's a foreigner? A foreign hippy, come to say good-bye to his best friend.

"My sympathies."

The older policeman looks him in the eye with painful insistence.

"Your embassy told me when the plane was leaving. I didn't know if you'd be here. I'm Lieutenant Guérin. And Lambert here," pointing to the tall blond man, "is my deputy."

Guérin glances across the deserted car park, checking that no one else was expected, and opened the car door, inviting John to get in.

Guérin and Nichols sat in the back, Lambert at the wheel like a chauffeur. The traffic got slower as they approached Paris. By Saint-Denis, it was bumper to bumper. The heat rose, and the bright light made the car windscreens flash. Lambert glanced at the French national soccer stadium, the Stade de France—another thing kids like.

Alan's death was obviously filtering a set of people out of the mass, holding in its mesh some ill-assorted fragments: Hirsh, Bunker, Königsbauer, Ariel, himself, and now these two detectives, a comical complementary pair, but with a stale whiff of death about them. The one beside him had an evasive expression, constantly looking about him. The placid junior balanced his boss's nervousness. Two more extraterrestrials for Alan's funeral procession.

"Did the embassy tell you to keep me under observation?"

"No, they just gave me some information."

"Do they want me out of town?"

"I assure you, I have nothing to do with the embassy, Mr. Nichols. Can I ask you who you are?"

The lieutenant's eyes weren't moving, just his head.

"I'm just a friend of Alan's."

"Mr. Mustgrave's death, and your presence here, are not too popular at the American Embassy. Can you tell me why?"

John lowered his window, then almost immediately put it up again as the stifling heat from the idling engines was sucked into the car.

"How did you find me?"

"I went to the Caveau de la Bolée this morning. I met Mlle. Quéroy. She told me about you. I didn't know if you'd be at Le Bourget."

There was a note of disappointment in Guérin's voice. Who else had he been hoping to meet?

"Why did you go to the Caveau?"

"You don't believe Mr. Mustgrave's death was accidental."

"Is that what Ariel told you?"

"Yes."

The policeman had gone slightly red; Ariel and her sumptuous breasts must have wowed him. John imagined the surrealist encounter of the tattooed dyke and the little detective.

"Stop calling him *Monsieur* Mustgrave. Why are you so interested in how Alan died?"

"Who did that to your face, Mr. Nichols?"

"Call me John."

"Well, John, I think it may be in our interests to talk to each other. That's why I came to the airport. I'm just wondering whether the death of your friend might have some connection to"—he hesitated— "to my present investigation. I'm looking into a number of suicides. Or rather into murders disguised as suicides."

John somehow contrived not to jump.

"I don't know what you mean. It wasn't an accident, but Alan did kill himself."

"Why?"

"Because he was suicidal."

Guérin looked at him, amused by the absurd obviousness of his response.

"That's all?"

"Isn't that enough?"

"You're better at pretending not to be very bright than at telling lies, John. What's going on with the embassy?"

"You've spoken to Hirsh?"

"No, I was put through to a Mr. Frazer when I called them. Do you know him?"

"I've only spoken to him on the phone, the embassy secretary. I can tell you what I know, but I need you to do something for me in return."

"What do you want?"

"To talk to a dealer."

"The one who beat you up?"

"They were working for him."

"What can you tell me?"

"It's not going to be much help, because your story's got nothing to do with mine."

Guérin's head tipped slightly to the side, and his eyes widened.

"You and I have met each other, and the chances of that happening by accident are cause enough for suspicion."

Lambert drove under the *périphérique,* and they entered Paris by the Porte de la Chapelle. Guérin pulled off his cap and started to rub at some invisible incrustation. John looked at the scratch marks on his head, then out of the window at the streets, which seemed to worry the lieutenant.

"You think some people get their kicks out of suicides, go and watch them do it onstage? Is that your theory?"

At the word "theory," Lambert gave a start, and Guérin put his cap back on.

"Alan did his fakir act, he was a junkie, he was gay, and he slept with this guy at the embassy, Hirsh, who seems to have vanished from circulation. That's why the subject is sensitive. Okay, it's stupid to say that nobody's responsible. Lieutenant, I've written a thesis on this, and I'm not going to deny it. But when he was onstage, he was alone, and he knew what he was doing. Nothing can alter that."

Guérin smiled.

"You're lying more convincingly now, but your intelligence gives you away. I consulted the report on your friend's death. The procedure was rushed through in double-quick time, to put it mildly. Did you know that the Medico-Legal Institute conducted no autopsy or analysis? Very shoddy police work. Or the opposite. The inquiry had been totally blocked. You think something else went on that night, don't you?"

John looked at the faces of the drivers in the cars around them. He had the disagreeable and recurrent feeling that he had taken the wrong turning; that he had deliberately got himself into a bewildering maze. He was just going to tell another lie, despite this policeman who inspired confidence, when a cell rang. Guérin excused himself and replied. A nasal voice was saying something into the speaker. Guérin said nothing as he ended the call.

His cheeks had become hollow, and his eyes had retreated into their sockets. He had the pained and chagrined expression of a man who has had his worst fears confirmed. Lambert half-turned in his seat.

"Everything okay, boss?"

Guérin, looking cadaverous, said haltingly:

"We're going to have to leave you here, Mr. Nichols; we've got work to do." He held out a card to John. "Call me tonight. Forgive us. Lambert, please drop Mr. Nichols at the nearest *métro* station."

John said good-bye at Métro Marx Dormoy. Lambert had put the sun visor down. Guérin made a sign with his hand, and the car pulled away.

He had gone to the airport without knowing why, and as usual, the answer had come from somewhere else.

•

"Where are we off to, boss? It's a woman, is it? You . . . um, you look a bit upset."

"No, not a woman . . . look, youngster, promise me you'll look out for yourself."

"What do you mean?"

"Just promise me, look after yourself."

"Yeah, right, of course, I'll take care. But what's the matter?"

"Savane's dead. Killed himself."

"Boss, does . . . does that mean they'll be after you again?"

Lambert would have sooner bitten his tongue, but the idea came only after the words were out.

•

Lambert had his hand on his gun and was shaking from head to foot. Guérin, lying on the pavement, and scarcely breathing, had grabbed hold of his leg to hold him back. He was clutching his assistant's calf, groggily, incapable of speech. Lambert the faithful dog was showing his teeth; Roman was yelling. Shame was turning to rage, sullen hatred to violence, guilt into a show of honor. Three men, uniforms in disarray, were holding the beast back with difficulty, looking as if they wanted to turn him loose. The holstered Beretta, gripped by the tall, blond junior, was banging against his ribs. Lambert had said nothing, but was white with rage. He bent his knees and slipped his arm under Guérin's, without taking his eyes off Roman. Barnier had arrived and was trying to speak over Roman's yelling.

"Calm down, calm down, for Christ's sake!"

Roman roared.

"Get that fucker out of my sight, *now*!"

Blood was streaming from a cut on Guérin's cheekbone, and his head was shaking. Three uniforms dragged Roman toward a car, panting. His feet scraped the ground as he tried to get purchase to attack again. Lambert watched him wild eyed. Barnier was beside himself.

"Lambert! Put the gun down! Or I'll arrest you!"

Lambert yelled now, louder than anyone else. "Get that scumbag out of here! Take him away!"

Barnier decided to hold still, faced with the determination of this great fool, and took it out on a nearby fireman.

"Look after Guérin, why don't you? Can't you see he's hurt?"

Guérin clutched at Lambert's Spanish soccer jacket and leaned into the gutter to vomit. Berlion, who was still on his knees, was swallowing his tongue and holding onto his balls, his eyes popping out of his head. Lambert wore size 44 shoes and played soccer. Divisionnaire Barnier didn't know where to turn. So he shouted at everyone. His entire team had just imploded.

Savane, his arms and legs stiff, was laid out on his back in the middle of his living room. His eyes were open, his service revolver in his hand. Savane, a great big guy you couldn't shift, a statue pulled down by a revolution. On the whites of his eyes, alongside the blue irises, sat drops of blood that the fixed eyelids had not blinked away. Lieutenant Savane, a bullet through his forehead, was staring at his colleagues with eyes that were red, white, and blue, and nobody dared close them.

The compress wasn't staunching the blood streaming between Guérin's fingers. Around him the room was full of noise, murmurs, embarrassed movements. One or two people had left the room with expressions of disgust. Guérin knelt down beside the body, and some idiot muttered under his breath: *"What the fuck's he doing here? Kowalski wasn't enough for him?"* Guérin heard nothing, nor did he see Lambert stride across the room and plant himself in front of two men from Homicides. Ready to let them have it in the guts.

"Get the hell out of here."

Lambert had already laid Berlion out. He was frothing at the mouth. The halfwit obviously had teeth. The two men got the hell out.

Guérin, still on his knees was meditating on the pointless death of a police officer, worn to the bone by a job without a future, the absurd death of a perfectly good-hearted man who had been turned into a monster by a life he had hardly had time to understand. Out of all the suicides in Paris, it was inevitable that one day he would come across somebody he knew. The rarer possibility—that it should be someone he liked—made the experience all the more painful.

He unbuttoned his yellow raincoat, took it off, and spread it over the corpse. The gesture had an electric effect on the other people in the room. Relief at seeing that face disappear. The appearance of Guérin's unfamiliar puny outline. The shedding of his eternal yellow second skin, like an insect emerging from a chrysalis. The tenderness and gentleness of his gestures. The respect for privacy and for the passing of a man. A gift from the tiny Guérin to the cooling mastodon. A game of deceptive appearances that went right over the heads of the officers still present.

Guérin stood up, into a silence like that in church, hesitated, looking at the body that his raincoat only half covered, then knelt on the floor again. He pulled the yellow shroud down a few more inches, with a slow gesture and a smile . . . a promise.

He walked out of the flat, leaving behind a group of horrified colleagues now stuck in the room with the corpse. Savane's bloodstained face was once more staring at them with its red-spattered eyes over the top of the raincoat.

Savane had made a deliberate effort to die with his eyes open. Someone else would have to close them for him. The guys from the Disciplinary Division, perhaps, the same ones who had used whitehot pincers to tell him he was being dismissed from the service. Or Roman, who had informed against his comrade in order to save his own undercover job? Or Barnier, who had always thought him an idiot? Well, it wouldn't be Guérin, anyway, the only one who had spent a year trying to open them for him. Or the dealer from the Goutte d'Or, who had died in the night.

Savane had looked the bullet in the face, a moment of truth, and it was only right that his little pals should experience it, too.

Only it was now Guérin's job to bring down the whole show. A question of balance.

"Thank you for stepping in, Lambert. Drop me off at the office, then go and have a few drinks and put your thinking cap on. Things are going to get complicated, and you'd better give your career some thought."

Lambert handed the boss his cap, which Roman's left hook had sent flying.

"Boss, I never wanted to be in the police. I wanted to be a nurse. But my dad said that was a girl's job."

Guérin smiled and leaned toward his deputy, showing him the cut on his cheek.

"What do you think about this, then?"

"It needs stitches."

What connection is there between a man who weeps and a man who is angry? The weeping man wants to be a nurse; the angry man goes for the balls. And the only solution, the link, was Lambert. Not too bright, but in good working order. Guérin didn't try to ask why, around him, suicide was becoming a miracle solution that prevented people from looking for any others.

"Lambert, son, you're a mystery."

Lambert did not reply: he was absorbed in staring at Lieutenant Guérin.

●

Tenon Hospital, in the rue de la Chine, was the nearest place he could get stitches. A center for cosmetic surgery, as it happened, and the wound wasn't quite serious enough for that. The police badges persuaded a specialist on liposuction to take care of Guérin's cheek. "Nothing fancy," he had said, "just sew it up so that it stays put." But the doctor took pains to make a good job of it, under the curious eyes of lanky Lambert. He refused to write an invoice, saying that it was a pleasure to do something useful for a change. But he also gave Guérin a brochure about hair transplants, with an expression suggesting he might start with that.

Six stitches and a small scar for his old age.

Lambert slid behind the wheel and cleared his throat.

"Boss, I'm sorry . . . I, um, I just can't manage it."

"Manage what?"

"I'm sorry, I can't manage to shed any tears for Savane."

The man who could weep had finally delivered a kick in the balls. Two big tears ran down Guérin's cheeks.

●

In the office, the stain on the ceiling had dried up, the pink was paler, and the brown rings around it stood out more clearly. Lambert tore two pages from the calendar. Ripping off these two little pieces of paper made him feel as if time had speeded up, was getting out of control. He had forgotten his role as timekeeper these last days. The calendar had stood still on the day Savane had come to see them.

Guérin sat behind his desk and slid a trembling hand over his cap.

"Now then, young Lambert, we need some coffee."

His deputy went off, dragging his feet at his usual calm pace. Why did he still say "young Lambert" and call him "son"? He remembered his mother, who used to call him "my big boy," and the feeling that had given him that he had never grown up. By calling him "young Lambert," he was probably trying to say the opposite. He then turned his mind to Nichols, a more strongly built and intellectually sharper version of Lambert, if that comparison made any sense. The American was an empty shell, ninety kilos' worth of questions. His mother probably called him "my big boy," too. So perhaps there was a connection between going to a university and having a castrating mother. Guérin let his ideas run on for a bit before he dared to open the envelope. On his desk, in Savane's small and contorted handwriting, just one word on the crumpled paper: *Richard*. He looked at the door—Savane had presumably picked the lock without difficulty—then unfolded the letter.

There are some photos of Kowalski in Roman's place. Roman's so dumb he couldn't help hanging on to them. Now I'm dead, you can finish your investigation. Sorry I let you down. Don't worry about the memory I'll leave behind. If you bring down these shits you'll be doing what I'd have done if I'd had the guts. At least I won't have died still one of them. Goodbye, Richard. And thanks.

"Boss, they only had decaf. That okay?"

12

The teenager, fourteen or fifteen, and growing fast, arrived on a skateboard, slaloming between the pedestrians. Tight jeans, enormous sneakers, and a skinny T-shirt declaring *"No Current, No Sharks."* His Beatles bangs flopped over his forehead, and he was being a pain in the ass to everyone. He stopped his skateboard with a kick and tapped in the code of the big metal door. John went in behind him.

The young rebel, plugged into his iPod, looked him up and down, wondering what tribe he belonged to. A techno warrior? Homeless? A leftover hippy? The boy asked him who he wanted, with all the aplomb of a householder. John said he was visiting the woman on the ground floor, and the moptop boy blushed scarlet. Behind his dilated teenage pupils could be guessed the hours he had spent spying from his bedroom on the studio windows below.

"Patricia? I don't know if she's there. I can go and see if you like."

"I can manage."

The boy trailed around the yard on some nonexistent pretext, hoping to see the girl from the ground floor who took her clothes off all the time.

Patricia opened the door. The dark glasses could hide her eyes, but not her mouth. The manly kudos of having been punched on the jaw did not suit her as well as it did John.

"What do you want now? Go away."

John tried to see behind the dark glasses and his distorted reflection. "What happened?"

Black, long-sleeved, high-necked sweater, no skin showing. Comfort or camouflage. She'd had a bad time. She was trembling, bourgeoise and haughty to her fingertips, wearing her temporary bruises with the dignity of a ruined aristocrat.

"Get out."

"I want some answers, now."

She looked over his shoulder at the empty courtyard and let him in.

Today her style was low heels, tailored pants, black, too, and the sweater was skintight. These carefully chosen coverings were worrying in a woman who had few inhibitions.

"I went to the airport this morning. You didn't come to say goodbye to your friend."

"I was otherwise engaged, Mr. Nichols."

She took off the glasses. The left eye was black and closed. She had dressed to match.

"A problem with a customer. He didn't like the photos?"

"Alan told me you had no idea how to talk to women."

Her blonde curls seemed ablaze, atop the sexy black column.

"I live in the woods."

"*Really?* One would hardly have guessed."

"Black suits you. Are you in mourning for your business?"

The remaining eye was enough to put him in his place.

"I have no idea what you're talking about."

John blinked. An explosion went off in his head. There was no longer any lying, calculation, or game playing in Paty's voice. A cold shower. John P. Nichols was knocked out by one look. Bad call, wrong track. With one sentence, a fuse in the machine had blown and hit him between the eyes. Patricia Königsbauer blackmailing someone, playing the whore for money she didn't need? No, it was ridiculous. Alan. Him again. John walked around the studio, looking into the blank canvases for a confidence that he had already lost. With the first reply, like the first arrow. For months now, every time he drew his bow, he'd had the same impression: doubt. Fear of aiming at the wrong target: he'd had the same intuition in the car with Guérin. It was Alan who had landed Paty in the shit. That's what must have happened. Alan with his big grin. "Want me to stand in front of the target?" She had been beaten up on account of the fakir. As he had. Paty was a friend. Another friend. John had been jealous. "*You used him.*" Since the beginning. He had denied, thought, mulled over, invented a portrait of her to feed his own bitterness.

He tried to rescue what he could of appearances, so as not to have to backtrack too fast. But this time he knew, he would be the one who ended up stripped naked.

"Was it Boukrissi who did this to you?"

Go on, John, get in deeper.

"You really don't get it, do you?"

"Well, who then?"

"The important thing is *why*. I wasn't at the airport, because I was being beaten up, on your account."

Get the buses back on track, do the math, Nichols, stick the pieces together.

"Big blond guy, neck like a bull, American?"

"They told me not to talk to you. Get out, get out of town, take the money and disappear. That's all you can do now."

"But who are you talking about? Who's 'they'? The chauffeur? Hirsh?"

"Hirsh? Don't be ridiculous, Hirsh was just a plaything for Alan. I can't tell you any more. Just go."

"Tell me about the blackmail. Were you in it with Alan? Who else was there, that time I came here?"

"Stop inventing stupid stories. I was never in anything with Alan."

"Tell me what happened. I can protect you."

Her laughter, exploding from the black column, resounded around the studio.

"Protect me! Don't be ridiculous!"

"There was a policeman at the airport this morning. I can call him if you like."

"So you say."

He put Guérin's card down on the counter in the kitchen.

"Do you want to talk to him?"

"You disappoint me."

She folded her arms but looked at the card. She was trembling with fear. Her skintight clothes, John thought, were to hold in the fear.

"Who was here when I came before?"

"Hirsh."

"What was he doing?"

"He'd come to warn me."

"About what?"

"That the others would probably come. He thought it was because of his affair with Alan."

"Tell me, for fuck's sake . . ."

"They want the money and the documents."

John sat down on a stool, and she had the decency not to humiliate him further. She said nothing but went behind the bar to fetch a glass and poured herself a Scotch, which made him want one, too. As she had two days before, she turned and looked critically at John's portrait: *You're too big. You take up all the room on the canvas.* "Alan did this because of *you*. It's all your fault. Does this policeman really exist?"

"Yes."

"Why is he interested in Alan?"

"Just tell me everything."

She swirled the alcohol around the glass.

"Then you'll get out of my life?"

Choose now. The truth and then go? A lie and stay here? He knew fuck all about what was going on.

Go down with the ship. Get it over with.

John clenched his teeth. "You didn't sleep with Alan, did you?"

She sipped the whiskey, not sorry to end up confessing: "It was a lie, pure vanity."

"Why did you do my portrait when Hirsh was there?"

Her black eye opened a little, and the hazel iris shone in the middle of the bruise. A smile. The killer blow, John. Soon.

"It was a game Alan liked to play. Hirsh came sometimes, too. It wasn't *blackmail*, just a game. Alan liked a good show . . . the way the . . . He said it made him laugh to see these men's faces when I made them impotent. You probably think that's perverse, sadistic, whatever. Alan said you were straightlaced, naive; you were just into boring stuff."

"Alan said that? Why did you do it with me, then?"

"Alan talked a lot about you. One more of his games. I suppose he liked to get inside other people's emotions by proxy."

She smiled again and finished the sentence she had started two days before.

"Alan was in love with you; he'd always been in love with you."

"I know."

Each of them on one side of the bar, faces in the mirror, distorted.

"When he laughed, the truth was sad but beautiful." She turned her back. "I liked Alan's games."

Before he could say anything else, she made him leave.

•

Bunker was finishing his rounds. He had slept badly, with his joints and his scar aching. All day, he had prowled the park railings like a wild beast, Mesrine skulking at his heels. He had coshed a man, no doubt risking his life, and uncorked the volcano of anger that he had spent long years trying to bottle up. He could hardly say he regretted it, but he was afraid now that he might not be able to turn back the clock. The American had shaken his false sense of calm, blown a hole in his hard-won little island of security.

He had tasted once more the freedom that had sent him to prison. The gates were closing on him, and Bunker was gasping for breath. That kid was going to push him deeper in without realizing it. And the old convict would be asking for more.

He dragged his boots along the alleys of the gardens aiming for his cabin, with the impression of going back into the cooler. How long had it been since he had approached a woman, gone into a café, or been able to walk through the streets? All he knew was these fucking lawns, the park fountains, the pigeons, the minimarket in the rue Bara. How long since he had really seen his city? Had a life? 1994 had meant the cabin with its little fence. He had never counted the years. Time had stopped with the 1983 calendar and never started again. It was time to stop lying to himself. Getting on for fifteen years in a park . . . A double sentence.

Fear of opening the cage door. Prison had been following him around . . . he was beginning to admit it. It was right here, inside him.

The American was slumped across the step of the cabin.

Mesrine sat down at a safe distance, not attempting to come nearer. Bunker waved his hand and fetched the little table and chairs, a bottle of wine, and two glasses without a word. The shrink needed to talk.

It was a fine day, almost warm in the shade of this umbrella pine, surviving miles from the sea. Mesrine stretched out in the sun a few yards away.

"So you said good-bye to your buddy?"

John smiled. He was aware of having a mask over his face that was unlike him. A routine mask, expressionless and distant. With Bunker's ugly mug pretending to be happy with his lot, they'd have been a gas at a fancy-dress ball.

"Why do you always understand too late something you already knew? Know the answer to that, Bunk?"

"You wouldn't last long in prison, tell you that, son. Too much going on inside that head."

Visitors to the park strolled by, no doubt thinking they were witnessing a typical picturesque Parisian scene. An old reprobate, no doubt, with his glass of red and his tobacco, alongside a Yankee hippy smoking a cigarette, and a mutt that was clearly an enemy of the system. Bunker put his cap on the table and rumpled his hair. He filled the glasses. John took a long pull on his Gitane.

"I tried to say good-bye, but he came back again."

"No further on then?"

"Yeah, I am, but it doesn't make things any better."

"Spit it out, Mr. Shrink, I can't wait."

"Apparently all this has happened because of *me*. I can't think any different. She was right."

"You saw the girl again?"

"Here's looking at you."

The wine was working its benevolent magic.

"Alan met Hirsh at the cabaret. Hirsh liked all kinds of perversions, probably because he'd led such a sheltered life. Alan played games with him. It gave him a kick, this junkie who was into S&M, this Gulf War veteran, screwing Hirsh in his office at the embassy. If that wasn't so stupid, it would almost be funny. But that was just the last stage."

"Drink up. I got nothing to do but listen."

Like every time he talked about Alan, John's American accent was stronger.

"The CIA, NSA, and FBI, the secret services, they've always got cutting-edge technology, but that's not the only thing they're into. They're into psychology and social science as well. They call it 'intelligence.' *Bullshit.* Torture isn't the best way to get information. Eighty percent of stuff you get that way isn't reliable: pressure, lies, memory failure, phony confessions, anything to stop the pain. The things that really work are spying and truth-telling drugs. Torture's a form of psychological warfare. When people talk about gratuitous torture, they think it isn't to get information, that it's pure sadism. But really it's the opposite, it's the true torture. The idea is to demolish the enemy, then let a few go back home. To tell the tale. They demolish them, Bunk, so they won't give you any trouble in the future. You're going to build a perfect world of tomorrow, using guys who don't share your vision of democracy. And you let them loose like a virus, a virus of fear and silence. Torture means attacking an individual to terrorize a group. You create these lonely men, the walking dead, and they strike fear into people. And if you want to manufacture torturers, same thing. You take regular guys and transform them. You empty them out and then fill them with whatever suits you. You get a trained soldier, someone in the secret police, or a scientist who sees enemies everywhere. And around these guys, with films and newspapers, you build a world that tells them they're absolutely right, paranoid and ignorant. And to make it all work properly and efficiently, you need some specialists, intellectuals, people like me. Creating torturers isn't something you can simply improvise. Then, after that, you find some guys like Alan. That's not the hardest bit.

"He had no idea the Gulf War was about to happen. He only joined the army to get out of Kansas. He was recruited when he was still in the mud on Parris Island, the boot camp for the marines. Alan was good and ready for all this, a whole new custom-built family. Unbelievable what a man will do to get out of Kansas. His instructor, the one who found him, he was in the CIA, and he was heading up a new program. So Alan spent four months in a training center in the navy base in San Diego. At first he didn't get what was going on with this special job. They never tell you directly, it's all very gradually eased into place. You're an *intelligence specialist*. And he was a good pupil. To create a torturer, first of all you show him what the other side did—in Korea, Japan, Vietnam. And on the other side, of course, they're doing the same thing, showing *their* soldiers what was done in Korea, Japan, Vietnam. You want to terrorize your enemies, and the result is just the opposite: you get to be so goddam disgusting that you're the direct cause of the resistance. If they torture your father and mother, what do you do? Give them a hand burning the bodies? Don't laugh, Bunk, there are professionals in the military who still don't get it.

"Alan was in one of the first planes that took off for Iraq in '91, with the Intelligence staff. This was a new war, a new generation, new technology. Nothing original about it. Just perfecting the old ways. You give your victims a cocktail of drugs; you mess up their biological clocks, light, sleep; you put them in cages too small to lie down, too low to stand up, or boxes where you *can* only stand up, for days. You alternate the things you do, the kind of humiliation, depending on the people you torture; you adapt it for religion, or culture, or sex; you make threats, give them false information: your brother said this, your pal's confessed, your father's dead, that kind of thing. And the guys in charge, they watch their men as closely as the prisoners: they're sensitive machines . . . you've got to look after them.

You can't let it get out of hand, let the sadists go off and do whatever they want. The progress that's been made in torture these days, it's in the quality of the people doing it. Alan was very fragile before. Over there, he was one of the tough guys, a real asshole. He took it out on people's bodies. He told me that when he was doing that, he could feel in his head that his father was proud of him. Or so his instructor was telling him. This guy, his commanding officer, he knew Alan's whole life story. Successful torture is when you've destroyed the victim's ideology. And a well-trained torturer gets his own ideology inside the other guy's head. That's what ideology is, Bunk. A distorting mirror, where the enemy has the same twisted face as you. Alan's boss was just a machine for processing ideas that weren't his own. But who has their own ideas anyway? If you're a good subject, you can do everything they tell you to and even get the feeling you're free. Alan liberated himself in Iraq, you could say. But all the same, there was something inside him that put up resistance. A paradox. He thought the army had freed him from his past and that he could start living a new life afterward . . . his own life. So he got out. When he got back from the desert, he left the army. Well, what he did, he broke his contract; he deserted. But when he found himself out of the army, he couldn't recognize the world he'd had described to him, and that felt strange. Strange to feel like the men he'd sent away with their balls ripped off.

"So, Alan started to take heroin, because it's a drug that cuts you off from the world. He was already pretty hooked on drugs anyway, coming out of the army. And afterward he found it perfectly normal to be like the men he had tortured. To take his clothes off in the street, to roll on broken glass, not to sleep anymore, to have night-mares and to have sex with guys he felt nothing for. The army made a success of him, but the wrong way around: now he started warning Americans off going to war. That's what his fakir show was all about. A fight inside one man, between the victim and the torturer, in front of the public that had created him. He was doing what he had done to his victims the other way around. So we worked together to try and fix what my colleagues had broken. When he got to Paris, the worst was over. He'd become a kind of image of himself, and he was soon going to lose that. In the Caveau, when he met this embassy guy, Hirsh, he thought it was hilarious. Picking up a gay American diplomat who went to the same kind of hangout that he did? Another mirror image, another one claiming some kind of false victory. Having sex in Hirsh's office, I don't know how he managed it. It must have made him laugh so much. Then one day, meeting Hirsh at the embassy, he saw Frazer, the so-called secretary. That's not his real name. The man who recruited Alan back in '90, in South Carolina. He was with Alan in the Gulf. Frazer came to see Patricia this morning, and he beat her up. I've never seen him, but Alan told me about him. When she described him, I knew just who she was talking about. His real name's Lundquist. Alan went nuts when he recognized him. He started injecting again. He just collapsed.

"That was two months ago. That's when he came to see me. After that, and I know how, he blackmailed Lundquist. It's not Alan's dealer who wants me out of town, it's Lundquist, Samuel Lundquist. His name is all over my thesis. Alan must have used my work to blackmail him. Patricia said that Lundquist gave Alan some money. Three days before he died."

Bunker, looking somewhat stunned, had his glass to his lips but forgot to drink.

"And you know the funny thing? The reason I didn't publish my thesis was to protect Alan. The FBI contacted me when I'd done all the research, and they told me not to publish it, or Alan would go to jail. He had signed a contract with the army, *security clearance*. *Access to Sensitive Compartmented Information.* Compartmented! That's a real military euphemism. They were blackmailing me, they didn't want any of my thesis in the public domain. Well, I signed up to the deal, and told Alan to get out of the country, to go to France. He died because he went back on the deal that was protecting him. So Lundquist—and the people who must be behind him—will be wondering what I'm going to do now. All that stuff, the First Gulf War, it was fifteen years ago, but of course now we're into another never-ending war, with more torture. And in my thesis there are plenty of names of people still in post. When I was writing it, Alan and I, we'd decided we would spill the beans. I didn't respect scientific objectivity, as my profs would say. But that's what Alan wanted, and me, too. But, now, what am I going to do? I've no idea, no *fucking* idea at all."

Bunker waited for the rest. The kid's indecision didn't seem like a proper conclusion. John smiled and raised his glass.

"The girl, Patricia, she told me to get out of her life and never try to see her again. If that's what interests you."

"Ah. So she wasn't lying."

"Not this time."

"So she said the opposite of what she thought."

"Bunk, I called my mother in San Francisco. The FBI came and did a search in the house. They took everything, my laptop, my notes, all the work I had left there. And I called my thesis supervisor. Same thing at UCLA: they took everything."

The old keeper was twiddling his cap in his fingers, staring into the distance, over a playground, a tennis court, the park railings, and the rue Guynemer. His boyish smile had vanished, leaving just an ersatz fixed grin in contradiction to the anger in his eyes.

"Something there doesn't fit, son."

"The Aouch brothers . . ."

"Boukrissi's just an ordinary crook; it must be your Lundquist who's pulling his strings."

"He may have killed Alan."

"They know where I am. You've put a bomb under my cabin, sonny."

John dropped his gaze, breathed out, and then faced up to Bunker's thermonuclear expression.

"Um, it's not over, yet. I . . . I met this French detective and he thinks Alan didn't commit suicide. He wants us to share what we've got, work together."

The ex-con's jaw muscles clenched and unclenched. His gappy teeth ground like rusty hinges.

"Bunk . . ."

"Shut up!"

"I've got something else to ask you."

Mesrine had pressed himself up against his master's legs. Bunker's lips didn't move. The words seemed to come out of his forehead, from a swollen vein throbbing under the scar.

"Son, I told you to drop it. Your artist was right. Maybe you got your reasons, but you don't half go around dumping other people in the shit."

13

The cup of decaf reeked of pointlessness. Guérin fiddled with the stitches on his cheek to try to stay awake. He kept looking at his watch, checking that time was going past outside the room with no windows: 6:12 p.m.

Nobody in No. 36 was yet aware that the whole floor was smoldering away underneath them. Savane had relit the fuse by blowing his brains out.

The Big Theory was on the point of collapse, sabotaged by Kowalski's return. It was sinking, and Guérin along with it, in a tangle of obscure, isolated trails. The Caveau, Nichols, three ghosts, and Savane. The letter. An incoherent mess. One thought obsessed Guérin, a keystone with rocky foundations: he had to move in on Roman. And prove that the whole edifice was built on nothing. A precarious shell suspended from a set of illusions. Which he proposed to sweep away. There was no victory on the horizon. He would just have to introduce a wedge, and whatever the scale of the collapse, he would either be crushed or survive. Move in on Roman.

He stared at the door to the archive room, his arms folded, enveloped in a silence loud with questions. In his mind, he walked in between the shelves, revisiting the files, without remembering having ever found sufficient reasons for the suicides listed there. The dead have no way of justifying themselves, and the dossiers could never contain all the possible elements behind their choice. The reasons of the dead have to be looked for in the living. The choice made by Savane. Move in on Roman.

All he lacked now was some excuse to move into action; but he could find none. He scratched at his stitches, glanced at his watch again: 6:14 p.m. Why was he so reluctant to do what he had to do?

The telephone rang. Guérin sat without moving, deaf to the sounds of the telephone that was shouting an answer at him.

It went on ringing. Lambert looked inquiringly at the boss, and in the end he picked it up. He listened, took notes, using his elbow to anchor a slip of paper. His voice echoing in the office sounded like Guérin's.

"Car exhaust, underground garage, avenue Victor Hugo. Boss?"

Guérin was looking at Lambert with his head on one side: his face lit up with a friendly smile.

The little lieutenant took a deep breath and slipped Savane's letter into his pocket, not worried now about his career, or the consequences, or the reasons of the people who were still standing. Death, the leader of the dance, had just made a phone call. The answer had come from the catacombs, the foundations of everything, delivered by a Hermes in a tracksuit.

In his little world of the archives, what could he ever change except the past? His mistake had been to think that he would act for the future.

He stood up, in the name of the dead.

"Okay, let's go, Lambert, but I need to drop in at my place on the way."

Guérin slipped a few tools into his coat pockets. A set of skeleton keys, a flashlight, a small claw hammer, and a pair of gloves. Churchill said nothing. Just a bundle of feathers, crouching on his perch. The parrot's breast was now bare, revealing his sad, gray wrinkled skin. His clipped wings were mere stumps. The bird who had never flown was methodically pulling out his plumage.

Guérin put some seed in his dish. The bird gave him a baleful look and went back to work on itself.

Avenue Victor Hugo: a parking space in the basement of a stone building. The man had made it a point of honor to die gripping the wheel in the official driving-school position, hands at ten past ten.

De Rochebrune, a writer, journalist, economist, publisher, and essayist. Yes, he'd tried everything: the remaining possibilities must have seemed too trivial. His wife, talking nonstop, for fear of having to surrender to the evidence, insisted on telling her husband's life story in detail. She drowned her lack of understanding in sociological explanations, a futile stream of words that Guérin let flow without interrupting. This man had left a much longer suicide note than Savane's. A typescript of two hundred pages on the passenger seat. This couple were both wordy. Either he'd written something really good before dying or he hadn't and was providing an explanation for his death. Box checked off.

Guérin's notebook had not come out. Lambert was making some awkward jottings in his pocket diary. The two policemen were mournful, tired presences, communicating their gloom to anyone else in the parking lot not already depressed. Lambert muttered a few words of sympathy without conviction. They moved off, while the voice of the woman, now hanging onto the arm of a haggard fireman, echoed through the underground garage. Their departure made the atmosphere lift a little.

Lambert, dark circles under his eyes, stuffed his hands in his pockets, dragging his sneakers on the concrete floor.

"Back to the office, or will I take you home?" he asked, not really believing the day was over.

The boss wasn't listening.

It was getting dark outside. The stitches looked like flies on his cheeks.

Guérin called Information from the car.

Address and phone number, Frédéric Roman, Clamart.

The cell beeped, and a text appeared.

"Clamart, rue Barbusse, No. 13, Lambert."

Lambert did not reply or ask what they were doing.

They took cover in the southern suburb of Clamart, in a street lined with bungalows. 9:00 p.m. Guérin remembered reading Henri Barbusse's book *Under Fire*. Images of the trenches and of bombs tearing bodies to pieces came back to him. Pacifists make the best war reporters and monks the best writers about love.

A light was on in Roman's house.

Guérin tapped a number into his cell.

"Yeah?"

"Guérin here."

". . . What do you want?"

"Savane left a note. We need to talk."

"Fuck off."

"Either me or the disciplinary tribunal. In my office, in an hour."

"What about Berlion?"

"Looking for a scapegoat already? Savane not enough for you?"

". . . You can't touch me."

"One hour."

Roman emerged from the house ten minutes later, pulling on his leather jacket. He got into his car and drove off at speed.

Guérin put on the gloves.

"Keep watch, Lambert. Call me if you see him coming back."

•

He had about an hour. Time for Roman to get to 36 quai des Orfèvres, realize he'd been fooled, and come back. The garden gate was still open. It was a modest bungalow, bought for immediate occupancy ten years ago, the householder's pride having faded somewhat now. Guérin peered through the window of the living room and checked out the inside doors. No alarms. Noticing a decorative brick on the ground by a dead lilac bush, he decided not to bother with his locksmith tools and used a quicker and not too damaging alternative. He placed his cap against one of the panes, and hit it with the brick. The broken glass fell on the carpet. He put his hand inside and opened the catch.

Roman's place was a mess, when inspected by flashlight. Living room: racks for DVDs, American action movies or French comedies. A locked wooden desk. Empty beer cans on a low table, a shabby sofa. He broke open the door of the desk. Porn films, locked away from the kids. Guérin felt around among the DVDs, turned over cushions, opened drawers. He had a whole house to search, at least in the obvious places, hoping Roman wasn't a genius at hiding stuff. And that the photographs were still there. Drinks cupboard, look behind the bottles. Nothing in the living room. Kitchen: the neglected kitchen of a divorced man. Cupboards, drawers, on the units, under them, under the sink. The pool of light flickered hesitantly from place to place. Nothing in the kitchen. What about the hall? A cupboard with accordion doors.

More clutter, work tools, a sawed-off shotgun and cartridges, knuckledusters, copies of *Playboy* and *Target*, a new Browning rifle, a Mauser survival knife, well sharpened. Bullets, cleaning stuff. Old shoes, rusty sheers, gardening gloves, and a dusty box of toys. Nothing. Guérin put the claw back in his pocket and carried on, knife in one hand, flashlight in the other. Bathroom stinking of piss. Nothing in the tank.

Main bedroom. The stuffy smell of dirty sheets, feet. Under the mattress, in the wardrobe, under the bed: more porn mags. A framed poster, Dirty Harry under glass. What a cretin. Look behind the frame. Nothing. Cut up the mattress, open up the pillows. Nothing. Carpet: use the knife. Nothing. Guérin was sweating now. Spare bedroom. Bunk beds. Kids' room, neat and tidy. Toys in a chest, plastic guns, childish drawings pinned to the wall, Walt Disney duvets on the bed ends. Photos on the bedside table. Two boys, age about eight and ten. Miniature versions of their father. Graceless, tough looking. The family was low of brow. The room was orderly, and dust lay thick. The kids didn't visit often. Look around, cut up the mattresses, with some reluctance. But nothing. Roman at least had the decency not to hide photographs of corpses in the kids' bedroom. Bathroom. Rancid towels, peeling wallpaper, patches of damp. Guérin looked at his watch. Half an hour already. Dirty linen, shelves, cupboards.

Nothing. Under the washbasin, behind the bath, nothing under the bath. Ventilator grill. Knife out again. No, nothing behind it.

Back to the living room, open up the sofa. Nothing. Carpet, attacked again with the knife. Nothing. Back to the kitchen. Fitted cooker. More and more frantic, Guérin pulled the oven from its fitting. Nothing behind it, nothing inside. Moved the fridge, holding the flashlight between his teeth. No, nothing behind it. Had Savane got it wrong? Roman must have got rid of the photographs. Forty-five minutes. The kitchen smelled of grease, cooking oil, unwashed dishes. There was bound to be an attic, maybe a cellar as well. Guérin exhaled deeply.

●

9:30 p.m., sixteenth arrondissement. John put the visiting card back in his pocket.

He rang the bell of the building in the rue de Longchamp several times, waiting two minutes. No reply from Hirsh's flat. He hadn't really expected it. He hesitated, then pressed the concierge's bell three times. The big wooden door swung open a few centimeters, and an old woman's eye moved up and down behind the crack of light.

"What is it?"

"I'm sorry to bother you so late, but I was looking for Mr. Hirsh."

"He's not here. Are you from the embassy?"

John exaggerated his accent.

"Yeah, that's right, I'm a colleague of Mr. Hirsh's."

The concierge opened the door a bit wider. Dressing gown, slippers, smell of vegetable soup wafting out.

"Would you be Monsieur Trapper?"

John cleared his throat and smiled broadly.

"That's *right!*"

"He told me you'd be around."

"Ah. Good."

"He left something for you."

The old woman disappeared, behind the door, went into her quarters, which she had left open, and brought out an envelope. She had glasses on now and scrutinized John before handing it to him.

"What do you do in the embassy?"

"I'm in the cultural service, I, erm . . . deal with artists."

"Ah, I thought so. You don't look like the others. We've got two more people from the embassy in this house. Lots of them in the area. Here it is."

She passed him a white envelope. Handwritten: *John Trapper.* John smiled again and pocketed it as naturally as he could.

"Tell me, *madame*, when did Mr. Hirsh leave?"

The old woman's white eyebrows shot up above the spectacles.

"Didn't you know?"

"I knew he was leaving, but not so soon."

"He went the day before yesterday. Some people came to fetch his things today, removers. Two hours, and that was it, all done. He said he was going back to America. Promotion or something, but he didn't look happy to be going. I think he'll miss Paris. What a nice man, I'm going to miss—"

"Thank you so much, Madame. Goodnight."

John read the letter as he walked back.

Mr. Nichols,

As you will have gathered, my situation has become impossible in Paris. I have to go back to the States. My career's on the line, but I'm going to try to do what seems important from now on.

Alan asked me to send a letter to your address in the Lot, in case anything happened to him. I didn't realize then what it was he wanted to talk about. I should tell you that I posted it after we'd met at the embassy. A letter for you, from Alan. I don't even know if you're still in Paris, so perhaps you're already back home and have got the letter by now. Never mind, it's almost funny, even in these circumstances, to be getting out of town and leaving a mystery message. I hope you read this note that I'm giving my concierge to keep for you as a last resort, since I can't reach you.

Alan talked a lot about you, and I'm sorry I didn't get to know you better. I couldn't talk to anyone, except to Secretary Frazer, and that was not an enjoyable interview, about my love for your friend. It was a tragedy, but now I think, after all, that he must have wanted it that way. The letter to you makes me think he was preparing his death. You knew him better than I did, so maybe you will understand better.

Forgive my little trick over your name, just a precaution.

Good-bye.

FH

Alan certainly had a gift for casting. The lucidity of the torturer. John smiled wryly as he thought about the young diplomat. He hadn't really understood what he was getting into. A cheap thrill, slumming it with a hippy masochist. A little rebellion against Uncle Sam's establishment. He'd had a dodgy love affair while under the influence, but he'd played his part in it, too. Hirsh would surely get over it.

His cell rang. He jumped. Cold sweat. The screen lit up in the dark kitchen. Unknown caller.

Not Lambert, then. Roman? If the worst came to the worst, he could play for time. He breathed in and pressed *reply.*

"Lieutenant Guérin?"

"Yes."

"John Nichols."

"Who?"

"John, we met at the airport, Alan Mustgrave's friend."

"I can't talk now."

"I've got to see you."

"I haven't got time."

"We've got to meet."

"I'll call you back."

"I don't have a mob . . ."

Guérin had switched off, furious and high on adrenalin. Minutes lost, huge fatigue and nerves on edge. His hour would soon be up. The house had been turned upside down. And now Nichols and his masochistic pal were blundering into the Kowalski sewer. He put the flashlight down and rested both hands on the work surface. He breathed in with his stomach, giving himself a minute to collect his thoughts. Sweat was forming on the bald cranium and trickling down into his eyes. The acrid smell mingled with the odor of stale fat. He shone the flashlight on the hood over the hob, and pressed the on switch.

The extractor fan didn't work. He jumped back and dropped the knife. The blade bounced on the tiled floor and shrill tones suddenly burst on his ears. The cell again. Still not Lambert. He waited for it to stop ringing and picked up the knife, his heart pounding furiously. He pulled the grid out of the hood. Sticking to the grease-drenched filter was a plastic bag, and inside it a big brown envelope. He slipped his hand inside, teeth clenched on the metal flashlight.

His cell registered yet another message, and the wretched beep made him jump again. Yes. This was it. Color photographs. Corpses laid out in the morgue for autopsy. Kowalski. Abruptly, Guérin vomited, a burning stream that sent the flashlight skittering across the kitchen floor. He ran from the room, skidding on the pool of sick on the floor, jumped out of the living room window, and got into the car with Lambert. He collapsed on the seat, deathly pale, clutching the envelope in his trembling hands.

Lambert, alarmed, put his foot down.

"Where to, boss?"

"Your place."

Guérin listened to the message on his cell in a daze. It was the American again.

"Lieutenant, it's John again. I'm in a phone booth. I'll wait half an hour. Please call back, it's urgent."

"Nichols?"

"Yes."

"What do you want?"

"I've got to see you, now."

"Where are you?"

"Lambert, go to rue de la Pompe *métro* station, we're picking up the American."

"Boss, what's all this about. What were you getting from Roman's place?"

"Evidence, my son, that the worst is always yet to come."

"And this hippy, this American, what's he got to do with it?"

On the avenue de Paris, they met Roman coming the other way, sirens screaming. Lambert shrank back on his seat.

•

John got into the back of the car. No one spoke. Lambert let him close his door and then drove on. John noticed the stitches on Guérin's cheek but asked no questions. Their faces were starting to match.

"So, Monsieur Nichols, you went on searching. And what did you find?"

"Alan's got nothing to do with your case."

"Still just as sure of yourself, are you?"

"There are people after *me* now, the same ones who were after Alan, but they've got nothing to do with your investigation."

"So why are you here?"

"Alan was blackmailing Frazer, the secretary in the embassy. Frazer headed up this unit in Kuwait in '91. A specialist in interrogations. His real name's Lundquist, and he was with the CIA. Alan was one of his men, a protégé. I think Frazer used Boukrissi, the dealer, to kill Alan."

Lambert sighed deeply. The American was even nuttier than his boss.

In Lambert's studio apartment, there was no room for the three of them to squeeze in alongside the immense TV screen. Twenty square meters, including the shower, the kitchen units and the hot-water tank. They remained standing, as the young man brought out a folding chair from a cupboard.

Twelfth floor, a fantastic view through the only window onto the City of Clouds housing project in Nanterre. Tower blocks with round sides like they built in the seventies, decorated with trompe-l'oeil skies and clouds, in faded tones of red and blue. Magical under a gray, half-full moon. At the foot of the tower blocks, gangs of youths were fooling about and smoking under the streetlights. The lamps were wreathed in mist, like vaporous islands on which the teenagers were huddled.

In the distance was the great illuminated window frame of the La Grande Arche de La Défense, these days more and more hemmed in by the new towers, cranes, and buildings in Puteaux, shooting up like mushrooms.

John turned away from the window.

"Want a drink? I've got some beer," Lambert suggested.

Guérin shook his head, the American accepted a Kronenbourg, its damp label smelling of Camembert.

Guérin took out his notebook, and Lambert, following the boss's lead a few seconds late, took out his diary.

"Okay, Monsieur Nichols, we're listening."

"What?"

"Tell us about Monsieur Mustgrave."

John drank half the beer, with his back to the window.

"In '90, when he recruited Alan, Lundquist was a little over thirty. He was in Army Intelligence, and the CIA had taken him on. He belongs to that generation of Americans that regrets having no more commie bastards to fight. The Cold War was just over, the Gulf War was just starting. That was a stroke of luck for guys like him, patriots."

An hour to tell them everything as he paced about the tiny room. The story of the hemophiliac fakir raised no laughs. John let it all spill out. The Jim Beam bottle, Alan, his PhD thesis, Bunker, Boukrissi's two henchmen, Königsbauer, and the money, Hirsh, and the message he had found earlier. An hour to unroll the whole story, from Venice Beach to Paris. Finally he fell silent, grappling with a sickening feeling that his story was a pack of lies, invented to impress his listeners.

As a conclusion, he announced what was coming next.

"Bunker's taken the train down to the Lot this evening to fetch my thesis."

Guérin had taken a few notes. Lambert, who had filled the pages of his diary up to August, asked the first question.

"Want another beer?"

Guérin crossed his legs and looked directly at the American.

"Why did you come to France, Monsieur Nichols?"

John went to the window and looked down at the lampposts twelve stories below.

"After Alan left in 2006, the CIA got in touch with me. They put this proposal to me: work on a program helping veterans, former special services personnel. Another deal, practically blackmail: we'll forget about Mustgrave, if you work for us. The U.S. always takes care of its enemies. I accepted. I didn't feel I was . . . what would you call it, selling out? I thought I could do some good, working with guys like Alan. Yeah, it was hypocritical, I know: the army giving therapy to the same guys it had destroyed, so that everything could stay under wraps. Well, I accepted all the same. But I soon realized they were using my work not so much to treat people as to perfect their own training practices. So I resigned. I came over here, to the Lot. I stopped doing any research. I wanted to forget the whole damn thing."

John smiled at his reflection floating over the Paris suburbs.

"Stupid, isn't it? You never can forget stuff like that. For six years, I'd been saying to Alan, look, you've got to talk, get it out of your system. And then I went to earth in the woods myself. He was braver than me. You see, I'd signed all the same confidentiality agreements as him. Maybe that was really all the CIA wanted: that way they'd got me pinned down. If ever this affair gets out, I'll never be able to go back to the States, because I'll be a traitor. Alan didn't know about that. Do you still think your suicides have anything to do with him and his act?"

Guérin looked disappointed with the question; he sat up straight, as if to explain to this slow-witted pupil.

"They're all the same cases, only from different points of view. The same as Kowalski. Death onstage."

"Kowalski? Who's that?"

The lieutenant opened the envelope and took out the photographs, laying them one by one on Lambert's coffee table.

Corpses, in various positions lying on autopsy tables, or on gurneys belonging to the morgue, like the one on which John had seen Alan's body. A naked man, the same one in all the shots, was having sex with them. Corpses of both men and women, before or after the autopsy.

"That's Kowalski. He used to be a *good* guy. But a fakir too, like your friend, a torturer, and a self-torturer. I thought the evidence had gone up in flames when his house burned down the night I went to pull him in for questioning. Suicide, sleeping pills, and gas. These photos have just come to light, after another man killed himself. For two years now, people have been accusing me of driving Kowalski to suicide by running a completely fictional inquiry . . ."

His eyes focused in empty space, Guérin was talking to himself. Lambert was sipping one of the Camembert-smelling beers, saying nothing. John blanched as he looked at the photographs, a mixture of French and English running through his head.

"Maybe someone killed him, too, like Alan. Whoever took these photos perhaps?"

"They were done to order . . . commissioned. The real killer's always the audience."

"The Saint Sebastian Syndrome," John whispered in English.

Guérin snapped out of his reverie.

"What was that you said?"

"Pictures of Saint Sebastian. The archer. The one who watches, the spectator. He's the executioner."

14

Looking through the train window, he could see only his own face reflected in the dark pane streaked with the lights of the suburbs. As the train picked up speed, he had watched flash past first the modern illuminated buildings of the new Paris, then the less well-lit suburbs, finally the deserted streets of dormitory towns, with their rows of unlit villas. Then after Les Ulis, the wide, dark plains. Behind the glass, you could sense the countryside by the deep silence that had overcome the passengers. A silence like the desire to sleep. His face had become sharper now, imprinted on the invisible background. This was a journey where all you could do was contemplate yourself, moving across landscapes you had to guess at. If only they didn't get panic attacks all the time, ex-convicts would make good travelers.

Night train.

He had had to take the *métro*, and before that, so as not to look stupid in front of the kid, to haul his old ne'er-do-well clothes out of their mothballs. A two-piece suit that had already been difficult to squeeze into in 1991, and it was even worse seventeen years later in the hut. But it was good quality, and he had sucked in his stomach, encouraged by the idea that he looked like someone else.

The suit of a man-about-town. A musketeer from the chic underworld of the 1980s. The suit spoke of past glories, fast living, and nightclubs. Of course it was well out-of-date, dark brown, a color that used to be fashionable but was unlamented now.

Between two spells in jail, Bunker had lived the high life, at a time when other reprobates had chosen the more austere pleasures of politics. Bunk had been a frequenter of casinos, and his dog, Mesrine, summed up what he felt about revolution. Especially when revolution was a rallying cry for psychopaths. Nutters like that weren't so bad to chew the fat with in jail, but they went too far sometimes. Accusing the authorities of injustice when you got your own kicks wielding a submachine gun was a joke that wore off quickly. Some of them had pure hearts and violent ideals; others were just evil bastards to be distrusted. He had lost his own freedom three times and gritted his teeth. He hadn't tried to justify his own armed robberies by Marxism–Leninism. Maybe he was on their side, sort of, only doing it his way. This guy once in Fleury Prison had told him he was a structuralist. Well, fuck that. Anyway the suit didn't look reactionary now, just old-fashioned.

Mesrine, tail between his legs, sniffed the pants with their smell of camphor. When Bunk thought about it again, the suit had given him a panic attack. He had been wearing it in '83, and again when he came out, eight years later. It wasn't reassuring to let it see the light of day again. He had considered wearing his park keeper's uniform but in the end decided that would be even worse.

And before that again, he had had to put up a bit of resistance, making it plain to the kid that he wasn't going off full of the joys of spring. It had only lasted a few minutes; then he had found some arguments himself. Bunker had been grateful for the chance, but he hadn't told the kid, feeling a bit ashamed that he hadn't got to this point before under his own steam.

"Just for two or three days, okay? Anyway, gotta lot of leave coming to me, haven't I? City Hall owes me . . . Mesrine can come in the train, can't he? I'm only doing this to do you a favor, son. Get that straight for starters . . . No one'll notice if I take a few days off. Blimey, nobody noticed when I went away for eight years. So how do I get to your place? . . . Got a train timetable, have you? Got to change anywhere? . . . You better do me a drawing, I won't find your camp just like that, heck, make it bigger, kid, I can't hardly see anything with those squiggles . . . Saint *what*? Oh shit, look at this suitcase. Have to get another. Can't get on a train with a case all tied up with string. And what about Mesrine's food? Where am I going to find some dog food? . . . At the grocer's in the village? . . . Opposite what? . . . There's a café? Well, that's the first bit of good news. How old is she, Mme. Bertrand? . . . Oh, forget it. Got a bit of string? And where are these papers anyway? I'm never going to be able to find your place . . . You don't seem even to know where it is on the map . . . What? Not on the map? Oh, fuck this for a lark, I give up . . . What! Take that back, kid, or I'll set Mesrine on your ass . . . I am *not* scared! And it is *not* natural. I just need to figure things out; you can understand that, can't you, for God's sake."

In the *métro* on the way to the Gare d'Austerlitz, he cursed the American shrink. He felt too hot. Mesrine flipped every time the doors opened. When he had to change at Denfert-Rochereau, the string on the case had broken, and his bottle of wine had shattered in a corridor. He had scraped together his things, red faced, and while he was trying to fix the case again, Mesrine had taken off. Ten minutes to find the dog. Mesrine had got into a train heading for Robinson in the southern suburbs. He had just had time to grab the scruff of his neck before the doors closed. Another ten minutes to find the right connection. He had got to the mainline station dripping with sweat, his throbbing carotid vein thrusting at the top button of his shirt. The woman at the ticket desk wasn't much of a looker. But she was the first woman he had asked anything from in fifteen years, and she had been helpful. He had been hurtling along like a scalded cat, only to get there an hour early.

Under the great glass roof of Austerlitz, Bunk had drunk a beer, in a café from which he could see the platforms. The rear ends of the trains with their greasy axles and shock absorbers looked as if they were turning their back on him, as if they couldn't give a damn. Their destinations, exotic places like Vierzon, Châteauroux, or Moulins, sounded classy enough to make him feel small. The second beer tasted like dishwater; the old man was getting morose.

Twenty minutes. Just twenty minutes to get from the park to the station. In fifteen years, he had escaped for no more than half an hour. His anger had worked on his scar, because he was obliged to blame himself and no one else.

Fifteen lost years; when you were sixty-six, it was a lot. Hell, not minutes, years, another fifteen living in the shadows. A quarter of a lifetime, then another—he hadn't gone on counting.

He had been tempted by a ham sandwich but gave half of it to the dog without regret.

The fashions, gestures, colors, and shapes around him meant absolutely nothing to him. He was from a completely different age: twenty-five years too late. He thought: I kept my regrets warm, I built walls thicker than the prison's. I was a coward. I just didn't face them, and I thought I'd got rid of them. And then along comes this kid with his rotten backpack and his pal who sticks needles in himself . . .

He had to take a decision, right. Not dead, and not sick, at least. But he couldn't admit it was possible, in just one second, staring down the station platforms, to start living again and forget the past. The fire inside, the furious determination to refuse compromise, had seemed to be extinguished. Bunker's shirt was soaked with distress, with a desperate desire to go home to the Luxembourg Gardens. He had pulled down his sleeve to hide the tattoo on his hand: he had the horrible suspicion that his grotesque appearance was upsetting people, that his stink of prison cells and mothballs was spreading all over the station, getting up the noses of people who knew how to catch trains, who knew how to put everything behind them and just take off. He had been watching them, those people, and resigned himself to never being a complete human being. The travelers sitting near him all looked tired, but they felt free enough to slump in their chairs. Everyone else seemed to know where they were going and where they were coming from. The waitress depressed him too. A young woman of North African origin, who looked as if she wanted out but was zipping about in a series of straight lines between the round tables. A common-sense Fury, with aims as solid as his doubts: serve the customers, clear the tables, take the money, give change, bring up her kid, find another job for the weekend. She made him feel dizzy, with her quick movements and her certainty invading his fear of existence. Not a single wasted gesture, every last second used up to the full. Thirty perhaps, or a bit less, hair tied back so as to speed through the air more quickly. She had whipped away his empty glass, then knelt down to pat Mesrine's head, a quick pause for tenderness between two swoops.

"What sort of dog is he?"

The direct and sudden address of a kid who has learned to get straight to the point, no messing. The accent of the suburbs, and eyes as deep-set as her tracks through the café.

"Mongrel, found him in the street."

"A mongrel, that's cool. What's his name?"

"Mesrine."

"Like the guy in the film? Someone told me it was all true, but I don't go for that."

Bunker gave the ghost of a smile, thinking of the kid. By the time she had finished petting him, Mesrine's hair was standing on end, like a punk.

"No, it's true."

The waitress stood up again.

"You know about that, the olden days, Mesrine and stuff?"

"Yeah, did know them."

Bunker had dropped his voice not to be overheard. The waitress was speaking loud and clear as she wiped the next table.

"So where you off to, then?"

"Place called Saint-Céré, in the Lot."

"That'll be the Toulouse train, 21:58."

She must spend her life looking at the back end of trains.

"Yeah, that's the one."

"I get my holidays in August, and I go to Royan. Do you go there often, the Lot?"

"First time."

"Is it nice? Countryside?"

"Dunno."

"You don't know where you're going?"

She laughed showing her sharp little teeth, good for biting apples, and was gone in a trice.

Bunker had realized what had happened as his confidence was coming back. Even if he probably reminded her of her grandfather, she had given him a smile. And she wasn't a mommy in the park, or a teenager, or a student from the Luxembourg. A real woman, in her natural background, had smiled at him, a free man. Out of the fish tank into the ocean.

All he'd had to do was open his mouth without being afraid of drowning, or of the air ripping painfully into his untried lungs.

A happy sort of apprehension made his hair stand up on end: "Attention please. The train now standing at Platform 17H is the Express Teos 3624 for Toulouse, departing at 21:58. Calling at . . ."

He counted his money quickly, taking it out of a pocket that had once been full of hundred-franc notes with Pascal's portrait on them, those big banknotes that snapped like no others. Not that he gave a damn; riches had brought him nothing that lasted, and a man his age still had a right to some love. He left a three-euro tip on the table, a small fortune, but cheerfully spent.

Bunker snatched up his case. Mesrine came bounding behind him, and they approached Platform 17H. Bunker gripped his ticket in his hand, counting the carriages and muttering their numbers over and over at each door until he reached the right one. His hand on the steel handle, his foot on the step.

Night had been a good excuse not to panic. The American had given him a hug in the rue de Vaugirard, like an old comrade, or like a son sending his elderly dad off to the countryside as the war reached the city. Not a son, a friend. A real friend, who had landed him in the shit.

Sitting in his seat, watching his own pale reflection, it seemed to Bunker that the details of the Gardens were already vanishing from his memory.

•

He didn't sleep, didn't want to. At Vierzon, contrary to expecta-
tion, he had found something to look at, even from the train door.
Passengers getting off or on, sleepy faces of people waiting to meet
other people. He had sniffed the air, trying to recapture the scent of a
hardworking provincial town that had long been a Communist Party
stronghold. He remembered stopping at Vierzon in the summer of
'72 or '73, driving back up from the Côte d'Azur in a Renault 16,
with his pockets full of money. He had sat at a café terrace, it must
have been the days he used to drink Fernet-Branca. The train moved
off after a minute, under a metal bridge painted in strange colors.
A nocturnal monstrosity that made his heart leap with joy. Mesrine
had calmed down, Bunk was thirsty, and they went off in search of
refreshments.

The drinks guy was taking it easy in a reserved compartment in
the middle of the train. His red uniform tie looked as if it were stran-
gling him; as he was a heavily built forty-year-old with the forearms
of a welder, the three dots tattooed in a triangle at the base of his left
thumb probably had something to do with it. Bunker bought two tiny
bottles of wine from him at an exorbitant price, trying to cover up
the cross on his own hand. But the ex-con sandwich salesman, probably taking part in some rehab program, had already spotted it. An
unwelcome recognition, which came with its own codes and attri-
butes. Distrust at first. Because they were both wild creatures and
might have friends or enemies who were incompatible, both inside
and outside. Then the connection, the fucking connection, that all
the ex-cons in the world have between them: not being ashamed, as
you were with other people, of having been behind bars, and a sort
of stupid pride when you met someone who knew what it was like,
that value judgments inside weren't the same as outside, and how hard
it was, even if you couldn't admit that to yourself. But above all, it
was the recognition of fear in the look they gave each other. The cold
fear of people who know that freedom is a conditional gift: keep a
low profile. Bunk wanted to grab his wine before starting the ritual

exchange of pedigrees, breaking the tradition of ex-cons always having to speak to each other, even if only a few words. Because you had
to establish a hierarchy, weigh every word, every gesture, whereas all
Bunk wanted to do was speak normally and smile rather than have to
clench his teeth.

He turned away abruptly.

"Hey!"

This wasn't the first ex-con he'd met, but this one made him
uneasy. He left a trace of prison behind him wherever he went, and
had done so since the day he got out.

Bunker clenched his fists; Mesrine was showing his teeth.

"Your change, sir."

The voice of a kid from the sticks, overlaid with inner-city vowels,
unmistakably someone who had done time.

The guy held out some coins. Bunker pocketed them, and the man
pressed another little bottle of wine into his hand.

"Go on, take it. I don't like talking about it either, but I never
know what to do." The salesman rubbed at his tattoo with his thick
fingers, the hands of a man who now had a vegetable allotment and
felt happy with it. "And bon voyage."

Bunker stood like an idiot, trying to say something, the best present he had ever had in his hand, but the man had already retreated
into his compartment. *Bon voyage.*

At Brive-la-Gaillarde, he had to hang about for two and a half hours
on the platform in the middle of the night. Sitting on a bench, with
his coat collar turned up, the old bear listened to the hand of the station clock tick every minute. He had sipped slowly at the last bottle
of wine and smoked his roll-ups as he waited for the train for Saint-
Céré. Departure 5:57 a.m., arrival 7:49 a.m.

Mesrine was curled up on his feet, asleep with one eye open. At
5:50 a.m., three youths, no more than twenty years old, in the last
stages of drink, rolled onto the platform. They chucked beer cans at
the rails to watch them explode. Bunker went on watching the clock.
Mesrine was now sleeping with one ear cocked.

The local train, a rusty old diesel, had only two cars. Bunker let the youngsters get in and chose the other one. No other passengers. The roisterers had slumped across seats in their car, taking up two places each, pushing and shoving one another. Bunk put his case beside him, his tattooed hand flat down on it. Fatigue was beginning to make his eyes sting, but he waited until the three lads had gone to sleep, worn out with their night on the tiles, before he pulled down the blind.

He was awoken by the stillness as the train came to a halt in the little station of Bretenoux. Bunker's reflection was no longer visible on the pane now: the gray dawn was lighting up the deserted platform, and he could see through the window. The youngsters had disappeared. He took from his pocket the directions the American had written for him. They included a list of all the stations between Brive and Saint-Céré. Bretenoux was last but one. His watch said 7:30 a.m. He felt like sleeping some more, but the fire in the sky to the east held his attention. An orange glow, outlining a low range of mountains on the horizon. Without taking his eyes from it for a second, he watched the sun rise up out of the earth. It was his first horizon, his first real sunrise since . . . Bunker hadn't visited the seaside when he had left jail the last time. It was the favorite fantasy of longtimers, the subject of endless discussions on nights when your morale was in your boots: "I'm going abroad, way away somewhere," "smell the sea air," "get as far from here as I can." A dream one distrusted, that some men wouldn't admit to or even entertain, because it was too good to be true and the time dragged even more slowly after that. From Fleury, Bunk had taken the bus straight to Paris, without searching for the horizon. So did everyone else.

He set foot in the Lot by stepping down onto the platform at Saint-Céré Station. The ground felt as hard there as everywhere else. As the two-car train rattled away, he listened. Silence. A few cars on the other side of the station building, just to remind you they still existed. Insects. Crickets, like in the old days in the Paris Métro, when they used to feed on cigarette butts. The air here had its own scent, not marked by pollution.

In his immigrant's costume, clutching his suitcase tied with string, and with his mongrel crouching by his leg, Bunker felt like staying there for a few hours: no need to move. An early morning breeze, already warm, ruffled his hair. He could feel emptiness all around him for a radius of several kilometers, the absence of humans crammed together.

A taxi was standing outside the station.

"I'm going to Lentillac . . . know where that is?"

The driver, who looked like a cross between an ape and a tractor, glanced at him curiously.

"Why wouldn't I? I'm a taxi man!"

Shit, these natives had a different accent from him. Bunker had not realized he was so far south.

"Okay for my dog?"

"Wouldn't want him to run behind now, would you?"

The driver got out and opened the trunk, taking Bunker's case without missing a beat or looking askance at his suit, which was probably still rather avant-garde for these parts.

The café tables were only just being set out on terraces, the iron curtains of the shops just being raised. Saint-Céré didn't really wake up until about nine or ten o'clock.

"You going to the hotel, then?"

"Eh?"

"I said, going to the inn at Lentillac, are you?"

"No, the shop. What's this river?"

"The Bave, of course."

The road took them uphill, through a narrow valley, green and twisting. Below it ran a river, a few meters wide, sparkling and rippling. Bunker lowered his window and let the air blow across his face. Mesrine remained obstinately crouching on the carpeted floor of the cab.

The road parted company with the river as the valley widened out. The old man tried to glimpse the track that would take him to the American's camp.

"How far to Lentillac?"

"Four kilometers."

A minute later, he spotted a dirt track cutting steeply down to the right, toward the bottom of the valley. He unfolded the kid's plan, with a drawing of the road, wavy lines for the river, a cross marking the church and village, the track going off on the right, three kilometers before Lentillac. That must be it. A long walk, though.

On the way to the village, they had met no other vehicle. It was 8:20 a.m. Bunker paid the driver, who dropped him off in the main square.

War memorial, church, bar, shop, post office. An old geezer on the church steps, leaning on a stick. Mesrine sniffed the air timidly, still sticking close to his master's legs.

Bunker swayed back and forth in his clumsy shoes and looked carefully both ways before crossing the road. Mme. Bertrand, of indeterminate age, was an antidote to love, and her shop was a museum piece. He filled a basket with cans, some bread, a bag of crunchy dog food, and three bottles of Cahors, good stuff, not rubbish. The bottles were heavy, and he had a long walk ahead, but it was downhill and he was thirsty.

He dug into his savings to pay the old woman. The American had given him his train fare plus some ten-euro notes for expenses. But he intended to use his own money before he started on that. He had to pay out of his own pocket if the shrink's therapy was to work. Mme. Bertrand wasn't as indifferent as the taxi driver. She looked at him suspiciously, wondering what this decrepit snob was doing, drifting about this dead-end place. She didn't miss the tattoo on his hand either, when he put his money down on the counter.

The old man in front of the church had multiplied. Two granddads were now squinting at him from under their cloth caps.

The door of the Bar des Sports was open. The sugar bowl was in the shape of a soccer ball, there were trophies and photographs of soccer teams everywhere, plus the firemen's calendar, Formica tables. It was cool, dark, and deserted. A refuge in summer from the heat. The barman was a nostalgic soccer fan, but his playing days were over. Seventy years old and still looking good, except for the giveaway strawberry nose.

Bunker asked for a coffee with a shot of Calvados. He no longer felt frightened since setting foot in Saint-Céré. He'd got here, he'd identified the forest track, the place was calm and lovely. The barman, a pro, just went about his business as his customer sat drinking. Mesrine had remained on his feet, his nose pointing at the door.

"You open this afternoon?"

"All day."

They set off on foot along the road. The two old men watched as the stranger with his dog, his cardboard suitcase, and his shopping bags disappeared in the distance.

Jacket over his shoulder, feeling warm after climbing up the incline, Bunker put his load down in the grass. Nicest cell he'd ever laid eyes on.

Mesrine was already sitting, his tail wagging in the grass, his paws shaking, and his eyes on his boss. Bunker looked at him, his own lip trembling a bit, too. "Go on! Go, boy!"

The dog didn't budge but was getting more and more excited and apprehensive.

Bunker waved his arm in the air.

"Go on, off you go!"

The old mongrel stood up and rushed straight ahead for about ten meters, stopped, looked all around, his two hundred million olfactory cells exploding with joy. He followed his nose in all directions, gave a few barks running, stopping, and running the other way. Bunker gazed at his dog, without daring to inspect the tepee, or the careful arrangements the American had made for his solitary homestead, the hammock suspended from two trees, and the sunny valley opening out at his feet. He sat down at the top of the log steps, and Mesrine joined him. The dog snuggled up to the old man, and they both looked down at the valley.

"Dog, tell you what, we're going to like it here."

15

Guérin hadn't gone home. He had stayed up all night at Lambert's. The first time in two years that he hadn't slept in his flat on boulevard Voltaire. Churchill would no doubt be screaming insults down into the courtyard, unless he was sulking in silence.

Lambert had driven the American back to the Luxembourg Gardens and returned at five in the morning to lie down on the divan. Guérin, sitting at the window, had watched the gray dawn come up, shedding light on the City of Clouds, gradually revealing its faded colors. A pale sun pierced the urban mist, and the radio alarm started up at 7:30 a.m., with the headlines from Radio Luxembourg. Aggressive news bulletins that had rudely awakened trainee officer Lambert from his sleep. Lambert started to move about, embarrassed by his boss's presence in his flat. He hadn't changed out of the Arsenal tracksuit in which he had gone to sleep. The coffee maker began to spit. Guérin looked up gently at Lambert and accepted the steaming cup he offered.

The photographs were still lying on the coffee table, dimly illuminated by the morning light, relics of a hideous orgy, rediscovered on waking, and enough to bring a retch to the throat. The two men's eyes were red rimmed with fatigue as their bodies and clothes embarked on a new day without having shed the weariness of the previous twenty-four hours.

Once he had drunk his coffee, Guérin switched on his cell. A few bleeps indicated messages he had failed to pick up.

The little lieutenant rubbed the top of his bald head, letting his fingers run over the pink scars where he had picked off the scabs. Stripes of new skin, soft and tender to the touch. Another line of reconstituted flesh, with its stitches still in place, ran across his cheek in a long black stripe.

"Now then, young Lambert, this is when you have to make up your mind."

Lambert had rubbed his face and pinched his big nose, standing in front of a bookcase and the shooting trophy. The objects in the room were still only vaguely outlined, drowned by gray light in a mass without contrasts. The decision was fraught, but in the end inevitable.

"Boss, I already said, I'm not going to walk away from you."

"What about your career?"

Lambert zipped up his jacket.

". . . Well, I wouldn't carry on without you, anyway."

Guérin seemed to want to say something, but Lambert had stopped listening and was looking at the photographs. The young policeman's features had sharpened. Lambert had grown up overnight.

"Guérin, what the fuck is going on? Roman called me in the night, he says you've wrecked his house! Even his kids' bedroom! What the devil's the matter with you? Isn't there enough of a mess already?"

Barnier had evidently not slept either; his voice was sharp.

"I've got to see you, *commissaire*. I'll explain."

"I should bloody well think so! In my office in an hour, and it had better be good."

"I'd prefer to meet you somewhere else."

"You're finished, Guérin, don't try and impose conditions on me."

"I could call someone else."

"You're crazy . . . Where do you want to meet?"

"Doesn't matter. Let's say . . ."

10:00 a.m. Montparnasse Cemetery, a whole neighborhood in itself between the boulevard Raspail, the rue Froidevaux, and the Gaîté quarter. Above its walls loomed the huge Montparnasse Tower and other tall office blocks, vertical projects looking down on this immense horizontal expanse in the middle of the city, safe from real estate developers. On the Paris map, it looked like a green space, but in reality it was uniformly gray. An underground city, a reverse reflection of the 1970s Maine-Montparnasse development. Most of the names on the graves were unknowns, a few celebrities from between the wars; it was less of a showbiz graveyard than the one at Père-Lachaise. Among the nonfamous, one could easily slip in a few obscure policemen. Thousands of tombs, but no indications of the cause of death. Old age, accident, illness, passion, crime. How many suicides? Better not to know, perhaps: the number might interfere with the beauty of the place.

Guérin walked to the middle of the central alleyway, turned left, and counted the rows. Eleven. It had the grid-plan simplicity of an American town, he said to himself, as he came to a stop in front of the grave. All you need is the intersection of two numbers.

A name and two dates, some plastic flowers decorating a rarely visited tomb.

Guérin pulled out his cell.

"*Commissaire*, a slight change of plan. I'm not at the bottom of the tower, I'm in the cemetery. I dare say you remember the way . . . That's right."

Barnier arrived in front of the grave ten minutes later. Guérin wasn't there. The divisionnaire turned on his heel, scouring the horizon bristling with tombstones. A few elderly visitors were bending down to pick up faded bunches of flowers, carrying shopping bags, their wrinkled faces reflected in the polished granite. Barnier was holding his hat in his hand and leaned down to look at the grave. His bulky silhouette, well wrapped up in a three-quarter-length gray overcoat, suddenly convulsed.

CHRISTOPHE KOWALSKI 1966–2006

On the flat slab were the usual trite messages: "To our valued colleague"; "To our friend"; "Everlasting regrets"; not much real

affection, but plenty of respect, and four plastic flowers, rather discolored, in a little tin vase. But behind the flowers, was an enlarged
photograph of Kowalski, naked under strip lights, in the act of taking
a woman's corpse from behind.

Barnier stood up abruptly, bending his spine as if under an
invisible whip. He looked around the horizontal expanse of the
cemetery again and saw young Lambert, hands in pockets, a few
rows away from him. Lambert was leaning up against a Gothic
tomb and watching him. Barnier wheeled around as he heard steps
on the gravel.

"Morning, *commissaire*."

Barnier put his hand to his chest to press his madly beating heart.
Lambert made a move toward his armpit, thinking he was reaching
for a gun. But the boss's boss was simply panic stricken.

"What's all this about, Guérin? Where did you get this . . . this
photograph?"

"Does the place suit you, sir? A bit dramatic, I grant you. Do you
know what the connection is between this grave and yourself?"

"This is no time for riddles, Guérin. Did you find this at Roman's
house?"

"Between necrophilia and the Homicides squad?"

Barnier's voice quavered, high up above the tombs. "Stop this
nonsense now!"

"Between a pervert and the people watching him?"

"Guérin, you're in no fit state. You're out of control. Maybe you
were right about Kowalski, but it doesn't change anything. You're
barking up the wrong tree. Kowalski committed suicide, and nothing
can alter that."

"Between suicide and murder?"

"What is it you want? Do you want someone to apologize to you?
Don't expect anyone to give you a medal. Nobody wants all this shit
to come to the surface again."

"Between a photographer and a parrot?"

Barnier put one foot on the gravestone, leaned over an,d picked up
the photograph, tearing it to pieces without looking at it.

"Roman will be sacked, if that's what you want. But there's no question of taking this any further to the Disciplinary Division or anywhere else. Is that what you're after?"

"Between a divisionnaire's head and an ordinary policeman's skin?"

Barnier threw the fragments of the photograph at his feet.

"What do you think you're going to do? Think you can come out of this smelling of roses? Reckon you can destroy our entire squad, with the blessing of the Ministry of the Interior?"

"*Commissaire*, somebody has to have taken these photos. Somebody must have been protecting Kowalski and his pals. Even if they were well out of order, *someone* had to be in charge, someone had to cover for them when they had gone too far, so that they'd go on doing the job expected of them. Don't you agree? You haven't found the answer yet, but it'll come to you. Let's say we're an oddly civilized organization that can't yet manage without certain necessities. It needs people like you. Excuse me. Like us. It's a heavy weight to carry. For some people more than others."

Guérin was staring beyond his commanding officer, his head on one side, calculating future trajectories between the tombs.

"Being out of control, as you nicely put it, is inevitable. It isn't a paradox that anarchy, or at any rate anarchy of the mind, is found among people whose job is to keep order. Kowalski must have been just one link in a chain of command. To think someone like him can exist and do all that in a vacuum would be ridiculous. *You* had to be there, to protect them, to turn a blind eye to a few little peccadilloes. Do you think your rank protects you from the rest of the world? Giving orders, *commissaire*, means you're the last person who can disobey them. It isn't the great man's burden; it's just a pathetic illusion of power. You need obedience like you need a mirror, with devoted servants to maintain the illusion. It's asking a lot of a man to place him at the crossroads of duty and disgust. Perhaps there were tastes and distastes that you shared with Kowalski? Am I wrong? But after all, Kowalski didn't kill anyone, did he? No, of course not. Other people did that for him. Once things had got that far, all that was needed to guarantee the stability of the whole structure was a fuse that could be allowed to blow if the unexpected happened. In other words, a scapegoat. Remember what you said, *commissaire*? *"Guérin, Suicides is you now."* You made me your excuse, locked inside a room that was full of them. But with one difference: I'm still alive. It's easier to get the dead to talk than to make the living shut up. You were right. Suicides *is* me. But murders, in this cemetery, that's you."

Guérin smiled; Barnier took a step backward, hitting an invisible barrier.

"I've got about fifteen of these photos. I needn't describe them to you. You know what they're like. Whether Berlion, or Roman, or you, took them doesn't matter. It doesn't matter either, which one of you turned on the gas taps at Kowalski's house. All I want is for you, and the others like you, to draw the right conclusions from all this. Make your choice freely, on your own. No more chain of command. You just have to account to yourself, nobody else. Other people will take your place, but it's a good thing sometimes for the cogs in the machine to think about what they've been used for. If the idea of killing yourself crosses your mind—and it will, believe me—think carefully before you act. Do it for the right reasons, *commissaire*. The shit, as you so aptly put it, doesn't need to come to the surface. It's smeared all over everything already. Take a breath of air, taste the lonely joys of anarchy: all you have to do is search your own conscience."

Guérin, stooping now, stepped over the shredded photograph. He went past his deputy, nodding to him. Lambert watched the divisionnaire leaning over Kowalski's tomb for a few minutes. The chief was mumbling something, alone among the alleys. The young policeman looked up at the sky, searching for an unlikely break in the clouds, detached his shoulder from the tomb, stretched, and walked off after his boss. He turned around as they left the cemetery. Barnier had fallen to his knees in front of the grave. Lambert felt no particular emotion.

16

Bunker found everything he was after among the American's things. Matches, newspaper, kindling, logs, an Italian coffee pot and some coffee. It took him some time to get a fire going all the same, on all fours in the grass, blowing on the flames until he felt light-headed. He had exchanged his crook's costume for a more rustic pair of pants, a T-shirt, and one of John's shirts with its sleeves rolled up. He had fixed up the electricity again, following the directions he had been given. John obviously organized his camp according to the same logic as the old man. It was a little world of manic simplicity, slightly paranoid even, built on the freedom of having nothing but the bare essentials.

Mesrine was running around the camp in ever-widening circles, exploring his new territory and marking it by lifting his leg every few meters. Holding his mug of coffee, Bunker whistled to the dog when he disappeared for longer than a minute.

He looked into the dregs of the coffee, then stared ahead of him, every time letting his eyes wander a little farther afield. Bunker was sending his intimidated gaze into the far distance as his lungs filled with fresh air, making him feel dizzy. No more park railings, no more swept paths, no more tourists. Silence, a little breeze coming up from the valley, fluttering the leaves. The coffee tasted awful; the American had no sugar in the tepee. Bunker still made it last as long as possible.

The fatigue from his almost sleepless night made his legs feel heavy, but he didn't care. Mesrine made a rapid reappearance, then dashed off again chasing some wild creature such as he had never seen before. Bunker leaned over the bound pages.

The Saint Sebastian Syndrome
The victim and the punished
By John P. Nichols
UCLA 2006

Under the title, someone had written a few sentences in English that he couldn't read. The rest of it was in English, too. He flipped through the pages with his big fingers, impressed by the quantity of words, astonished that someone could write all this, just to say in the end that man was a bag of shit and not to be trusted. Behavioral psychology, he couldn't care less, but he knew that in this pile of paper there were the names of some men who meant business. They had to be taken seriously, and one had better be afraid of them. He put the thesis down and refreshed his eyes by looking down at the stream running below. The leaf mold and sediments made the water look a golden brown. Bunker's nostrils dilated as he tried, like Mesrine, to rediscover the smell of bathing in the wild. The sun was strong but felt good. Bunker thought of himself taking all his clothes off and plunging his backside into the cold water. The old man hesitated, out of both embarrassment and fear of the cold.

He checked the time on his watch, swallowed the last of the coffee, and whistled to the dog. Mesrine trotted beside him as he went along the narrow path with his carrier bag. The sun warmed the broom flowering at the edge of the track; foxgloves waved in the breeze, and Bunker remembered his grandmother telling him when he was a kid that these elegant flowers were poisonous. He stepped cautiously to the side so as not to touch them, holding his breath, despite the uphill slope. A big grasshopper shot past his head with a whirr, and he gave a start. He stopped walking, to listen for mocking laughter. But he was all alone and smiled. Fifteen years in jail, no knife had ever frightened him, and here he was, terrorized by an insect.

He had been walking back up the road for about a kilometer when a tractor pulling an empty trailer stopped alongside him. An elderly hippy, with a beard, long hair, and a headband, was driving it. Presumably a back-to-the-land survivor from the sixties, with a smile as happy as an evening spent smoking weed.

"Going to the village?"

"Yeah."

"You're coming from John's camp? Isn't he there?"

"Nope."

"Jump in the back, I'll drop you off."

Bunker blinked. This guy's casual manner disarmed him. He put his foot on the wheel of the trailer to hoist himself up and sat down, his legs dangling from the back. Mesrine started yapping. Bunker thumped the floor of the trailer; the dog crouched and sprang up. This cool dude seemed only too happy to have passengers in his rattletrap. He nodded to Bunker, giving him a thumbs-up, and the tractor started with a snort of its exhaust, suggesting a speedy takeoff, then trundled along at all of twenty kilometers an hour. Bunker was bouncing around on his backside. Wisps of hay flew around his head, lodging in his hair.

The dude introduced himself as he let him off by the sign for Lentillac.

"I'm Bertrand. Me and my wife, we're in the farm, just a bit down from John's place. Feel free to drop in if you want. We're just starting haymaking, but you call around after six, we can always have a drink."

The hippy looked about sixty. He leaned out of his smoking heap of rust, stretching out his hand, and Bunker shook it.

"Édouard's the name. Thanks for the invite and the lift."

The Bar des Sports was open and deserted.

The barman had had a go at the red, as could be seen from his eyes. Bunk put his bag on the counter and ordered a glass of the same. Drank it straight off, looked at his watch, and asked for another. At 2:00 p.m., the telephone rang. The owner picked up, listened in silence, then brought it over to him.

"For you."

Bunker nodded thanks and turned to face the tables, putting the receiver to his ear.

•

John had slept until late morning in the Luxembourg Gardens. A disturbed sleep, but his bad dreams hadn't wakened him. His face had almost returned to normal. The black eye hardly showed now. His ribs and stomach were still sore, but he could live with that. After coffee prepared on the hotplate, he lit a cigarette. A feeling that something was missing persisted in spite of the nicotine. It was the time of day he usually practiced with his bow. But the park was full of visitors, so he abandoned the idea, with a slight feeling of relief. He had taken up archery at the same time as starting his thesis. Maybe it was time to give it up now, even if he was replacing it with cigarettes.

At midday he left the park and walked through the streets: to the Pantheon, the place de la Contrescarpe, the rue Mouffetard, just another American tourist. When he reached the Gobelins, he bought some more cigarettes. He went on down the avenue de Choisy and crossed the gardens at the end. Trees and lawns were hardly sufficient compensation for being here. At Tolbiac, he went into a telephone booth. He got two numbers from directory inquiries. He left no message on Patricia Königsbauer's answering machine but called the Bar des Sports in Lentillac.

Bunker's voice sounded far away, but it was reassuring.

"It's me here. You okay?"

"Yeah."

"Did you find everything?"

"Yep, the lot."

"Got something to write with?"

John heard Bunker asking for a pen and paper from the barman.

"I'm listening."

"You need to post the thesis to this address: Richard Guérin, 74 boulevard Voltaire, Paris 11."

"Who's he?"

"Cop who handles suicides."

"And you really trust him?"

"Yeah, I do. And something else, Bunk. In the post office, there should be a letter for me from Alan. You'll have to sweet-talk Mme. Labrousse, the postmistress, to get it. I'll call you back in half an hour, and you'll have to read it out to me."

"That all?"

"Yeah. How do you like the tepee?"

"It's like my hut. Only better."

"Half an hour then."

John went to sit on a bench in the park.

Bunker paid for his drinks and set off across the square.

"Sit, boy! Wait here."

Mesrine sat down outside the post office.

An old guy with a stick was hanging onto the counter, his nose to the glass and his mouth against the plastic screen. Bunker prepared to wait, but the old man moved aside at once. He wasn't there to collect his pension, just to chew the fat with the postmistress, the aforementioned Mme. Labrousse. Cast-iron perm, flowery blouse, and pebble glasses. The old man developed a sudden interest in an ad for life insurance with his ears flapping two meters behind him.

"I need to send this packet."

He put the American's thesis on the counter.

Mme. Labrousse weighed it and gave him a bubble-wrap envelope.

"Regular or special delivery?"

"Express."

Bunker wrote Guérin's address in the space provided.

"Mr. Nichols asked me to post this for him. What do I write where it says sender?"

"Mr. Nichols, the American?"

"That's the one."

"You put his name, then Le Bourg, Lentillac, 46200 Saint Céré. His mail comes in here. The postman doesn't go down to his camp."

"Oh, er, by the way, he asked me to pick up his post, too."

"I shouldn't really."

"He's expecting something, news from a friend in Paris."

"He hasn't given you anything, a note or something?"

Bunker flashed her a racing-driver smile, revealing his gappy teeth.

"He just said, 'Ask Mme. Labrousse, she's really nice, you'll see.'"

The woman blushed behind her thick spectacles.

"Well, as it's just for you. Yes, there is a letter from Paris for him."

Mme. Labrousse rummaged in a plastic crate and pulled out an envelope, patting down her perm.

"That'll be eight euros twenty for the express post. It'll get there tomorrow morning."

Bunker laid on the charm again, directing a final, devastating wink at his bespectacled friend.

"If you want, I can put a table outside for you, then you can smoke in peace. Bloody antismoking laws, what a waste of time."

Bunker was rolling himself a cigarette as he leaned on the counter.

"Don't bother, I'll do it."

He dragged a table and chair outside and sat on the pavement at the edge of the main road. Across from him, on the steps of the church, the ancient mariner from the post office and another old chap were pretending to be busy with something. Bunker raised his glass in their direction, and the ancestors looked at him without reacting.

He was halfway through his third glass when the telephone rang.

"It's for you again," the barman called.

"Right, I've mailed your book, and I've got the letter."

"Can you open it and read it to me?"

Bunker pulled the envelope open with his thick fingers.

"There's a checkroom ticket and a note. But it's all in English. I can't translate it, kid, no idea what it says."

"Try and read it all the same."

"Shit, are you kidding or what?"

"Go on."

"*Bigue John, I am sorree I did . . . didenet*, with apostrophe t, *inveete iou for mai laste shô.* I can't make head or tail of this; can you understand it?"

"Carry on."

"Shit, kid what are you making me do? *Tank iou for evereetingue iou deed. I doh eet vit no regrett and eet ees betteur zate iou are not eer: in ze public terre* (with h) *vill bee onlee peeple zate are not mai frend. Iou dont* (apostrophe t) *beeulongue terre* (with h). *Ai love iou, mai best frende. Taque carre ande for-give iou . . . iourselfe. Alan Must-e-grave. Alan must go ome.* Fuck, this is driving me nuts. You getting this?"

"Yep. That all?"

"Just one more line, wait a bit."

"*Iou vill find ate tisse* (with h) *place, a bague vit a little present frome mee. Notingue* (with h) *important compare vit vat iou dide butte somtingue tou mak iour life easee. Go travele, John, doo eet for mee.* That's it. The end. And don't ask me to read it again. Kid, you still there?"

"What's the checkroom ticket?"

"Wait, it's kind of a receipt. There's a date, April 10, 4:30 p.m. There's a stamp on it, shit, I can't read this. The Encas-something . . . 43 avenue Gabriel, 8th arrondissement, in Paris. Mean anything to you?"

•

John recognized the waiter and the waiter remembered him: the big backwoodsman with his bow and his Indian blanket. He explained. He'd lost his ticket, but he had forgotten one bag in the cupboard. He'd had a problem, and couldn't get back here before.

"It's against the rules."

"Look, I'm not going to make a big deal out of this, but your racket here isn't particularly honest either. That doesn't bother me. I just want my bag, and I'll leave you a tip you won't forget."

The waiter thought for a bit, without making much of an effort. "Okay, go ahead, the boss isn't here. But be quick about it."

John pushed open the door of the luggage room. Still the same collection of backpacks, suitcases, wine crates, and cleaning materials. It was only dimly lit. He shook the bags, moved the cases around. Between a pile of Coca-Cola bottles and a bucket of floor cloths, he found a black canvas bag. The zip opened easily. A couple of hundred-dollar bills, pulled out at random, shut the waiter up. John went out fast. He passed the embassy without turning around and walked as quickly as he could without running. In the Tuileries Garden, he sat down and opened the bag. Bundles of dollar bills, some in fifties and some in hundreds. He counted out one bundle of each. Ten thousand in the hundred-note packs, five thousand in each fifty-note pack. At least sixty packs in all, just chucked in the bag, with rubber bands around them. Between four and five hundred thousand dollars. Half a million bucks.

He stared at the pond in front of him, where kids were launching model boats. He smiled, thinking of Alan throwing this heap of cash into the scruffy cupboard, a few yards from the embassy. Even at two euros an hour, he could have let the interest pile up a bit.

Guérin replied at the third ring, and a screech drilled into John's eardrum: "Telephooooone! Telephoooone!" Then he heard Guérin asking who it was.

"Nichols. I need to see you."

"What's going on?"

"I've found something important."

"You've got my address. Saint-Ambroise *métro* station."

In the *métro*, he clutched the bag close to his body. The train was full of people, all probably dreaming of a fortune like this. John felt like dumping the dollars down the nearest drain.

He rang the bell at Guérin's address.

The décor of the flat was as minimalist as its furnishings. Everything was clean, despite a suffocating smell like the inside of an aviary. In the living room, on a perch covered with crap, a repulsive parrot was screaming: "Haaarder, come on, sweetie! Haaaarder!"

"Shut up!"

The creature had hardly any feathers left except on its head, and its flaccid flesh was gashed in many places. Once it had stopped shrieking, it began pecking at what remained of the skin on its claws.

"His name's Churchill. Don't pay any attention to him."

John looked first at the bird, then at Guérin, with his scabs on his head and his long scar. The lieutenant wasn't wearing his coat, and John was taken aback by the fragile, misshapen figure.

"Not at work today, then?"

"No. But you seem to be busy."

John passed him the bag. Guérin opened it. The money had as little effect on him as on the American.

"Lot of cash."

"Alan died for this. Doesn't seem much to me."

"No, obviously."

"Say, your bird doesn't look too good."

"He's depressed." Guérin lowered his voice. "Since my mother died." John ran a hand through his hair, puzzled.

"But he's on the way to killing himself. Can't you do anything?"

"I can't bring her back."

"Find him a mate?"

"I think he's too old."

"It's never too late."

Guérin rubbed his head.

"It would take someone special."

"Could be found."

Each of them, one hand scratching their heads, looked at the parrot, which offered itself up as a martyr to these two human wrecks. John turned to Guérin.

"That yellow raincoat, it belonged to your mother, right?"

Guérin leaned his head to one side.

"No, not at all. What gave you that idea?"

"Nothing, I just thought. You haven't slept? You look tired. I dreamed about those photos last night, this morning I mean. So what's happening about that Kowalski guy?"

Guérin looked at Churchill.

"The news will filter through. I left Lambert by the phone. He'll keep me up to date if anything happens. I don't think it'll be long."

"What?"

"The end, John, the end, of course."

"You've got them?"

"By the balls, if you'll pardon the expression. But it doesn't make me particularly happy. I only did this for Savane."

John rubbed his two-day stubble with a rasping sound.

"Okay. And the suicides, your theory?"

"That's different. One mustn't hope too much for an end to that. Do you want something to drink?"

Guérin took him into the kitchen, a pretext for getting away from the parrot, who was eyeing them evilly.

John explained his idea, sitting on the work surface. Guérin had his back to him, staring out of a window overlooking the courtyard. He moved his round head at regular intervals, a rotational movement, neither approving nor disapproving. Guérin was taking mental notes, or perhaps thinking of something completely different. He said nothing for a minute after John had finished.

"So where do you want to arrange this meeting?"

"Not a lot of choice. In the Caveau de la Bolée. You think that perhaps . . . too theatrical?"

"Noooo."

But Guérin was uneasy.

"I'll call Lambert. He might be needed, if this man is as dangerous as you say."

The little detective wasn't put out, but he was anxious.

"You're afraid something might happen in the club?" John winked. "Or to Ariel?"

Guérin's neck and scalp blushed scarlet. He cleared his throat.

"Do you have a gun, Monsieur Nichols?"

"What? No. But I can get hold of one. You think that's necessary? But I don't know how to handle a gun."

"It's not for you, John." Guérin stood upright. "It's for me."

The American creased into laughter.

"You don't have a gun? You're the *police*, and you're asking *me* to get you a gun?"

"I've never had one."

"You will help me, then?"

"You can use the phone in the other room."

John went into the main room of the flat with caution. The parrot, rocking to and fro on its perch, stretched its neck out toward him with a fixed stare. John dialed the embassy number.

"Can I speak to Secretary Frazer, please? This is John Nichols."

The switchboard put him on hold, to the strains of Louis Armstrong singing "What a Wonderful World."

When Frazer answered, Churchill extended his neck at full stretch and screeched "Haaa! Assaaassin!," the veins on his bare neck standing out.

On the landing John shook Guérin's hand.

"Thanks for all this."

"Forget it. Do you know what Churchill once said?"

"He said a lot, didn't he?"

"He said in wartime the only real enemy is the truth."

"Yeah, well, he was a politician and a soldier, so I guess he knew what he was talking about."

"Till tonight then, John."

•

Bunker was walking back down the road, after having hung about a while in the café. In fact it was almost six, and he had been soaking up red wine for getting on for three hours. His mission was completed. He was on vacation in the countryside now. The *vin ordinaire* at the café was fine, he had no timetable, and he didn't need anything else. He had drunk until he didn't feel like another mouthful. In the end, the barman had opened up. Between four and six, they'd been matching each other, glass for glass. Roger, with his balloon-like red nose, had told him all about the village. Bunker inspired confidence in professionals. He didn't go into a bar to play chess, to a brothel to have a chat, or to a casino to write a book. When he stood leaning on the counter of a bar, the barmen facing him felt they existed for good reason. Tea pissers can get lost, as Roger remarked after their eighth glass. A customer of Bunker's capacity pleased him. Once he was

launched, he was unstoppable. He told Bunker about when he lived
in Cahors and played soccer, the "honor division" of Montauban after
the war, and how he had got married. He poured out his life story
with the impression that he was having a proper discussion because
Bunker listened with his granite face. In fact, the old convict had said
hardly anything. He simply nodded, asked the odd question, setting
the barman off again when he looked like drying up. One question
per glass. Until he was now fairly well tanked up.

"Another one, Roger, please? So you know the American?"

Roger filled the glasses, without bothering to wipe up the spillages.

"Old story. I wasn't here then, but I heard about it."

Bunker raised his glass.

"Cheers. What's it about then?"

"Oof" (intake of breath). "Goes back to the days when there
was this commune here, a whole bunch of hippies. They lived
down in that valley, this was before I came. 'Bout twenty of them,
all young, I think. And there was this American guy with them.
Some say he fell in the river and drowned, some say it was an accidental overdose, and some say he did it on purpose. Nobody really
knows. Anyway, after that, they all left. There was this woman,
she stayed on a bit. The dates, people don't agree about, but she was
certainly pregnant. Then she left, too. So when this new American
came back here, you know the big blond one, not the other, the old
people around here said he was the spitting image of the guy who
died. Well, 'course, he was his son, wasn't he? His father's buried
here in Lentillac. Bertrand's the only one left now of all of them,
the old hippy. He's got a farm. One night when I'd been here a bit,
Bertrand, he'd had a few. He was sitting right there, just like you
are. And some hunters came in. He doesn't like 'em. Well, I don't
know how it came up, but he started to talk about guns and all
that, and he said that was what was wrong with the world, weapons made everyone stupid fools. That's what he said: 'stupid fools.'
And he got a bit carried away, and he told me the Yank who was
here, the one who died, he'd been in Vietnam, and it had done his

head in. Wars, hunting, nuclear weapons, the Holy Trinity—he mixed everything up. But I remember him talking about it. And I've got some buddies who were in Indochina, and I can tell you, they weren't too good when they came back neither. If you want any more, you'll have to ask Bertrand."

Bunker allowed the conversation to drift on to other less interesting subjects, knocked back a few more glasses, and left to go back up the road.

On the way out of the village, he pushed open the gate of the cemetery. A few dozen graves in the evening sun, an ancient lime tree, and a view out over the valley. A nice place. He found it quickly. No flowers, just a simple headstone and a dusty slab.

PATRICK NICHOLS

1948 AUSTIN TEXAS

1974 LENTILLAC FRANCE

Bunker sat on the edge of the Michaud family tomb, opposite that of John Nichols's father.

Mesrine lay at his feet, indifferent to the scenery, because the ground was warm.

Bunker, chin in hand murmured to himself.

"Stupid little fool."

Without knowing whether he meant the father or the son.

When he reached the track, he wondered whether to go on down the road as far as Bertrand's farm. But he was pretty far gone already and had learned more than he wanted to know. He decided to put it off until the next day. There was plenty of time. Mesrine was already bounding in the direction of the tepee.

"Okay, dog, we'll just be *chez nous* tonight. We'll have a bite to eat." Bunker set off down the track, wondering what was happening in Paris. He was slightly annoyed with himself for not telling the kid how much he was enjoying himself here. He hadn't thanked him, or even told him to take care of himself.

It was still warm. Encouraged by the wine, Bunker promised himself he'd have a dip in the stream.

Mesrine rushed up the next incline. The sun was slowly sinking behind the northern ridge, bathing the southern slope in a golden glow. Bunker could see the big oak tree. He was back in time for his first real sunset in twenty-five years.

17

The cook, as hirsute and pale-skinned as before, had exchanged his apron for a black T-shirt. He didn't really have the build of a bouncer but was perfect as doorkeeper for an S&M show. A well-dressed couple went in, thirty-somethings, the woman pretty and blonde, the man a smooth type in a suit, ill at ease in a place where no one cared how much money he was making. The Gorgon with the Gauloise held the door open, without paying them any attention. As he saw John approach, he raised an eyebrow.

"Tonight, super show. Boss'll be pleased to see you. She's on edge, first show since that night with Alan."

"Lots of people?"

"We'll soon be turning them away."

"A friend of mine should be coming, man with a walking stick. Is he here?"

"Not yet. But I'll see he gets in." He moved aside to let John pass. "*Enjoy the show,*" he said in English as he glanced distrustfully down the rue de l'Hirondelle.

John went in, clenching his fists.

The hangings had been pulled aside. On the stage there were some accessories, dimly lit. A table, some skewers, hooks suspended in the air, a knife, bottles, and flashlights. The room was packed, the audience squeezed up in the aisles. A hundred, maybe more. Electro-rock music was playing from side speakers, pulsing away in a heartbeat rhythm. Some people were crammed together around tables, others were standing. The coat racks were overloaded, and clouds of smoke from the red candles on the tables wafted under the lights. It was as dark and as stifling as an oven.

Most of the faces were young: gelled hair, tattooed arms, piercings. Goth pinup girls in long black coats, with boots covered in buckles and smiles etched in black makeup to match their nails. Some of the guys wore makeup, too, looking like a mixture of owls and crows. Night birds, their pupils dilated by pills and powder. Vampires who flocked to see fakirs in this place with its antique stone walls, white-faced disciples of morbid poetry. Disguises, masquerades, eternal teenagers under long, shapeless coats, their flesh either hidden or covered with cosmetics: originality and conformism, a perpetually chewed contradiction. Men watching men, women watching women. They merged together, a mass of bodies.

The audience sitting at the tables was older, less noisy, all wearing black, too, but more soberly dressed. John Lennon glasses, post-Goth-punk intellectuals, waiting in silence. Women with tightly pursed lips, grinding their teeth instead of laughing. Habitués of extreme conceptual art. They liked watching S&M shows with timid little pats on the bottom, to pass the time intelligently and relieve the boredom of sex. They had come to watch a man suffer without complaining, although they themselves probably moaned all day long, boring their shrinks, their partners, and their friends to death with their egotisti-cal agonies. They had come to watch a real-life actor, a living man, piercing his skin. A plucked parrot, a Saint Sebastian in search of his *amour propre*. Self-love was what the audience came looking for. Giving yourself a scare by watching a man suffer was one way of getting through to your inner self.

John laughed inwardly. and his laugh turned to a grimace. Sebastian, they said, survived the arrows because the archers loved him too much. They dared not aim at his heart. Fakirs and martyrs have to consider the public's love for them as their most serious hope. The path to holiness on one condition: persuade them that you are dying in ecstasy under the blows. It's a show.

But that evening in the Caveau, it wasn't love that had drawn them along. They were there because of death. The death they had either missed or wanted to see again. How many of these people had been present when Alan died?

John unbuttoned his shirt and wiped the sweat from his chest. How many of these were making a return visit?

Saint Sebastian had survived the arrows and then died when he was beaten to death by a less scrupulous public.

The guy onstage was going to need a stiff drink.

An Asian waitress in a bra and skirt, tattooed to the eyebrows and with the muscles of a karate specialist or a ballet dancer, was gliding between the customers, holding a champagne bucket above her head. She put it on a table just in front of the stage. John watched the well-dressed couple from the door sit down there, joining another wealthy pair of Parisian bourgeois. The women were sexy in a classy way, with maximum slit skirts and décolleté, clothes that if they had been red instead of black would have made them look like whores. They had highly polished nails and whitened teeth. They exchanged greetings without looking each other in the eye. The two men, in casual shirts and dark jackets, shook hands in an exaggeratedly virile way. What a jolly start to the evening. Later, after the S&M act, they would have a little coke in a nightclub full of people like themselves, till the sweat poured into their eyes as they discussed bankers' bonuses; then some partner swapping; the exchange of like for like in a penthouse with mirrors, brought together by their possession of capital that would soon, after all, be exhausted.

The most expensive tables, up by the altar, were occupied by addicts of the chic frisson, the ones Ariel had talked about. Aficionados of "this incredible act, you've just got to see it," which would make their anesthetized libidos explode, liberating the well-calibrated fantasies of a sterile class obsessed with its own preservation. An animal crowd all around them, so they could slum it a bit. And a front-row seat for the smell of blood,

Leaning on a wall to right of the stage, bending his head because of the low ceiling, Lambert was wearing a yellow tracksuit, the only splash of color in the whole room, but one hardly noticed him. His long form melted into the wall as he leaned on an old poster for white magic. The tall, fair-haired policeman raised his gaze slowly toward John, and their eyes met. Lambert was no longer wearing the happy smile of a kid watching planes taking off. It must be his new face that allowed him to merge into the mass of the Caveau. Lambert slowly turned his head toward a table on the other side of the room. John followed the direction of his gaze.

Guérin was sitting down. Ariel, in a tank top, her arms glistening with sweat, was serving him a glass of beer. She was watching him intently, part mother hen, part she-wolf. Guérin was looking around, perhaps for a table with three people. A blonde woman and two men. He looked like a choirboy who had wandered into a brothel.

The *patronne* slipped between the tables and crossed the room in her leather pants, rubbing up against people as she passed. She was either trying to get the clientèle aroused, or looking for a little warmth in the icy furnace. She arrived in front of John and stood on tiptoe, straining to make herself heard.

"I kept you two seats like you asked. That little table there, just behind your pal. Where did you dig him up from?"

"What?"

"Never mind."

Ariel was indeed on edge. She glanced around the room, as disgusted as when it was empty. "What's all this about? Alan still?"

John nodded. Ariel dropped back onto her heels again and tugged up her bra straps. She grinned, to give herself confidence.

"Go and sit down. I'll bring you a drink. It starts in a couple of minutes."

John made his way across the room, apologizing to people, trying to shrink his shoulders so as not to jostle into them. But the bumps were hard, the bodies he met unyielding. He sat down at the table. On a card alongside the candle, Ariel had written *Reserved for Saint John*

Pierce. John picked the card up to look closer. He turned his back on Guérin, who did not see him smile.

"What time did you tell him?" asked the lieutenant, without turning around.

"About now."

John looked toward the door. The cook was pointing at him, indicating the way to Lundquist.

Forty-five, short dark hair, a smooth jowly face. Handmade suit, tie, average height. Lundquist strolled across the room as if he owned it, or had organized the whole evening. He could have been a critic at the private view of an artist whose career he was about to destroy. In his hand he held a cane but did not lean on it. An accessory that suited neither his age nor his physique, and which he was holding just under the pommel like a scepter.

John was surprised to see him alone. That made no sense. Someone must surely have arrived ahead of him, someone in the room who already had him under surveillance. Hard to tell in this crowd. The music slowly faded away, and silence fell. All heads turned toward the stage, except Lundquist's. He was looking toward John. The lights dimmed, the stage was lit up, and Lundquist sat down at the table.

His back was rigid, and he used the cane to sit down. He had had a fall from an army vehicle in Afghanistan and fractured several vertebrae, or so Alan said. This was the man Patricia had described. The stiffness of his body added to his cold manner. His eyes were like drills, piercing anyone who looked at him, turning them into an adversary.

A harsh electronic composition, somewhere between twelve-tone music and New Age, started to play. The single candle on the table lit Lundquist's brutal and unmarked face from below. People held back from applauding as an anxious excitement rippled through the audience. On the stage, a young man with shaved head and ponytail bowed soberly, holding three needles twenty centimeters long in each hand. John remembered the plucked wings of Guérin's parrot, ending in the stalks of the vanished feathers. The fakir smiled and planted the first needle in his forearm.

Lundquist read the card on the table, then looked around the room, with a smile, He spoke in English.

"Funny place this."

John chose to speak French.

"You think so?"

"So it was here that Mr. Mustgrave and Mr. Hirsh . . ."

"Stop being a fool."

Lundquist's smile vanished, replaced by a much more natural expression of animosity.

"Mind your language, Nichols."

"No point wasting time. I don't want to sit here with you longer than I have to."

Ariel put a beer in front of John and asked the man from the embassy if he wanted a drink.

He didn't reply. He was watching the stage. The fakir was now pushing a needle into his tongue. Ariel moved away silently, after an anxious glance at John. Lundquist glanced at her retreating buttocks, twiddling his cane in his fingers.

"So, what is it you want, Nichols?"

"Alan's dead. The blackmail's over. I'll give you back the money. And in return, you don't take any further action. I don't want the FBI harassing my mother. And you can tell Boukrissi to lay off and leave me alone."

The fakir now put a needle through his cheeks, which crossed with the one already in his tongue.

"Boukrissi?"

"You know perfectly well who I mean."

"Are you taping this conversation by any chance?"

"No. It's just between ourselves."

"I don't understand what kind of deal it is you want, Nichols. What can you offer me? This young man is amazing," he added, looking at the stage again. The show amused him, as if he were a romantic poet visiting the music hall.

"I know what you were up to in San Diego and Iraq. I've got dates, names, details. Alan's dead, but there are plenty of other witnesses I could call on. He wasn't the only one under your command. I'll be able to find the others, I've got their names."

Lundquist looked more and more amused.

"You don't have anything. Just the ravings of a junkie who's dead, a mythmaker and a paranoid self-harmer who was never even in the U.S. Army."

"You can destroy all the files you want, and it won't make any difference. All it needed for the whole world to find out about Abu Ghraib was for some cretins to post up pictures of what they were doing on the Internet. I've got four hundred pages of evidence. Don't you think that's enough? At a time like this."

"I thought you said the blackmail was over! You don't have the means of your ambitions, Nichols. I'm sorry about your friend's death, but I had nothing whatever to do with Mr. Mustgrave."

"I don't have any ambitions. I'm just saying you'll find it hard to cover up your past. It could be the end of your diplomatic career in France, *Frazer*."

Lundquist put his cane flat on the table. The fakir, still bristling with needles, had now put hooks through his nipples and was hanging weights from them. His skin was stretched, and he walked across the stage. His smile had lost its brilliance and a little blood trickled down to his belly. In the front rows, hands clenched the stems of their champagne glasses more tightly. The audience had fallen quite silent. Only the dissonant music was there to cover Lundquist and Nichols's voices.

"I could call the police in, over Boukrissi. He might have an interesting tale to tell."

"Watch it, Nichols, you're playing with fire."

"You told Boukrissi to cut the dope with something else, didn't you? What did he put in it, to make Alan hemorrhage? You know your drugs, Frazer, I'm well aware of that. You provided the dealer who would kill Alan."

"Mustgrave was a wreck, a degenerate, like Hirsh. He got what was coming to him. There was no need for anyone to give him a push. It was your job, not mine, to help losers like him."

"You really are a piece of shit. A trained poodle who thinks he's a psychologist. You're a sadist and a coward, an impotent one, what's more, with your stupid conductor's baton. Your superiors gave you an honorary job here in Paris because you're an embarrassment. Your ego makes you a time bomb. They won't hesitate to get rid of you, like Alan, if you start making waves."

Lundquist's hands whitened as he gripped the cane. Behind the diplomat, at the next table, John noticed a man looking at them. The only other person in the audience who was not watching the show. Not the embassy driver, but it could have been his twin brother. The heavy-duty chaperone was in the starting blocks.

Lundquist's face had stiffened and twisted. His voice went up an octave, and the civilized varnish exploded in a second.

"What about you, Nichols? You got your rocks off looking after a queer like Mustgrave? A little bungler who reminded you of the daddy you never knew, the Vietnam vet with post-traumatic stress disorder? Another junkie *he* was, too, a stupid idiot who did himself in as well, I heard. So who are you working for, Nichols? Your mom? Did she tell you to go in to sort out her problems for her? How long did it take you to screw up the courage to come to France? You even sent Mustgrave on ahead. Am I wrong? Tell me, you shit-faced pacifist, who's the real coward here? If I'd waited any longer, I wouldn't have needed Boukrissi to pass Mustgrave any dope. He'd have killed himself without any help from me. In fact, that's what happened. He knew perfectly well what he was doing. That pervert Hirsh told me, and he was in the front row. Your pal, the homo, he *let* himself die. And where were you when that was going on? I bet you were relieved when you heard that walking disaster had hit the deck at last. It's true, isn't it, Nichols?"

The fakir, now pierced all over and laden with weights, was unrolling a blanket covered with crushed glass. He took a few steps on the shards, barefoot, then let himself fall heavily to his knees. A crunch of broken glass and excited gasps from the audience.

John pressed the cane down with both hands, crushing Lundquist's fingers. Behind him he heard Guérin stirring.

The colossus behind Lundquist was moving, too. Then he seemed to hesitate and sat back down. John hadn't noticed Lambert slip into the middle of the room. The young officer had put the Beretta to the back of the bodyguard's neck, while apparently still absentmindedly admiring the show.

"You're the one who doesn't get it, Lundquist. The CIA is more interested in guys like me than in sickos like you. You're ten a penny, and so was Alan. I could ask them to break you if I agree to work for them."

Lundquist's arms started to tremble, and he pulled at the cane with a grimace. Onstage, the fakir had stood up, was unhooking the weights and taking out the needles. John suddenly let go, and Lundquist, caught off balance, fell back against the chair.

"You can't touch me, and don't think you can!"

"Witnesses. A dealer the French police can question. If that isn't enough, I'll sell my thesis to someone else, one of the people whose names are in there, the ones who've had brilliant careers since Desert Storm, not phony diplomats like you. I don't think they need asking twice. Especially since I won't ask a lot for it. All I'll ask for is Frazer's head, and they'll give me it on a platter. But if you just drop it all, you can bury the whole thing. That's all I'm asking, and I already told you, I'll give the money back. Otherwise, it's the police and the media. I don't give a damn about going back to the States, Frazer, it's your country, not mine now. I'm not one of your protégés; you've got nothing on me."

Alan used to say that Lundquist had tics. When he was furious, when he lost control of one of his men, or when he went into the interrogation room. His eyebrows were knitted, his nostrils dilated, and his shoulders twitched with a movement that communicated itself to his stiff spine.

"Police! Who do you think you are! The French police can't touch me, I'm a diplomat."

John moved his chair aside.

Guérin turned around slowly toward their table, calmly, with his strange manner of looking beyond the present. Lundquist had no idea what this grotesque apparition could mean, this man with a scarred face and a hydrocephalic head, balanced unsteadily on its neck. Guérin waved his tricolor badge in front of his eyes. In his other hand was a little digital recorder. John lifted the card labeled Saint John Pierce and picked up the wireless microphone underneath it.

"Lieutenant Guérin, Paris Criminal Investigation Department. Your diplomatic passport will indeed protect you, Monsieur Lundquist, but your compatriot here, Mr. Nichols, has persuaded me to take the opportunity to ask for a favor I'm owed from people higher up. Just by chance, it happened this morning. The Minister can't refuse me anything at the moment. I'm quite ready to question you about the death of Mr. Mustgrave, as well as about a dealer, a Monsieur Boukrissi."

Lundquist was jerking with spasms and looked back over his shoulder. John leaned across to him, almost breathing him in.

"Forget it, Frazer, your bodyguard is being watched."

The fakir had now attached two hooks to the skin over his shoulder blades, attached to ropes running up to pulleys in the vaulted ceiling. The Asian waitress was acting as his assistant. She pulled on the ropes with her dancer's tattooed arms. The public gasped again, and a storm of clapping broke out as the fakir rose into the air. His pain could be seen on his face, deforming a more and more fixed smile. Not exactly holy ecstasy, but he was certainly getting a good round of applause.

Lundquist was frothing at the mouth, but his pale eyes did not express defeat, only rage.

"Without your thesis, you can't do a thing. We've got all your papers, Nichols. If there's still a copy left, I'll soon have got it from . . ."

The fakir spread his arms wide in a cross, throwing out his chest.

The audience rose to its feet clapping hysterically.

John cried out:

"*What!* What did you say?"

Their table was surrounded by people; Lundquist made a dash for it, hitting his way out with his stick. John leaped up. He saw

Lambert's Beretta, held by the barrel, come down hard. A sound of breaking glass and the bodyguard collapsed between the tables. The fakir was still hanging on, trembling more and more now. The Asian girl weakened and relaxed the cords, which were vibrating, the music stopped, and the audience was screaming with joy. Lundquist thrust aside the cook at the door, and John burst out after him, elbows and shoulders thrusting his way through, Lambert at his heels.

There was another guy waiting outside, a hundred kilos, tough, fists at the ready and no hesitation. Lundquist had certainly not come alone. John's nose burst open, and he fell to his knees. The gorilla prepared to have another swing at him, but Lambert raised his pistol three times. The barrel of the Beretta was covered in blood. The second bodyguard rolled into the gutter, bleeding from the head.

Lundquist was hopping up the road: his fractured spine prevented him from running, so he used his cane as a pivot to provide speed: a three-legged insect, damaged, escaping down the rue de l'Hirondelle. Lambert crouched in firing position, as in the gun club. Facing front, both hands gripping the Beretta's slippery handle, his legs flexed and apart.

"Police! Stop or I'll fire!"

Lundquist stopped dead in his zigzag flight and wheeled around. He was holding a handgun. "Shit," Lambert whispered and smiled.

Bubbles of air and blood were spurting from the bridge of John's broken nose. His head was whirling. He wiped his eyes, brimming with tears, got to his feet, and saw the two men standing in the street, both armed.

Everyone hit the wrong target

John sprang to cover Lambert with his body.

Lundquist fired twice.

"Empty shells" was John's last thought before he felt the shock, and a bone shatter somewhere in his body.

The door of the club opened, and cheerful voices spilled out into the street. Guérin saw a man in a suit stretched out on the ground. Lambert and Nichols were a shapeless mass in the middle of the street. Lundquist was still pointing the smoking gun, his eyes staring.

Guérin took one of the Aouch brother's pistols from his coat pocket, slowly and with regret. He aimed for the legs.

Ariel came out, pushing aside the open-mouthed crowd, which was now spreading into the street. She looked at the last man left standing. Guérin, his big head to one side, was already searching for possible explanations.

18

Juliard didn't get the call from Paris till 6:00 a.m.

Three motorcycle gendarmes left first, while the others loaded two vans and a four-by-four. Bullet-proof vests, heavy arms and action stations.

Michèle, the blonde, insisted on coming. They didn't let her drive.

At the top of the track to the camp, one of the motorcyclists was waiting. He was picked out in their headlights through the haze which was dispersing as day dawned. Juliard leaned out of the four-by-four.

"Well?"

"They're on their way back up, commandant."

The two others were scrambling up, still wearing their crash helmets and out of breath.

"There's a car parked at the bottom of the track, commandant," said the first. "We didn't go beyond. No sound, couldn't hear anything."

His colleague, bent double, hands on knees to get his breath, confirmed: "Hired car, Paris plates, sir."

Juliard got out and went to the first van, where Verdier, the sergeant with the gray mustache, was at the wheel.

"We're going in on foot."

The gendarmes got out of the vehicles, and Juliard gave them an emergency briefing.

"Right. The call came from a lieutenant in the Paris police, CID. We've got a fax from the backup legal authority as well. But we don't know exactly what's going on. He said that there should be someone staying at Nichols's place at the moment, a man called Bunker. About sixty, white hair. The instructions say find him and bring him in. But he may have been taken hostage. We don't know who could be down there with him, or how many. Paul and Philippe have seen a car parked down there. Bunker came by train. So there's got to be someone else there. Paris says the suspect or suspects are probably armed and dangerous. So we won't take any risks; we're just going to take a look, that's all. If we find a problem, we put the barriers up and wait for reinforcements from Cahors, understood? This isn't just some drunk driving offense, so watch out."

The first rays of the sun were just reaching the peaks above the valley. The damp night air was condensing into a light layer of dew. The helmeted men started to creep down the track in groups of three, their hands gripped tightly around their guns. They moved silently, sending out steaming breath. Juliard, up in front, crouching in the wet grass on the side of the road, raised his arm and made a fist. Everyone stopped. He beckoned Verdier, who joined him. Juliard gave orders in a low voice.

"Verdier, you know the spot. Have a look first with your men. Call us when you can see the camp."

Verdier ran his fingers over his mustache.

"Whatever you say, sir."

Juliard looked at him for a moment, feeling vaguely anxious.

Two minutes later, Juliard's radio crackled. He took the receiver from his shoulder. Verdier spoke in a whisper.

"Nothing here, sir. Can't see a soul. Not a sound."

"Don't move, we're coming down. You others, Martinez, Blanchet, stay by the car."

Juliard stood up, motioning to the others to join him.

Two men advanced down the log steps, weapons at the ready. Three others covered them from the top of the incline. There was no one inside the big tent. The sun's rays were now reaching the deserted encampment.

"Shit," Juliard said. "The car's still here. And someone seems to have settled in. But where are they?"

The acned junior gendarme piped up:

"Sir, when we came to find Nichols the other day, we found him up in the woods, shooting his bow."

"Verdier! Take four men and go and look up there."

His radio crackled again.

"Commandant? Martinez here, I'm down the bottom, I think you'd better come take a look."

Juliard told his men to wait and went down, stumbling over the ruts in the path. Martinez pointed toward a hayfield, at the bottom of the track, running down to a water meadow by the river. The hay was still standing here; it hadn't been cut. But the grass had been trampled, in a curving track toward the bank. Someone had walked across the field to go to the river. In the distance, the water sparkled golden brown.

"Anyone got binoculars?" Juliard asked.

"Back in the truck, sir."

"Never mind."

Juliard put his hand up to shield his eyes and peered ahead. "There's someone by the water."

They went down in a group of six, each one making a fresh track across the hayfield as they walked in parallel lines. Juliard was in the middle, following the original pathway. Halfway to the river he stopped. At his feet lay the body of a black dog, curled into a ball in the grass. An old dog, its teeth showing in a grimace, its skull shattered. Looking toward the river, he could now see the naked torso of a man with white hair leaning against a tree. Juliard raised one hand, and the men stopped. He blew out then took a deep breath, taking his Sig Pro from its holster.

"This is the gendarmerie! Put your hands up and identify yourself. Stand up slowly."

A warm breeze ruffled the tall grass, matching the ripples on the river. The man leaning against the tree didn't move or reply.

"This is Commandant Juliard speaking, from the national gendarmerie! Put your hands up! State your name!"

The white hair blew a little in the wind, like the stalks of grass heavy with seed. Still no response. Juliard stepped over the dead dog, and the men went forward with him, gradually moving closer together. The six paths converged toward Bunker.

The body of a man in a suit was lying at the old convict's feet. A man with a blond crew cut, a bent nose, and cauliflower ears. The face of a former boxer on the neck of a bull, but strangely out of shape. The gorilla's throat was crushed and twisted, his top vertebrae out of line. The head lay at an odd angle and was already turning blue; the shoulders and the arms, thrown wide open, were submerged in about ten centimeters of water and swaying slightly in the current of the Bave. His open mouth was full of water, and a blackened oak leaf was floating in it. At the end of his right arm, lying on the sandy riverbed, was an automatic handgun with a silencer.

Bunker was naked, sitting at the foot of the oak tree, his legs stretched out and his head against the trunk. From a black hole in his belly, an impressive quantity of blood had flowed, down across his genitals and on toward the river without quite reaching it.

Juliard crouched down beside the old man. He considered, with awe, this massive body that had taken hours to die, the strong heart pumping out liters of blood, offered to the earth. The old man's hair was not wet. Either it had had time to dry, or else Bunker hadn't had time to go swimming. His green eyes were open.

With two fingers, Juliard touched the old man's carotid and found no reason for hope. Even worse. The body was almost warm. A matter of minutes. The officer took off his helmet and wiped some sweat from his brow. Bunker's mouth was fixed in the shadow of a smile.

Juliard asked himself why this ancient pile of muscles had not tried to drag himself up to the road. The old keeper of the Luxembourg Gardens had stayed there all night, by the river, oozing blood. What was he waiting for?

He looked at the tattoo on the hand, the fiery cross, then followed the direction of Bunker's last gaze, turned toward the field, the tepee on the side of the hill, and the sun, now already high in the sky.

19

John P. Nichols

John Nichols had stopped only one of the two bullets. It had gone in through the shoulder, shattering the humerus, and exited through the base of his neck, breaking his left collarbone. The pain from the wounds had been short lived at the time. It returned as he emerged from unconsciousness.

When he woke up, the man with the round pebble head was sitting in a corner of his room. The little lieutenant had brought his possessions for him: a backpack, the bow, a quiver of arrows, and a small black canvas bag. John had turned his head toward the window and looked out at the sky. He had no wish to talk.

Nichols did his reckoning.

Two men, each coming to the end of their road, had died on the banks of the same river. A Vietnam vet, Patrick Nichols, and an old ex-convict rebaptized with the name of a writer. Between these two, he would have to try not to go under himself. And between the two of them, there was Alan Mustgrave. John kept his mouth shut, for fear that too many words, or too few, would spill out.

The little lieutenant came in every morning, bringing news that John listened to without replying. He looked out of the window, waiting to be able to leave Paris. Guérin had accepted the situation from the start, with a nod of his head.

On the fourth day, a tall blonde woman had come to visit. He had turned toward her and said a few words, the first since the rue de l'Hirondelle. He had apologized, explained, and said he would be convalescent for some time. The woman had held his hand, talked of a former friend, and wished him a speedy recovery. After she left, he turned back to the window.

A week later, he had used the telephone in his room. He had called an undertaker and an ambulance company. He had left an envelope on the bed, signed his own discharge, and was driven out of Paris lying on his back in a white medical transport.

●

The burial plot had been bought in perpetuity with a handful of dollars. Under the big lime tree, facing the morning sun. On top of the coffin was another, smaller box.

John had thrown a few accessories into the grave to accompany Bunker and Mesrine on their journey. A bow, some arrows, a packet of Gitanes and a few thousand dollars. Enough for Bunker to get by, whether in hell or paradise.

The other people at the funeral were a gendarmerie commander in civilian clothes, a café proprietor, and three old men in cloth caps who had invited themselves along. A delivery man had put a wreath alongside the grave and given a card to John, who smiled as he read it. The epitaph on the grave would be a sober one:

BUNKER AND HIS DOG MESRINE

2008

KEEPERS OF THE GARDENS

Now they could keep an eye on the graveyard and the valley.

John had watched as the gravediggers threw earth on top of the two coffins. His last memory of Bunker: a suitcase done up with string, a suit from the 1980s, a spruced-up old convict whom he had taken in his arms in the rue de Vaugirard. Bunker was scared, yes, but happy. He had left freely. No need to go back over it and start fretting now.

John had walked over to his father's tomb a few yards away to put some wildflowers on it.

At the cemetery gate, Juliard had waited for him. Three men, groaning discreetly, were unloading a granite slab from a pickup truck.

Juliard had offered his condolences, and John smiled again. This time, Juliard had not wriggled out of his duty. He seemed to be moved. The commandant explained to Nichols where they were with the inquiry, its conclusions, and consequences. The American Embassy had put pressure on for everything to be dealt with discreetly, and as fast as possible. Some diplomats had arrived from Washington the day before and wanted to get in touch with Nichols. John laughed at this, saying the gendarmerie had become his secretariat.

John P. Nichols left a message to be passed on.

"They'll call again, to make me a proposal. You can tell them to go fuck themselves."

The two men said good-bye, and Juliard did not ask where he was going next.

John had walked as far as the farm where Bertrand and his wife lived. His arm in a sling was aching. He had sat down with them in the farm kitchen.

Two days later, Bertrand and his wife were finishing loading the tepee, the wind turbine, the PVC tubes and batteries, hammock, camp bed, and books into John's new small van. Bertrand kissed his wife and sat at the wheel, adjusting the bandana around his forehead.

"Time was, I'd have suggested dropping some acid. So where are we off to?"

"Do you mind driving? I'll tell you when to stop."

"Which way?"

"Up the valley to start with, and tell me about the night you pulled his body out of the river."

20

Richard Guérin

The Caveau affair was dismissed as a paragraph in the newspapers, all the principal actors having vanished: Nichols, Lambert, Guérin, and Lundquist. A shooting outside a club with a dodgy reputation. The cabaret was closed down by the authorities. Two days later, a private jet took Lundquist out on a stretcher. Guérin had aimed for the legs and succeeded in his risky shot. The diplomat left from Le Bourget Airport very early in the morning. Guérin did not go to watch the plane take off.

He had reported to his superiors, given them all the explanations, with evidence and witness statements. He wasn't expecting anything from them, just to get a hearing. Kowalski, Mustgrave, Lundquist. None of these affairs had anything to do with one another. Guérin gave up trying to prove they were linked.

Barnier was asked to take early retirement, a decision communicated to him in a private interview with the Minister: a dignified departure, with noises made about the Légion d'honneur. He had not yet committed suicide. Perhaps he was waiting until he was no longer on the force. Berlion had been transferred to Lyon, Roman to Organized Crime in Paris, where he would have new colleagues.

Kowalski's memory remained immaculate. The office had not blown up; indeed it had hardly trembled. At least in public. In the cupboards of the prefecture of police, a new skeleton was spreading a filthy and degrading stink, reeking of guilt and unanswered questions. Certain people regretted the truth having come out, because in the end it had not done anyone any good: they rearranged their consciences, waiting for the memory to fade away.

Nichols had disappeared from his hospital bed, leaving a note for Guérin.

Thanks for everything. Hope Lambert is recovering okay. Tell him if I'd had any choice, I'd have done it better. That raincoat did belong to your mother. When you've found an explanation of how we met, try to find me, and we'll see if it makes sense. Till then.

John

Guérin had ordered a wreath to be delivered in the Lot for the old park keeper's burial. He had put in a card for John.
A reassuring quantity of pure coincidence. Bon voyage. Guérin

He had refused promotion, which had been offered with some embarrassment in exchange for his silence. He wanted to stay in Suicides. His request was accepted. Guérin, though more than ever a thorn in the flesh of headquarters, had become untouchable.

Churchill had died a few days after Nichols's departure. Guérin had buried the old parrot in a corner of the courtyard, at four in the morning. The disappearance of the old bird had relieved him. But Churchill had abandoned him to a corrosive solitude, in which his old demons would soon start stirring. Churchill, the featherless macaw, leaving his master an orphan, at the mercy of his nightmares, a prostitute's son with no father. The Ministry had no need to worry about whether he would keep quiet: he would cloister himself in silence without any pressure from the outside.

Weeks passed. Guérin returned to his office. Hundreds of hours among the dusty shelves.

Lambert's desk was covered with piles of files, boxes from the archives that were starting to take over the whole room. Guérin went on answering the telephone, taking public transportation to report on suicides. He ticked boxes, contemplated the corpses with a pensive gaze, then returned to his real work under the eaves.

The summer had passed in a strange atmosphere, without his counting the days or feeling the warmth. Then autumn came. He began to use the service stairs only.

Winter arrived. Guérin was working weekends, nights, and public holidays. He was adding to his prosecution file against the world without letting up. He had become silent in other people's presence, neglecting his appearance, and eating only when absolutely necessary, when he could stand up no longer. His colleagues came to regard him only with pity. The Kowalski wound was closing up. And Guérin's very existence was becoming nothing more than a rumor that people did not bother to pass on. His loss of weight made his head look even bigger, and his black coat had become too big for him. He talked to himself at night, in the archive room where he sometimes slept on the floor, curled up in a ball. Guérin's head was an suppurating wound, infected from his constant scratching and hidden under a greasy cap.

On Christmas Eve 2008, a cold and rainy night, he sat at his desk without knowing what the date was. The calendar had not been updated since the night of the fakir show. The files were piled up against the walls, the wastepaper baskets were overflowing, and the strips lights were crackling. Looking up, he contemplated the stain on the ceiling. Its amethyst rings had grown monstrously; the plaster was cracked and bulging, threatening to come down in chunks. The brown circles had grown, covering almost the whole surface of the ceiling.

Richard Guérin thought about the Caveau again and of that night when, he felt sure, everything had almost fallen into place. For months he had hardly thought of anything else. He could memorize every face, every gesture of the evening, everything he had seen. Gradually in his waking dream, the faces of the living had been replaced by those in his files.

A show put on for him. The Caveau. Inside his stricken brain, he arranged clues, tracks, ideas. His personal archive, in which he took refuge for days on end, abandoning his office, the quai des Orfèvres, and Paris. A place free of material contingencies, where his reason reigned supreme. Guérin's mind freed itself from the real world to achieve its ends. Under the vaulted ceiling of the Caveau de la Bolée, he reorganized to suit himself the distribution of the audience, choosing new clients for the tables, new conversations, imagining links and meetings between the dead. He could question them, push them to answer his questions, talk to them without having to explain his hunches. Guérin was free. The world was at last moving at the pace of his understanding of it.

The imaginary, theoretical and dreamlike space into which he had escaped had gradually become his prison. As he explored it, every time staying a little longer, his return to the real world was becoming more difficult and inspired greater disgust. And fear. When he came around, he looked haggard, his cheeks hollow and his eyes feverish, a lost soul among his fellow humans to whom he could no longer speak. He had become afraid of not knowing which world he lived in now, the one in his mind or the more solid one of material reality. The satisfaction and frisson he felt on escaping it, he now sadly recognized as the dangerous pleasure that he might have got from drugs.

Until the day when he stopped worrying about coming back, when reality itself became a dream, a poetic and incoherent chaos, causes and effects that obeyed no law. Until the day when he no longer recognized himself in the mirror.

Inside his head, every element, every person, slotted into a place he chose for them.

They were all there: Paco, Nichols with his bow and arrow, Kowalski with his ashen face, Lambert with his gun, Ariel, and his mother encouraging him: "That's it, big boy, go on, you'll find them. They must be there. Keep looking." He moved the furniture around, reorganized the spectators into categories, added some new ones every day, tried every possible combination: he was king of his wax museum, free to put together, divide up and move the elements around to fill the last gap. The last black space in his memory, still unfilled. Because he had not been able to see everything that night In a dark corner he must have overlooked a table for three. A blonde woman and two men, the only living beings in the room that he had not been able to identify, distracted as he was by the necessary hazards of the Mustgrave affair.

Nichols had drawn him into the place of all coincidences, and the solution had to lie there. There was no other possibility. Somewhere inside his mind lay the answer.

Guérin looked up at the stain, that rainy Christmas night, as he walked around the vaulted room, going from table to table, an amiable maitre d', inquiring if everything suited the customers. A man was hanging up by hooks, blood was running onto the stage, and that was the only sound he could hear, apart from the rain on the roof. He went toward the stage, the last table, laid in front of three empty chairs. He was coming to greet the absent ones, the guilty ones, those he never saw, but who were there. The people he was waiting for, and who one day would come toward him unmasked, their faces showing.

Guérin was looking up at the stain, his head back and his throat stretched out. Around it a rope was tightening, and his shattered voice whispered in the deserted office: Goodnight.

There they were. A thousand absent people, drinking champagne, and laughing at the hemophiliac fakir. Guérin sat at the table, suddenly deserted, to watch the show. He was waiting for someone to come sit at his side.

The telephone rang. He picked it up with a smile

A new guest had just arrived.

21

Francis Lambert

Francis Lambert, born in Nanterre, had grown up at the same pace as the skyscrapers around La Défense. At fourteen, he already looked like a leaning tower himself. He reluctantly signed up for a baker's certificate. It hadn't been his idea to start working so young. At sixteen, he was an apprentice in the *boulangerie* where his father worked. Francis trailed around in the flour of the bakery and seemed never to stop growing. In the Cité des Nuages, he was considered a decent defender, though rather slight in build. When he wasn't at work, he was playing soccer. Outside his job, the housing project was his world. He never went beyond it.

His father was a common, or garden-variety, racist, defending his right to what he had: his right to a decent life as a French citizen. For him, being French meant being honest, hardworking, and—depending who he was talking to, usually in the café—white. Not Muslim, anyway.

A defensive racism, which fluctuated with the unemployment rate and the number of drinks he'd had. Lambert's parents had split up when he was little, and his mother had disappeared from sight. Francis lived among Arabs, blacks, and Asians as his natural milieu. He didn't feel any anger or frustration at living where he did, only boredom. While his job didn't interest him, at least he had one. The parents of other kids on the project thought him a good role model. He had seen his friends slowly get sucked under. Drug dealing, delinquency, fighting, and self-segregation. He didn't blame them. Some managed to escape; others got deeper in. Nothing to do with their IQ: the dealers on his block were probably brighter than he was. If you don't have any choice, being clever is not enough.

The bakery had to let him go once a local supermarket started baking its own bread. The boss kept his father on but let Francis go: at nineteen, he had more of a chance of finding a job. He was unemployed for a year. He spent it playing soccer, in between visits to the job center.

A career counselor asked him if he wanted to retrain. Lambert asked him how he could get to be a nurse. The guy smiled. His father guffawed. A month later, the agency sent him a suggestion: they were recruiting for the police. Lambert replied to the letter.

He passed the first-level exams. His image in the neighborhood changed, but he was still liked: policemen who came from the housing project were respected.

His new status allowed him to rent a studio apartment a couple of blocks from his father. He left early in the morning, storing his uniform in the cloakroom overnight. He was posted to the station at La Garenne-Colombes.

He worked there for two years, preparing for the exams to become an officer. Failed, twice. He asked to be moved to the Paris HQ, because it seemed like a nice idea to work in the CID. He enjoyed his new job, which got him away from his housing project. He banged away at the law books, conscientiously and laboriously. They ridiculed him at the station in Colombes.

Then a year later he got a new posting: the quai des Orfèvres, the Paris HQ. He was twenty-three and couldn't believe his luck.

It was hard to see at first why Barnier had plucked him from his little commissariat in the sticks. He was told to go to Suicides and had not the faintest idea of what the work would actually be. He found himself alone in a tiny office with no windows, on the top floor of a building at the far end of the Île de la Cité. Well, so what, he was out of his suburb, and he was a trainee in HQ. He stayed there, listening as a telephone rang and rang. He had been told not to touch it. He pushed open the door to the archives, glanced around at the shelves, and shut it again. A week later, Barnier reappeared, accompanied by a guy wearing a shabby yellowish raincoat.

"This is your new assistant," Barnier had said to the little newcomer and vanished without saying anything to Lambert.

Lieutenant Guérin had introduced himself and told him he needn't bother to wear his uniform to work. The next day Lambert turned up in a tracksuit. And then he found out why he had been chosen. At the coffee machine, an officer from the Vice Squad had called him "the new puppy for that asshole Guérin." Lambert had learned to live with the scorn everyone expressed for his boss, some of which rubbed off onto him.

Little by little, doing small favors, he had built up a network of acquaintances: other junior employees who appreciated his simplicity. Lambert, with his long legs and his basic niceness, had become a link between his boss and the rest of HQ.

Guérin took care of him, without treating him as an imbecile or pitying him. The boss was incredibly intelligent. Lambert didn't care what the others said about him. As for the work, he found some affinities with the suicides: these dead people reminded him of his tower blocks, no doubt because he always arrived too late to save them. And then there were the families. The families had always loved him, and Lambert had found a way of reciprocating.

The boss treated him not so much like a son, more like a woman would a child who was not her own. The first time Lambert had found Guérin in the archive room, tearing away at his scalp, he had realized that his job wasn't all that far removed from nursing after all. They looked after each other, without anything being said.

Lambert was happy. The office was a watertight chamber, a cell in which for hours he could think about anything he liked: his future promotion, the soccer results, gossip. He watched the stain on the ceiling change color with the seasons. He fetched the coffee, picking up tidbits of news in the corridor, and brought fragments of outside life into the office. When the telephone rang, he was ready. He got up to follow the boss and drove the car.

He had taken up shooting, leaving soccer and his housing project behind. This solitary sport, like his life at the quai, suited him fine. He had become good at it, although he didn't really like guns. Lambert thought that the decision to pull a trigger had to be taken too quickly, without giving you time to think. To compensate for the fear he felt for his gun, he never loaded it. The chamber of his Beretta, except when he was at the club, was always empty.

Nichols had tried to save him. Lambert was touched by that, even before he felt the impact.

When he woke up in the hospital, Guérin was there. The lieutenant was holding his hand.

The first thing he said, when he was able to speak, was to apologize for ending up in the hospital: "Not loaded, boss, it's never loaded."

Lundquist's second bullet, the one that missed Nichols, had done more damage.

Lambert's stomach was perforated, and the bullet had lodged between two vertebrae, cutting the spinal column. Lambert came out of his coma after three days and went straight into surgery.

In the post-op recovery room, with tubes and catheters everywhere, he had panicked. He had regained consciousness but was unable to speak, move, breathe, or swallow. There was a tube down his throat, he was on a respirator, and his hands were strapped down. He couldn't feel his body at all and had no idea what his condition was. His eyes filled with tears. Guérin had put a hand on his forehead, spoken gently to calm and reassure him. Guérin had lied. Lambert guessed as much and gave a sad smile.

The surgeon came to see him.

The boss was still there with his faraway gaze, the one that stopped Savane in his tracks, the gaze that anticipated the future and made Lambert seem transparent. But that day, the junior guessed what Lieutenant Guérin was thinking. He had no need of a surgeon to explain.

He had stayed two months in the hospital before being allowed home. Guérin was still there and had fixed up the flat, overcome by all the sneakers and tracksuits, which he had stuffed away in cupboards.

Lambert would never run again. He would never trail along the corridor with the sound like waves on a beach. The surgeon had not been able to save his legs.

He got a pension, and social services paid for a caregiver: a young student who came mornings and evenings to help him out of bed, to get into his wheelchair, to take a shower, have a meal, and go back to bed again.

His legs had gradually wasted away.

Lambert would sit at the window, looking down at the housing project he had returned to.

Sometimes he took the elevator, propelling his wheelchair between the tower blocks. People said hello; he chatted to friends, the ones who were getting on okay, others who were in trouble. His wastepaper basket was full of brochures for vacations by the sea or in the mountains, for people with reduced mobility. Going to the mountains in a wheelchair. He didn't give a damn about going on vacation. What Lambert wanted was to be able to drag his feet through the bakery flour or along corridors of the quai, then flex his knees and stand, feet apart, holding a loaded gun to Lundquist's head.

Guérin came to see him less often. The boss was turning into a wreck, becoming incoherent. Or perhaps Lambert was just not listening to him anymore.

The visits disturbed him. He surprised himself by hating Guérin, who was still chasing his ghosts, while he, Lambert, was stuck in a wheelchair. In November, Guérin stopped calling altogether. Lambert went out less and less often.

The caregiver tidied the flat every morning, clearing up the mess created by Lambert in fits of rage that were getting more and more violent. He wasn't bothering to eat. He drank a lot of beer and pissed himself sitting in his wheelchair. The apartment began to stink. Lambert would belch, roll himself over to the window, and yell.

He had a nightmare. Always the same, in black and white, and it scared him so much he became an insomniac.

His father occasionally paid him a visit. One night they were drinking lager and watching TV, his father on the couch, he in his wheelchair. After the film, his dad got up to go home, a couple of blocks away. The old man was a bit drunk. He hesitated on one foot, not knowing what to say. He felt sorry for his son but couldn't find the right words.

"Want a hand to get to bed?"

"No."

He shook Francis's hand, hesitated, then bent down and kissed him on the forehead. As he closed the front door, he said to himself, well, at least his son didn't have to work; he was supported by the French state.

Lambert dreaded going to bed; he was afraid of the dream.

A pack of beer on his thighs, he pushed his way to the window and looked out. The housing project was deserted. There were lights on in the apartments, but no one on the streets. Lambert threw an empty can on the floor and opened another.

Three teenagers came out of the building opposite and went over to a lamppost. They were sharing a joint. The rain had turned into flakes. It was snowing.

At first the dream had been the same: the cars, the crashes, and the skinny young man running with his arms spread wide. Then the scene changed and now it was himself, Lambert, who was running between the cars, going up the ring road with long strides and smiling.

The dream terrified him and enraged him. Because he could feel the asphalt under his bare feet, the wind on his skin, that marvelous weariness in his thighs, and the regular rhythm of his breath as he ran. When the truck came hurtling toward him, he would wake up screaming and banging his lifeless legs.

A few weeks ago, the dream had become a vision, and staying up drinking no longer protected him. He couldn't get rid of it. For whole days, with his head thrown back looking up at the ceiling, eyes open, he was running up the *périphérique* into the traffic. The naked man was smiling, and Lambert was weeping. He had stopped sleeping altogether.

He pushed his wheelchair over to a cupboard. His jacket in Brazil's team colors was stiff and smelled of mildew. He threw his half-full beer can at the shelf, splashing his Zidane T-shirt and knocking over his shooting trophy.

He was a good shot. He wouldn't have missed him, standing in the correct position as he was. But Lundquist had a loaded gun. Being nice wasn't an option with shits like him. Wasn't his life worth more than Lundquist's? Guérin had aimed too low. Lambert wouldn't have missed, firmly planted on both legs.

●

The youths, two white and an Arab, had met up at the bottom of the staircase, escaping from family meals that went on forever. They had gone out to hang about under the streetlamp. The hall with its broken windowpanes was no warmer than outside; might as well get some fresh air. A joint was passed around; the talk was about the evening, films, vacations in the mountains they would never take. Kids having a bit of fun. Snowflakes started to fall, as if suspended in the halo of light from the streetlamp.

"Shit, man! It's really Christmas now!"

They let the little flakes cover their hoods, looking up at the sky. No snowball fights yet, but it made them laugh. The flower beds around the apartments started to turn white.

The young Arab wiped the snowflakes from his eyelashes and raised his arm, pointing a finger in the dark. His voice alerted the others.

"What the fuck's he doing?"

They all looked up.

"Can't hear, what's he shouting?"

A man in a yellow jacket was contorting himself, twelve floors up, on the windowsill. The top half of his body was already hanging into the void.

ANTONIN VARENNE traveled a great deal and completed an M.A. in philosophy before embarking on a career as a writer. He was awarded the Prix Michel Lebrun and the Grand Prix du jury Sang d'encre for *Bed of Nails*.

SIÂN REYNOLDS is the translator of Crime Writers Association award–winning crime novels by Fred Vargas.